latest accessory

latest accessory

TYNE O'CONNELL

review

Copyright © 1997 by Tyne O'Connell

The right of Tyne O'Connell to be identified as the Author
of the Work has been asserted by her in accordance with the Copyright, Designs
and Patents Act 1988.

First published in Great Britain in 1997
by HEADLINE BOOK PUBLISHING

A REVIEW softback

10 9 8 7 6 5 4 3 2 1

All rights reserved. No part of this publication may be
reproduced, stored in a retrieval system, or transmitted,
in any form or by any means without the prior written
permission of the publisher, nor be otherwise circulated
in any form of binding or cover other than that in which
it is published and without a similar condition being
imposed on the subsequent purchaser.

All characters in this publication are fictitious
and any resemblance to real persons, living or dead,
is purely coincidental.

British Library Cataloguing in Publication Data

Demy softback ISBN 0 7472 7691 9

Typeset by Palimpsest Book Production Limited,
Polmont, Stirlingshire
Printed and bound in Great Britain by
Clays Ltd, St Ives plc

HEADLINE BOOK PUBLISHING
A division of Hodder Headline PLC
338 Euston Road
London NW1 3BH

For Eric, S.P., Cordelia, Zad and Kajj

.

ACKNOWLEDGEMENTS

So many barristers and City people deserve a serious thanking for the help they gave me, not just in legal and financial advice but in the serious shopping they went through for the good of fiction – not least of all Martin Gibson, Rupert Wilkes, Kevin Arnold, Tony Dymond and Helena Braddock; I must also take this opportunity to thank the builders who aided and abetted me in the emotional roller coaster ride that ensued when I decided to gut a factory in the City while still living in it with my unsuspecting family: Paul, George, Ted, Pat – brave men all – I tip my hard hat to you; my devoted children for sticking with me when thousands of other children would have changed their name and packed themselves off to boarding school; Eric and SP for learning how to use an espresso machine; my long suffering mother and father for taking my calls when I needed to whinge about the English and their weather; Darley Anderson and his gorgeous assistants and Geraldine Cooke and the astonishingly capable Kirsty Fowkes.

Naturally any errors of judgement in this work of fiction must be blamed on the people I've just mentioned particularly Martin Gibson whose guidance I have always taken in all things.

CHAPTER ONE

it's called joining the property market – and it shits on war for stress.

It was a hot June morning and any sane person was on strike or skipping work and taking the nearest charter flight to a sandy beach. This was a safe-sex-and-Campari-in-the-sun kind of morning. But here I was stressing my way to premature crow's-feet. I had major accessory problems that no Retinol A, AHA or Prozac-enhanced panacea was ever going to sort.

Every modern woman knows the importance of careful accessorising. It's seriously vital stuff after all – the breakthrough of the century. If you want to understand a woman don't study her – study her accessories. Coco Chanel would back me up here. Forget analysts, horoscopes and bank balances, I figure I can pinpoint a woman's personality, profession, marital status and future by a glance at her jewellery, sunglasses and shoes.

This year, like most of the gorgeous young things in London with an overdraft and a Harvey Nichols' store card, I was doing Prada handbags, Gucci loafers, thinking about a pierced navel and saving up for a jacket by Alexander McQueen. Then all of a sudden, before I had given the slightest consideration to the idea, the latest nineties' accessory was mine. And I hadn't even queue-jumped to get it.

One morning I simply woke up and he was there – my stalker.

And not just a variation on the theme either. I mean this bloke had serious cliché cachet. The whole bit – doorway lurking, large felt hat, trainers, trench-coat and knock-off Ray Bans. I wasn't quite sure how to deal with this. For a start I didn't have a clue as to why he came to fixate on me. And – without wanting to downgrade my ability as a kick-boxing black-belt or an independent woman in charge of her G-spot – I was terrified!

I mean I know it's supposed to be like really cool and all – Madonna and Princess Di are hardly seen anywhere without a stalker or two. But let's get real, a stalker of stars is one thing, but what kind of weirdo, no-life saddo wants to follow a relationship-challenged barrister with serious debt status? I had a brown bob for God's sake! This guy had big problems. The word *danger* began to take on a personal significance.

The daylight hours weren't a problem – all he did was hang around outside chambers like a good little obsessive accessory. But alone at night it was a different matter. At first I thought, yeah sure, he'll get cold or bored and go home to his own bed eventually. But he didn't.

Night after night, day after day, he was there. For the last one hundred and twelve hours, actually, this bloke hadn't slept. I know it's a stalkers job to, well, stalk, but this was taking vigilance a bit far. Was he an insomniac or had he just had a lot of practice at dance parties?

I took a peek out the window. Short, heavily built, Littlewood's mac – this bloke had makeover needs that not even Giorgio Armani himself could sort. He didn't look like a party animal either – wrong shoes. Ipso facto my legal brain deduced he must be on some kind of radical upper!

I started to neurose.

Well actually no, I had started to neurose months ago. Going back a bit, it wasn't as if the stalker was the only thing playing havoc with my biorhythms. I had entered a world that no one with an evolved sense of *joie de vivre* would touch with a

2

bargepole. It's called joining the property market. And it shits on war for stress!

Because once you're through the loan application and the gazumping and the mortgage documents and the deeds of sale and you're thinking, phew, well that was ten years off my life but at least it's all over – it hits you. You need to get the builders in.

I was starting to forget what life used to be like before I had half a dozen Irish chippies constantly under my feet. I couldn't move without a 'Bejesus watch where you're stepping, woman'.

Space. That was the word the estate agent had leant on heavily while he flogged this loft to me – as if good old-fashioned 'room' was too outdated, too unhip, too suburban for the Inner London property market. The development brochure spoke hypnotically about light and architectural ambience – glossing over the bit about no kitchen or proper bathroom. There were slick snaps of hip loft-livers in cafés off Clerkenwell Green, knocking back martinis like there was no tomorrow. I was seduced.

The plan was that moving nearer chambers was going to make my life easier. OK, so it cost me every penny NatWest were prepared to lend me, but I believed the bloke from Hartnell Estates when he told me 'proximity is all'.

I thought that even after nights of bacchanalian martini excess, I was going to fire out of bed like one of those human cannonballs – minus the sequins – and notch up litigation and arbitrations like nobody's business. I guess I hadn't counted on the bloodymindedness of the marketing genius who sold me this slab of lead called a futon.

Anyway you looked at it, I had gone into debt for a lifestyle people forge passports to avoid. My clothes and make-up had nowhere to hide and every inch of my two thousand square feet of minimalism was covered with a film of plaster. Every morning I woke up with amnesia. Was this really my life or had I fallen into an Irvine Welsh plot? If so where were the narcotics necessary to face it?

Seriously, this stalker bloke was like the last thing I needed on my plate.

I went to see my GP to increase my Prozac dose. I actually hate my doctor. My grandmother used to call our family doctor her pusher. 'Don't give me your Tin Pan Alley advice,' she'd tell him. 'I want drugs – hard ones!'

The only drugs my last GP had wanted to prescribe though were antibiotics. Doesn't the twentieth century suck? If ever there was a period in history you need sedation to get through, this is it. My new GP wasn't much better. It didn't matter whether I had a broken arm or a belligerent pimple, he didn't even bother to take my temperature before writing me a script for antis. 'Don't you know you're destroying the herd immunity?' I told him.

Anyway, after quite a few battles I finally broke his spirit and he is now pretty pliant about scribbling down words like Prozac and Analgesic on his prescription pad just to get rid of me. I refuse to take over-the-counter drugs such as paracetamol now because I hear they can wipe out your liver, and I am radically receptive to gossip. Basically if you can't buy it outside Paddington station it's either useless or will end up killing you, that's my philosophy.

So anyway, while I was at the doctor's, I decided to do a bit of research on my stalker and his insomnia. I asked casually about drugs that might be used to keep you up at night and about the side effects of lack of sleep. After telling me I wasn't fat enough to warrant diet pills and taking my blood pressure, Dr Dickner wrote out a script for Ritalin.

I had created a monster.

I explained that I didn't want to take Ritalin or any other kind of amphetamine on top of Prozac. 'You need a reality drug,' I told him. 'Even those gypsy women that sell heather at Victoria station can tell you that I need adrenaline *depressants* not stimulants. I live with a scary amount of stress! If I wasn't scared of needles I'd be mainlining Valium.'

Eventually I got him to confess that continued use of drugs like the ones he had just prescribed for me, or even continual lack of sleep, could produce a frightening array of symptoms:

loss of appetite
perspiration
constipation
violent mood swings
and – scariest of all – a short fuse.

That was when I decided to do what any girl with high expectations for the future and end-of-the-millennium neurosis would do. I gave up the fight to stay calm and reasonable. We were hurtling towards the millennium without adequate preparation. I had a man outside my door with the profile of a psychotic killer. Paranoia didn't come close. I started scanning newspapers for stories of stalkers and discovered that I was part of a growing movement of women scared out of their wits because of some loony bloke's fixation. My clerk blamed the Internet.

I stopped going out and stayed home to twitch the blinds and listen to noises. I was too afraid to go out in case his short fuse reached snapping point while I was putting my key in the lock. These were my golden years, I would never be twenty-seven again and I was taking on a lifestyle popular amongst the over sixties. I could hardly sleep. My imagination grazed free-range through horror scenarios Tarantino would pay to option.

Every time I looked out, there he was – lurking, staring through his Ray Bans into my architectural ambience. Basically, my life was being paralysed by a perspiring, constipated bloke prone to violent mood swings. 'So what's new?' my girlfriends said.

My girlfriends Sam and Charles are a lesbian couple I used

to live with when I was going through my 'all men are bastards' phase. I have now officially entered a new stage – my 'all men are bastards but so what some of them know where my G-spot is' stage. The girls asked if I wanted to move back with them. I declined – well they had a kid called Johnny now and my old room had become the nanny's room. At twenty-seven I was too old and too overqualified for sofa surfing.

'What does he want from me anyway?' I asked them. 'Doesn't he have a home to go to?'

'Maybe that's his point – he wants yours?' Sam suggested. 'Like those tramps that stare at you through café windows, you know, dribbling until you can't take it any more and walk out – leaving your pasta for the tramp to nip in and eat. It happened to me the other day in Soho at Café Bohème. Maybe it's like that, only this bloke's after your loft pad not your pasta. Maybe he plans to drive you away – or even kill you – and then squat in your loft!'

So much for friends.

The other piece of advice I received was to call the police. It was a real comedown for the original vigilante kid. Police and lawyers have an unsatisfactory relationship at the best of times. As a criminal barrister working for the defence, I was pretty proud of my ability to break down police evidence in three questions or less. The day I walked into Islington police station was the day they got their revenge.

'You should be flattered, love,' the desk rookie joked.

I told him to look in my eyes and watch his life rushing through my synapse. I was eventually upgraded to a sergeant who had his sympathy stripes. First he got me to admit that my stalker had never attempted to approach me or attack me or insult me. He hadn't even sent me a note. Then Sergeant Plugg looked genuinely disappointed as he told me that my stalker wasn't committing a crime.

'You're telling me that lurking isn't a crime? Go and take a look at him yourself,' I said. 'That Littlewood's mac he's wearing is a crime.'

'We are still waiting for legislation,' he explained.

'Well that's a comfort. What if he takes to me and stages a frenzied attack with an axe in the meantime?'

He agreed that a direct assault on my person with an axe was a police matter. He told me that in that instance I should give him a call. 'In the meantime we can have a word with him but at the end of the day it's not a crime to watch other people.' He raised his eye-brows as if to suggest that this freedom was the equivalent to the first amendment.

I rang up my analyst.

'Try to keep it in perspective,' she told me. 'Until the guy actually does something you really have no need to worry.'

'But I'm a panicker not a waiter,' I told her. 'I'm impatient, vulnerable and sensitive. You charged me money to tell me that stuff, you idiot! Stuff like I have an innate fear of men causing me pain. Well, one of them is outside on the street now, ready and willing to cause that pain this very minute.'

She then diagnosed me as suffering end of the millennium neurosis again and hung up the phone.

I rang her back and told her she was fired. The bill arrived the next day. It had a sticker on the corner – one of those smiley faces that you get on Ecstasy tabs and a small note on a *with compliments* slip saying that she was sorry that my destiny was not cooperating with my dreams. This philosophical gem took me half a bottle of vodka to digest.

By day ten I was having trouble talking to people about anything other than my stalker. I knew I was driving potential allies away but I couldn't help myself. I was his obsession and he was mine. I rang up my parents in Australia a hundred times but I hung up as soon as they answered. I didn't want to worry them, after all what could they do? But I did want to worry someone.

I guess the fact is that tea and sympathy are thin on the

ground in London, a city that's got its hands pretty much full with terrorists, tourists and a dilapidated tube system. Some people even hinted that I should be grateful for the attention. Some people asked me what he looked like. When I assured them that Hugh Grant had nothing to worry about, they reasoned that the guy was probably just an admirer and completely harmless. I should be flattered. You're moving up in the world, girl – inner city loft apartment and the accessory of the rich and famous.

The QC in chambers, Candida, hinted that she could have had a stalker many times over, but in the end she couldn't be bothered.

'We're talking about a stalker here not something you can buy from the Harrods' pet department!' I reasoned with her.

Anyway I think it was clear I was running low on options, which is the only justification I can offer for the absurdity of my next action – ringing up my ex for an argument. Somehow I reasoned that if I could get the stereo back off my old boyfriend it would at least be a victory of sorts. Then I could drown out my fear with the sounds of my generation. I would blast my stalker off the block with the music of Pulp, Sleeper and Oasis.

CHAPTER TWO

i was fighting above my disputation weight.

The bastard said no.

'Have you got PMT or something?' he patronised.

I reacted like the sane, professional, assured woman that I am and totally flipped. Ouch! I hate it when men get technical with my hormones. Information like that should be classified. What sell-out bitch ever told men about our periods anyway? They use this kind of info like women use a kick to the groin. The thing was he was right.

The first tear fell – and even though I'm normally as dry-eyed as your average sophisticated girl, I thought to hell with it. Let them fall! I mean, it wasn't as if I'd applied my mascara yet.

Actually, getting down to it, I hadn't applied very much at all. Apart from a bit of chipped nail-varnish, I was stark-ovary-naked, at the far end of my loft shell, on the toilet to be precise, on my mobile with nothing but the disembodied voice of the ultimate super-bastard for company. And now as the tears trickled down my face, I discovered I was also bereft of loo paper.

Get a grip, Evelyn, I told myself sniffling back the tears. You've read *The Feminist Mystique*. Let's face it I've read more books about being a woman with a clitoris than you can shake a phallus at, thank you very much. So why was I empowering this man with my vulnerability then?

I was a woman on the edge, that's why! Every long red nail I had ever cherished was broken, my hair was a deranged mess and a fine film of dust had settled into all my pores. On top of that I had a flat full of Irish chippies most days and at night I was being watched by a constipated bloke on uppers who could go bananas at any minute.

'And anyway I'll use *my* stereo how I like if you don't mind!' Giles summed up grandly, as if performing for a jury. He was a barrister too – only he had full cliché cachet, unlike me. When we were still together, we'd be at a party and people would ask him what he did. And I'd be thinking, you have to ask this man what he does? Isn't his pompous, tendentious demeanour enough? Do you honestly think this man could make his way in the world as anything other than a lawyer?

God, this guy was a jerk. My tears retreated. He wasn't worth wasting such valuable emotional artillery on. 'Oh right, so you bought Elastica and Pulp for yourself? Is that it?' I asked, thinking I had him by the testes. This bloke only listened to the William Tell Overture and Purcell – and then only when he was drunk.

And to think I once thought his musical predilections, or lack thereof, were eccentric and cute. I should have listened to Gran – nothing involving men with trumpets is *cute*.

I could tell by his silence that he was floored by this line of questioning so I grabbed at my advantage.

'Besides, I left you the television!'

'Rented,' he riposted smugly.

'Well, what about the curtains then?'

'They came with the place.'

'The toaster didn't!' (I was getting desperate.)

'My mother gave it to me.'

Basically I was squabbling with a mooting black-belt. This was a man who thought jurisprudence was fun, that the *English Law Reports* were light reading, who spent Christmas watching the O.J. Simpson trial tapes. You're fighting above your disputation weight again, I told myself. Move onto the emotional stuff – he's like a totally monosyllabic oaf in that realm. They didn't do *feelings* at Harrow.

Despite my better judgement I told him about the stalker.

He let out a groan and I knew what was coming before he said it.

'Well, why don't you come back here?' He used his kindly patriarch voice. He was like a truffle pig when it came to sniffing out a disadvantage. What he didn't know was that I'd rather eat a cow's spinal cord than go back to him.

'Gee what a great idea – I could sign over my vote to you while I'm at it, couldn't I?' I replied. A cold tear from earlier drizzled sadly down my belly.

'Oh, Evvy, don't be mad. Don't sacrifice your safety for this ridiculous quest for independence of yours.' I noticed the way he sort of choked on the last word – spitting it out like it was some kind of cyanide capsule he was paranoid would explode in his mouth and kill him.

His problem was he thought I was his true love. Which doesn't sound so bad until you put the emphasis heavily on the word *his*. Words like chattel didn't sound ironic when Giles said them. If I complained about being overworked it was always, 'Well you could always give up the Bar and look after me.' Gee thanks, nerd features. What a like absolutely riveting proposition. Why didn't Germaine Greer think of that?

Fact: Giles was a dated, self-centred nerd. Forget new-ladism, this bloke was an old fart. Everyone knew it but until I left him no-one dared say it. 'I wouldn't worry about it, even his name sounds like something you might find up your bum,' my receptionist told me supportively the day we broke up.

Maybe after all the macho posturing of Aussie men I was looking for a man with old-fashioned values – that was what my last therapist told me during one of our ninety-pounds-an-hour sessions. Obviously I sacked her too.

'Get a grip!' I had told her, jumping off the couch in her surgery. Besides the fact that she was wrong, I don't pay my analyst to give me advice. My hairdresser Stefan can do that. I pay my analyst to suck up to me and to pamper my baser nature. We Catholics call it our venial side. And after seven years of an on/off relationship with Giles, my venial side was getting pretty damn needy.

The parting of the ways finally came with his insteps. You know those foamy things nurses put in their shoes and osteopaths talk about with stars in their eyes? It just sort of triggered something off in me. He started wearing them because his feet got tired standing around in court all day. 'Give me a break! I manage to do it in six inch stilettos. You think my feet don't ache?' I asked him. No pain, no gain, as Gran always said.

Anyway, call me petty, but those insteps became the symbol of all the cloying boredom of our relationship. Soon after the insteps he started hinting darkly about children and I lost it big time. The thought of genetically reproducing this man with arch problems made my orifices curl up round the edges.

My trip down memory reclaim had to be put on hold though because I had heard a noise. A sort of thump – like my colon hitting the floor. I suddenly regretted that I hadn't taken up the Aid Abroad work in Angola while I still had the chance.

'Are you still there, Evelyn? Evelyn?' I heard Giles asking. But another loud crashing sound at the other end of my loft threw me into a verbal coma. I closed the phone and froze. Something was very seriously wrong.

Running over the seminal points in my mind – my present circumstances weren't all they could be. I was naked. I was sitting on the toilet with no loo paper – more noticeably with no surrounding walls. Outside was a man who hadn't slept or shat for a week. And all the while the banging sounds were getting closer . . . and closer. The mobile started ringing. I wanted to throw it but it was the only weapon I had. I had never felt so bereft of Mace in my life.

This was it – my stalker's big moment. He had finally taken one too many of those Ritalins and lost it. He was on his way to repossess. And here I was without so much as a built-in to hide out in – or even a window I could reach. I promised to start going to mass at the Brompton Oratory again.

I clasped my hands to my chest as the *bbrr-bbbrrrr-bbrr-bbbrrrr* of the phone alerted my would-be homicidal maniac to my whereabouts. I opened the mouthpiece and told whoever it was to fuck off because I was about to be slaughtered. Then I turned around to face the steel-capped boots of my attacker. Only it wasn't my attacker, it was my builder.

'Morning, Miss Evelyn, wonderful weather we're having for June,' he chortled cheerfully, as if finding his employer stark-ovary-naked, prostrate by the toilet on a mobile phone was all part of life's rich tapestry to the men of Kerry.

'Yeah right, Paddy,' I replied dryly. 'That's probably what some smart arse soothsayer said to Joan of Arc on the morning they lit the match.'

CHAPTER THREE

he was wearing a body-hugging psychedelic shirt over ball-breaking pinstriped vivienne westwood bondage trousers.

I'd had to knock back a week's worth of Prozac just to get into work that day. The recommended dose was one a day but Gran always told me only losers follow instructions – just the same I felt a bit queasy.

Vinny, our head bore in chambers, was loitering around the clerk's room hoping for a chance to make small talk. He's one of those blokes that's getting some practice in before he takes up his next position with the firm that provides all those mumbling mad people on the tube. He grabbed me in an ear-vice the minute I walked in.

Warren, our head clerk, was on the phone with one hand over his ear to block out Vinny's chatter. The football was on the radio – England were winning but I searched for diversion in Warren's phone call. He was selling our latest tenant, Orlando Porter-Meade, to Clifford Chance – extolling Orlando's virtues as a serious-minded counsel. This was madly far-fetched – the sort of stuff surrealist dreams are made of actually. Surely I'd misheard? Maybe it was the Prozac.

Candida, who'd taken silk after my last case at the Bailey,

hates Orlando. When I suggested once that he added colour to
our set, she suggested that a bleeding wound around his heart
area would add even more. She was nowhere in sight at the
moment or I'd have to pretend that Orlando was a stranger
to me – it being more than my life was worth to be caught
cavorting with her sworn enemy.

Candida constantly reminded those of us who would listen,
and even those of us who wouldn't actually, that there was no
place in 17 Pump Court for a man like Orlando. Which was
irrational anyway you looked at it. He was here – a fully fledged
member of our set – superglued to his tenancy like a Navaho
Indian to his moccasin.

But she was tenacious – it goes with the CV. 'We were
tricked!' she told us with alarming regularity. She'd whisper
it in his ear as she passed him where he was sashaying around
the library with his Walkman. And we had been really. He had
worn a sober pinstripe suit from Gieves & Hawkes throughout
his pupillage, before emerging from this chrysalis as a Ministry
of Sound bunny once we'd granted him tenancy.

We just took a cursory look at his degree from Cambridge
and his competition – a pimply graduate who shredded tissues
throughout his interview and a lady who lunched. In fact 'the
luncher' came within a hair's breadth of getting the place, but
in her final interview she explained that she only became a
barrister because her husband thought it would save him legal
bills (hee-haw-hee-haw!).

Even at that point we were still keen. She blew her chances
by mentioning that she wouldn't be available for court on
Tuesdays or Thursdays because that was when she met all
the girls at Daphne's – haw-haw.

Candida was in Monaco (with that mad, mad, extravagant
duke of hers) when we voted for Orlando and ever since she's
been trying to hatch a plan to destroy him. But he was going
to prove a tougher nut than me to crack – besides Orlando
had the backing of the rest of chambers. Warren liked him

because he had family links to Mossad which brought in a lot of work and everyone else liked him because he was so unerringly enthusiastic all the time.

He walked in now as I was sending off a fax to my bank – asking them politely to put off repossessing my loft. He was wearing a body-hugging psychedelic shirt over ball-breaking pinstriped Vivienne Westwood bondage trousers. Orlando wasn't so much high camp as high. Straight – but only sexually as far as I'd observed.

'Evelyn. You excellent woman!' he said, planting a moist kiss on my cheek the way old aunts do when they've been hitting the advocaat too hard.

I noticed Warren colouring visibly at our display of luvvie behaviour in the clerk's room.

'How are you, Orlando,' I asked, even though his answer was always the same.

'Inexorably, unutterably, superb, Evelyn. In fact simply superb.'

'So scrap the inexorable and unutterable part then?'

'Touché, Evelyn! An excellent touché!'

'Ah good, Porter-Meade,' Vinny interrupted. 'I was just telling Evelyn here about the remarkable advantage our Internet server has over CompuServe.'

'Piss off, Vins, there's a good man,' Orlando urged. He somehow manages to sound very in charge when he's not talking like an out-of-work Shakespearean actor. I was desperate to see him in court sometime to see which tone he used before the bench.

Vin shuffled over to have a sulky poke around the briefs on Warren's desk while Orlando led me aside. 'So listen, Evelyn, who's that shabby chap in the mac outside? I saw him following you down the street yesterday. He's out there now and looking damn threatening if you don't mind my saying.'

'Oh that's my stalker,' I said as breezily as I could given the fact that I'd spent most of last night in a lather of panic as his figure dipped in and out of the shadows of Clerkenwell Green. It was getting a bit embarrassing actually having this bloke tailing me like a bad smell around the Temple. People were beginning to talk. I was sailing dangerously close to getting a warning from Warren about him. For some reason, I couldn't seem to convince people that I hadn't got this stalker voluntarily, on mail order or something.

'You mean a real stalker? Like really glamorous people have? How cool! How inexorably excellent. What an unutterably outrageous accessory,' he drooled – like I'd just revealed the effects of a new drug to him or something. 'How'd you get him?'

'Well he came of his own free will but—'

'Cooooool!'

'It's not a bit coooool, Orlando, in fact it's all a bit bloody hairy actually. Especially at night. I hear every bump. And—'

Warren banged his hand on the desk. 'Do you think you could continue this discussion outside? I'm trying to discuss fees here and I'd prefer to do it with a bit of quiet.' There was a disappointed silence on the television as Spain scored a goal.

CHAPTER FOUR

dream on, your lordships.

Miss Candida Raphael QC, known to my friends variously as
The Anti-Girlfriend, The Super Bitch, The Virus or simply That
Cow, was in my room when I got there. Sitting on my desk,
peering at my private papers – as is her wont basically. I still
hated her like a vampire hates the sun but we'd settled on a kind
of détente since those early days when she'd tried to squeeze
me out of chambers with erroneous rumours about my being
a lesbian.

Candida's one of the old breed of women barristers who think
of the Bar as a gentlemen's club they had to claw their way into.
They don't fancy this new breed of female barrister who thinks
it's their God given right to be treated fairly. She had made my
time in chambers murder for the first few months – now she was
happy to settle for plain old Grievous Mental Harm – GMH.

Since taking silk, she's realised that instructing another
woman in the Royal Courts of Justice made for a formidable
team – especially when we're talking Mr Justice Hingewood
or Threep-Smith or any of the other major sexually challenged
wigs on the bench.

Those boys were sitting ducks for our charms. The bigger
their prejudice, the harder we batted our lashes and the higher
we wore our heels. By six inches, we were invincible – all they
could do was dribble. Not only does commercial law offer far
more financial incentive than criminal cases, there is much more
scope for a woman with flair.

With a jury you must stoop to conquer but in commercial law there's just a judge – usually old, quite often with gout, haemorrhoids or prostate problems – who thinks that life's challenges ended the day he sat down on the bench. Dream on, Your Lordships.

Watching their solemn faces collapsing into little puddles of perspiration as Candida's bouffant or, dare I say, my brown bob came peeking out from under our wigs was what I came to the Bar for.

Being of essentially soundish mind, I was happy to be *led* away from Snaresbrook Crown Court and ABH in exchange for watching the back of Candida's neck in the Royal Courts of Justice. My brief dream of quoting Keats down the Bailey soon dissipated after putting my life and soul into defending a man going by the name of Keith of Shepherd's Bush and then getting a cheque three months later that wouldn't pay a cab fare to Harvey Nicks.

I was young, I could take a knock, but being beaten about the bank balance by Legal Aid was more than I could bear. When Gran warned me that crime doesn't pay, it was an understatement. As soon as Candida cast off her old stuff gown for a silk, I said, 'Lead on, Candy baby!'

'So, Evelyn,' she purred. 'I've just had Matt Barton's solicitor on the phone. As anticipated, it's game on for the Mareva Injunction. Apparently the plaintiff has sent him a letter gloating. Bit mad, but there it is. He wants another conference to discuss it with us. So I suggested this afternoon.'

She was a woman who always looked like the cat who'd just broken into the cream carton so I didn't take particular notice of the way she was licking her lips and smiling lasciviously.

'So? Why's that require a con?' I asked stupidly. I was still thinking in terms of legal aid budgets where every meeting with a client has to be justified. I hadn't quite got my calculator around this commercial law game but the basic rule is that if the client's paying, he or she can have a conference as often as they like. Our meters were always running.

'Can't he just hand the letter over to his solicitor? Our next step surely is to apply to have the terms varied?' I was like the new prostitute on the block trying to talk her client out of wasting money on 'extras'.

I noticed that Candida was looking at me like priests do when you chew your host at Communion. Hello! her look seemed to say. We're talking about Matt Sex-On-Legs Barton here.

I blushed. Matt was our most beloved client. He was defending a private suit being brought by a woman – whom we suspected to be his ex-lover – who claimed that he had misrepresented the risks in failed unhedged investments he had made on her behalf. Her claim as plaintiff was that he had breached his fiduciary duty to inform her of the risk. Our legal retort was 'have you got a brain?' although because we were charging so much we were saying it in Latin.

Fraud is always a tricky one and in this case, where the facts were obfuscated by a relationship other than the fiduciary, it all came down to style. In short, it depended on our ability to charm the judge. Problem was, it was hard to focus on judges when the defendant was a walking talking Ken doll like Matt. I mean he probably had a brain too, but I had an IBM compatible for that. The fact was he was unattached and not gay. Which for a single girl in London spells 'tie him down and have your way. Quick!'

'Oh I get it,' I said, realising my mistake. 'Of course. Let's con our little hearts off. Get Warren to polish the room and get Lee to stick the Mouton Rothschild on ice,' I breezed. We giggled like errant school girls caught nicking underwear for a dare.

I knew I was committing the first error of dealing with Candida – relaxing. I was treating her like a fellow woman colleague and not the anti-girlfriend I knew she was. Big mistake. Huge as they say, but I was dizzy with the thrill of another meeting with Matt. I couldn't stop myself.

'He drinks claret,' she sneered eventually. I was well on the way to making a complete ovary of myself. Candida switched on my notebook and started reading my e-mail. I should have shut up, I knew I should, but I didn't.

'Oh, we had a boy in Kirribilli that drank claret on ice. He was gorgeous!' I gushed – all my barriers down now. 'When it was mid winter he'd wear his T-shirt and when it was a hundred degrees he'd wear a jumper.'

Candida looked up at me like she wished I would just swallow my tongue and die.

'It's called perverse psychology,' I expounded.

She gave me a smarmy look that my generation has to take third-world-debt loads of cocaine to perfect and then she looked out the window as if she was very, very bored. Following her gaze I caught a glimpse of my stalker eating a hamburger across the street and I found myself dwelling on his digestion again. What I needed was a Tardis or another century. That was my problem, I was made for another time, another era – a millennium where vulnerable people like me ruled and people like Candida, my stalker, and my ex-boyfriend swept the streets and gave me pedicures.

'Well, Evelyn, I'm afraid I just don't have the time to sit around and chat about your school days with you.'

That was Candida all over. My best defence was rigid formality at all times but whenever I was around her, I lost it. I tried to gather what was left of my self-esteem and adopted an overworked, busy pose with a pile of briefs. She tapped her blood-red, acrylic talons on the desk. I started undoing a pink ribbon and looked up at her with a look which was meant to say, Oh so you're still here then? But I may as well have dribbled and asked for a lobotomy for all the good it did me.

'You really should take a look in the mirror sometime, Evelyn. I don't always like to be the one to tell you that you look a fright.' She frowned, as if telling me I looked a fright was another one of the great burdens she carried. 'You look like you've just walked off a building site. And I mean it's not as if you have far to go. Heavens, I commute all the way from Hampstead – and look immaculate for my troubles, I might add. Whereas you . . . Well, just try and smarten yourself up before eleven.'

I pressed the Escape button on my PC and waited hopelessly for something incredible to change my life.

CHAPTER FIVE

my clitoris flew
through my g-string like a
ping-pong ball.

I could smell Matt's scent in the corridor before I even reached the conference room. Moschino – as in zany, sexy, alluring and rich, especially the rich part. This bloke wouldn't know a mortgage if he fell over one. I closed my eyes and breathed it in. Forget the fact that last time I smelt this perfume I had told the girl at the counter at HN that it smelt like the Edgware Road on a Friday night.

I don't know why I was so attracted to Matt – a man way beyond my age belt. God he must be forty or close to fifty even. Normally I go for men just out of Pampers – before they get into their full ego stride. There was just something about his languorous style that made my clitoris shoot through my G-string like a ping-pong ball every time I saw him.

I knew I shouldn't be having thoughts like this about a client, but it was pretty unavoidable where Matt was concerned. OK, so he had a ponytail, but I was prepared to give and take because he had something that neither his age nor his ponytail could take away. Matt was *suave* and there isn't a lot of that going around my generation. We were given vaccination shots against it when we were kids, along with chivalry and chastity. We were the unrefined generation, born raw and keen and prepared to fight for what we want.

Basically he was the ultimate manifestation of sex appeal

and I felt as awkward as hell around him. Like the suave, sophisticated gentleman he was he pretended not to notice. 'Yeah, I'll give it a berl,' he laughed when I blunderingly offered him sugar for his wine.

Nor was I alone. Candida and Matt's solicitor, Jackie Watters, her mouth full of the Fortnum and Mason biscuits Vinny had voted against at the last chambers meeting, were gog-eyed, mouths open as if waiting to receive the Eucharist. If this guy had undone his fly then and there, we would have been on him like a back of piranhas – no questions asked.

Poor, dear, deluded Matt thought we were spellbound with his case though. That's men all over – they think they're the only ones on the planet with a sex drive. Before the meeting was half finished my attention span was lost to the law. I may as well have studied card tricks.

By the time he had knocked back his second glass of sweetened claret I had developed X-ray vision and convinced myself I could see the Calvin Klein waistband on his undies. It didn't help that he had a really distracting habit of stroking things while he talked – his Camel Lights mostly. He wasn't so much a smoker as a stroker – they were his prop. My therapist calls it subliminal replacement. He thought he was stroking his cigs – I was fantasising he was stroking me.

When he asked me to explain what the Mareva Injunction would mean for him, I turned pathetically to Candida for help and said, 'That's, um, something to do with, er, thingamies isn't it?'

She didn't miss a beat. 'Interlocutory injunctions? Yes that's right, Evelyn. A Mareva Injunction ensures assets aren't spirited away before judgement is handed down.'

I tried to look involved by swinging my head around on its axis, like one of those plastic dogs on the orange-fur dashboards of Ford Sierras. He sipped at his wine and nodded. Pay attention, I told myself, this man is paying thousands of pounds for your attention, girl. Startle him with your jurisprudence, show him there's more to you than sugared wine and tongue lolling.

'Mareva Injunctions don't necessarily reflect the judgement and, given that you are not domiciled in the UK and considering the large sum of money involved, I'm not surprised that it's been granted. We can however apply to have the terms varied.'

'Yeah absolutely. We'll vary the, er, thingamies,' I added.

Matt looked out from under his sandy lashes and winked at me. He now had the Camel packet open and my eyes watered as he trailed his long brown finger seductively over the neatly aligned filters.

Tell me my hormones were mutating due to global warming, but the way he caressed those cigarettes made my cervix open up like I was about to give birth.

'Sorry, Candida, I was distracted. By vary the terms you mean?'

'Get you a larger allowance.'

'Well, Miss Raphael, you say the sweetest things.' He laughed, but he was looking into my eyes as he spoke. At least he made me feel like he was looking into my eyes, even if he wasn't.

'Like I said, money is not the issue with me. I'm a single man from the suburbs of Sydney. I can live on the smell of an oily rag if I have to. This case isn't about money.'

'It isn't?' we sang, Candida, his solicitor and I looking around the room for the camera.

'No. The reason Mitzy has brought this suit is because she's cheesed off with me for losing interest – in her, not her money. If I can be honest here?'

We nodded stupidly.

'I sell ideas not bonds. It's a social thing with me – I choose my clients, not the other way around. I like someone, I trade for them. I liked Mitzy, a lot. Well you've seen the letter.'

We all turned our attention to the letter, lying amongst the papers in front of his solicitor. It was covered in crumbs now. It was more a personally insulting diatribe than a letter actually.

Put it this way, I couldn't imagine wanting to rely on it in court. It made some pretty scathing comparisons between his bedside manner and that of a Guatemalan goat herd. If I was Matt I would have eaten it rather than shown it around.

'And you feel the relationship's failure is the reason she's brought this suit rather than financial losses?' Candida asked.

'That's right. I had total control over that account for months, I could have churned it for all it was worth.'

'Churned it?'

'Kept turning it over – as in pocketing commission – eventually exhausting it. Anyway there was nothing like that. But when I started to lose interest in her she started making unhedged trades, just to goad me I reckon. She did that on the advice of some sleazy Spaniard she met on a plane or something. I wanted to get away but she was talking about shit like writing naked calls, which is basically open-ended liability.'

'So you're saying she didn't lose her money on your advice?'

'No way. The opposite. I advised her strongly not to get involved. She was convinced it was fine but she didn't have a clue, she was acting on the advice of this Spanish bloke. He should be here now not me. I thought she was just trying to wind me up when she told me what she'd done, I didn't think even she could be that stupid.'

I knew that this was crucial stuff he was telling us but I was only watching his mouth and from lip-reading it looked like, 'OK, open your legs and I'll rim your vagina, Miss Hornton.'

I had to stop this lip-reading. For one he wasn't paying me for my lip-reading service, he was paying me for top-drawer legal advice. This was serious shit for him and the last thing he probably wanted was his barrister's libido taking her attention AWOL.

'I told her. "Look, Mitzy, this shit is gamma radiated, don't get involved. This Rico cove, what does he know? All he's got to sell are Italian bonds." But she wasn't interested. I mean, you've got to believe me this woman was gagging for it. Money I mean.

She wanted to do something reckless to make me sit up and take notice. You've got to believe me,' he told us emphatically.

'We believe you, Matt,' his solicitor assured him, giving his wrist a comforting squeeze which left a biscuit crumb bracelet on his sleeve.

We all nodded. 'That's right, Mr Barton, of course we believe you,' Candida and I chorused. Oh we believed him all right. We would have believed him if he'd said he was the Messiah and asked us to follow him down to the canyon to eat peyote seeds.

'Well, Mr Barton . . .' Candida started.

'Call me Matt – really, I can't be doing with this mister business. It gives me the creeps, know what I mean?' He gave us a knowing, guileless grin. 'Matt please! I'm a Sydney boy. Darlinghurst born and bred. Evelyn'll know what I mean here when I say "Mister's" not a term I'm entirely comfortable with.' I nodded sagely to signify I understood deeply.

I never thought I'd see the day when Candida fawned, but there we were – her eyelashes were flapping like cat-flaps and her lips had gone all sort of dissolvable. 'Of course, Matt, you clearly gave this woman all the advice you could, *caveat emptor* and all that,' she simpered. His solicitor nodded, her cheeks bulging with calories.

'We had a bit of a thing as you've no doubt worked out, but in the end it was only the money that mattered to her.' He sighed, looking pensively at the cigarettes. Our hearts went out to him.

He had slipped his forefinger under the cellophane wrapper of the packet. I felt my panty elastic strain. The moment was spoilt though when Mrs Watters started to gag on a biscuit and we were forced to sit in nervous silence for a moment, listening to a custard cream going the wrong way down her throat. 'Mr Barton has been emotionally stretched by all this,' she choked – a few biscuit crumbs scattering about her chin. We looked at her like she'd sprung a leak. I mean this was a man's feelings we were talking about not a lycra body.

'I think I'll bear up,' he chuckled, giving me another wink.

'Look, Mr Barton ... Matt, your case is this,' Candida explained. 'You had complete discretion over her account. She didn't give you that discretion without knowing the risks. As far as I can see she hasn't got a case. Notwithstanding the advice of this Spaniard chap, it would appear that she's taken her losses personally. I think this letter will satisfy the judge on that front. All we need to prove is that you gave full disclosure of all the risks involved.'

We all looked at Matt reassuringly. Candida was good at what she did although I thought she was barking if she truly intended to use the letter as evidence.

'I'm not in a position to give guarantees, Matt, but you are right to be defending this suit with everything you've got. This Mareva Injunction is unfortunately a fairly standard procedure – I'd be surprised if her lawyers didn't insist on it. We'll apply to have the injunction discharged but, regardless of that, we'll make sure that you are granted adequate living expenses according to your lifestyle. The aim is to freeze your assets so you don't squirrel them away, not to punish you before judgement is handed down.'

'Well, as long as I can still afford my Camels, I guess I'll cope,' he joked, giving me a sidelong glance. Talk about cool – this guy was dazzling. Here he was with this bitch suing the pants off him. By the sounds of it she'd already had his pants off, which amounted to a pleasure worth a few million.

As far as I was concerned this woman was the luckiest bitch alive. I couldn't wait for the showdown, I was going to have her ovaries in court. But Matt wasn't calling for her impalement, he was shrugging and nodding and taking this Mareva Injunction on the proverbial chin. What a man! I was so bloody moved I wanted to sing the Australian national anthem for him. Only I couldn't remember how it went.

Eventually his solicitor finished off the last biscuit and interrupted with a false cough. 'Well, I think that should do for now,' she said, gathering up her papers and shaking them free of crumbs.

Matt put his cigarettes into his jacket pocket as he stood up. His creased Nicole Farhi suggested a cool relaxed carelessness of which I heartily approved. Being objective, of course, I would have heartily approved if he'd worn a polyester safari suit, but, seriously, I don't like my men to be too obsessed about their looks. Or even about themselves really. I don't like men who take bubble baths for instance, or men that spend every spare moment at the gym – it denotes an arrogance, a self-interest that doesn't generally make for good sex.

I fell for a solicitor like that once – Mr Body-beautiful. He turned out to be gay – only slept with me as a favour. 'Welcome to the nineties,' my receptionist had said. 'All the sexiest-looking blokes are gay.' Yeah and all the sexiest woman aren't, my lesbian girlfriend added.

'Well, ladies, as always, a pleasure. Let's do it again some-time?' he teased, as if we'd just been on a date – well it felt like it. He shook our hands and turned towards the wall, as if he was considering walking through it.

This was it! I could feel it in my bones – any second he was going to turn around, throw his arms around me and declare undying love and stuff. I knew it, I knew it, I knew it. He pointed to the wall – well to this painting thingamie really. I'd never taken much notice of it before, our head of chambers' wife had bought it. She was on every art committee in this city and placed it on our *simply must have* list. Actually, I remembered the receipt better than the painting. It cost the equivalent of four pretty decent frocks – or two weeks' pay for my builders.

'Fiona Ray,' he announced finally.

'Are you an art lover, Matt?' Candida gushed.

'A connoisseur you mean? No, my taste runs to the slightly more eclectic. I like my art to shock me a bit more – you know as in jolt my focus!' He clapped his hands hard in front of her face.

Was he insane? No one did anything in front of Candida's face – hell, even breathing was a risk in front of this Lucrezia

Borgia. I hoped for his sake he had a taster. But then she laughed.

I almost fainted.

'I like that, Matt – "jolt your focus"! What an excellent expression, I must remember that. Jolt the focus – very good,' she enthused, virtually grafting herself to his body.

'This is a good piece though,' he went on. 'I saw it for sale at Waddington's last year in . . . October wasn't it? Yes, I considered it for my own collection. What about you, Miss Hornton – what are your thoughts on Fiona's work?'

Ah, now he had me. You know that feeling hostages get when the guard comes in with a machete – and it's not shaving day. Art? I mean wasn't he a Garfunkel? Gi'me a break here God – I don't do art. Now if he wanted to talk about graduated fees in the Crown Court or the law of precedent, I'd be right there, ranting on about constitutional procedure like there was no tomorrow. As in, get a life, you sad barrister.

I wanted to tell the truth and put my hand up for the Philistine Club, but I sensed that wasn't going to cut the grass with Matt. He was looking down on me like Moses waiting for the sea to part while I became vividly aware of how little attention I'd given my skin lately and how shabby my suit looked. OK so it was DKNY, but it needed an iron as much as I needed a crash course in contemporary art at this moment.

Get real, what would a guy like Matt see in a gangly woman with D-cups and about as much cultural finesse as a copy of Archbold? I had put sugar in his claret and now I was about to jolt his focus with the sheer all-encompassingness of my ignorance.

'Art? Phew! You've more or less hit on my favourite topic there, Matt. Hey, don't get me onto art or we'll be here all day. In fact my focus is still out after the last art jolt I gave it, so to speak.'

Matt put his head back and laughed. His Adam's apple, jiggling about his throat like a tea-bag in a transport café, gave me a clitoral hard-on.

CHAPTER SIX

i know the next millennium is just around the corner but I've only just this minute got my wardrobe ready to face the seventies.

I woke up on Saturday and remembered that I was in lust with Matt but as a client he was out of bounds. Matt The Out Of Bounds? I mean give me a break – it sounded like a horror film I might watch if I needed to terrorise my adrenaline. Not that I needed to pay for a fright with this stalker bloke watching me day and night.

In fact he was outside now as I was cleaning my teeth, lurking amongst the photo labs cum coffee shops, warehouses, magazine headquarters, art supply shops and BMWs that make Clerkenwell the area that it is. As usual he was adhering strictly to the etiquette laid down in the stalker's guidebook – trench coat, black felt hat and shadow lurking. Every rule except discretion that is – he may as well have been erecting a neon sign announcing his presence for all the attention he was grabbing. Passers-by were actually looking up at me to see what the fascination was.

But enough of my stalker. At least I was learning to live with *him*. It was Matt that had kept me awake the last few nights. I mean how could I jolt his focus without compromising my professional role as his counsel?

'OK, so tell me I've got it wrong again,' I had said to my girlfriends. 'Tell me he's wearing a placard reading "Beware of the Bastard – perpetrator of great evils at large".'

'He sounds great,' Charles had said, bouncing baby Johnny on her knee. 'It's about time you had some romantic distraction.'

A mobile rang somewhere and we stopped talking as we shuffled through our respective bags. I found mine first and embarrassed myself by saying, 'Hello! Hello!' a few times before realising that it wasn't mine that had been ringing.

'Oh yeah, like I haven't just managed to extricate myself from a romantic distraction for the last six months!' I continued while Sam wandered into the loo with her phone. Paddy had erected a makeshift screen after our last embarrassing meeting there.

'That's love, not romance, idiot,' Charles differentiated while Sam blabbered away frantically in indecent figures to some trader type person in the loo.

'OK, but how do I go about seducing him? He *is* my client remember. My professionalism as a barrister is at stake here,' I explained self-importantly.

Charles looked at me like I'd just offered to change little Johnny's nappy – a mixture of disbelief and fear crossed her face. 'Professional what?' she asked horrified. 'This is nineteen ninety seven, girl. Read the *Sun* – even QCs are doing it. Besides we are talking about sex, not arms dealing! He's being sued for God's sake. He's not been charged with anything. Get a grip on the millennium, girl.'

Charles was always saying stuff like that. It was all right for her – she had a grip on the millennium, she was born knowing what to do with a Pentium processing chip and stuff like that. I mean look at her hair, never a strand out of place on that bleached blonde crop. She was going to slide into the next century like an oyster down the throat of an heiress.

I groaned. 'That's my problem, Charles. I haven't got a grip on my era. I know that the year two thousand is just around the corner, but I've only just adjusted my wardrobe for the seventies. I'm not ready for the next millennium any more than I'm ready for the latest accessory. I'm not even sure how to use the remote control that came with the microwave. I pointed it at the thing the other day and made one of the Irish chippies' radio go off.'

She laughed. 'Chill out will you. All men like you. You're flaky.'

I slumped into one of the red velvet vulva chairs the girls had given me as a thank you for getting them the sperm for their beloved offspring Johnny. They had been worried about their baby slipping into one of the velvet orifices and getting stuck. Like, can you imagine the therapy bills in later life? 'Doctor, my problem is that my lesbian mothers lost me down a velvet vulva when I was a baby.' Serious!

Charles was sprawled out on a rug, holding Johnny above her – linked by a long trail of saliva. He kicked his chubby legs joyfully. I had one of those stabbing sensations of guilt that I get whenever I look at small children. The one that says I never want to have one. The one that competes with my DNA, screaming in my ear, 'PROCREATE OR DIE!'

'Well find a common interest and use it as a flirt tool,' she suggested.

'Take the testosterone host into my own hands you mean?'

'What are his interests?'

'Art. He said he likes to have his focus jolted,' I told her.

'His what?'

'His focus.'

'You mean like vertical hold?'

'I guess he means he likes to be surprised.'

'Well there you go. Surprising people is what you do best, Evvy. Just be yourself.'

'He's into art. I think he hangs out in that gallery scene.'

'So bluff.'

'Yeah right, and like I know enough about art to bluff. He doesn't want bluff anyway, he wants his focus jolted.'

'So tell him you and Damien Hirst used to drink whisky together down in Hoxton.'

'Where's Hoxton?' I asked and then I think Charles began to get to grips with my dilemma.

'You do know who Damien Hirst is don't you?'

'Er, he's a cutter for Alexander McQueen isn't he?'

The next day she dropped off some gallery guides and a few back copies of *Time Out* with relevant reviews circled. 'Remember, less is best when it comes to bluffing,' she warned. 'Go see like *the* most radical show in town, chat up the gallery owner, try and speak to the artist and make your limited experience sound really profound and vast.'

But art was a tricky one. This became clear as soon as I realised it might mean venturing further into the East End than Old Street to learn about it. Nonetheless I was determined to crack it. I just wished Matt could have been into Azzedine Alaia or something easier to get my enthusiasm around.

First thing that became apparent as I read and reread the reviews is that contemporary art is not a hobby to be taken on by girls who crave a quick fix. Your thrill expectation has got to be like exceptionally low! With clothes and shopping you know where you are. All it takes is an optimistic outlook, a flair for pronouncing Italian designer's names and a gold card. Glance through a few glossies, flick through the racks, learn a few well-chosen adjectives like ooooh and ahhh and charge it. *Voilà*.

On paper at least, art looked as dreary as law. I know that London's art scene is meant to be like the hippest thing around since Warhol's Factory but as far as I could see the people who wrote about it had degrees in tedium for tedium's sake.

We are talking Class-A terminology abuse, even a kebab became a seminal dialectic on the subjugation of women. There wasn't one show I read about that looked remotely jolt worthy. But I'm no quitter. After all, critics are renowned for being dry.

I had to get out there amongst it – drink whisky with Damien Hirst and explore Hoxton.

It was Saturday morning and I was in Armani jeans and white T-shirt (Donna Karan) and agnés-b shades, tanked up on half a bottle of vodka, a pint of tea and a few Prozacs, keen as a pre-pubescent girl waiting for her first period. My focus was ready and willing as I traipsed round the Saatchi collection, hoping to catch sight of Damien Hirst or even a bottle of whisky, and almost fell into a tank of oil.

That's art I guess – as Van Gogh and Gauguin found to their peril. Not content with your money, art wants human sacrifice – or at least bits of your anatomy.

Following the advice of Charles, I decided to get to know a gallery owner. I explained my fate to an extraordinary woman in Vivienne Westwood platforms at her gallery-cum-living-space in Bayswater, but my focus couldn't get a word in edgeways. Never underestimate a woman in heels higher than you'd dare wear yourself, Gran had always warned me, so I accepted her offer of tea. As she discoursed on space, housewifery and spa-baths, I thought I felt my focus subside just a little.

'Darling, if you want your focus really jolted you simply must go to the Mitchie Wanhato show!' she declared as she air-kissed me to the door.

Mitchie Wanhato was showing in a gallery near Regent Street which was now full of shoppers exercising their power to push up interest rates and I must say I felt very much the grown-up as I resisted the temptation to join them and climbed the stairs to the exhibition.

Before I'd even had to say installationist, I was standing in a white cubic den of claustrophobia with a stuck-up assistant who looked like a wax dummy.

She was looking down on me like I was a turd under her feet that she was too sophisticated to wipe off. I felt myself morphing into Edina in Ab Fab. Only I wanted sex not immortality and this bitch looked like she sensed that. I wanted to say something really cutting and harsh about her being a shop assistant and I would have got around to it, but a voice that was pure honey behind me said, 'Isn't the wax lifelike? Are you a fan of Mitchie Wanhato?'

Mitchy Wana-fucking-what? I almost said but I caught myself just in time. 'Yes a huge fan. Love these wax figures like nobody's business. Massive fan me! I've followed her career like a truffle pig,' I told her, but self-assurance is hard to fake when you've just realised you've been intimidated by a wax dummy.

'*His* career,' she corrected unfazed. 'This is just one of his wax "Buyer Beware" models – the rest can be viewed in *Tok-yo*.' She pronounced the word Tokyo with an inflection Emperor Hirohito himself would have been proud of.

'Oh right, I'll just like nip on over there now, shall I?' Give me a break, what the fuck was this woman on – techno acid?

'You can view them on the Internet in the office here if you like,' she explained in a voice so seductive, my sexuality was jolted.

'Oh,' I said a bit embarrassed. 'I'd love to.'

So Petronella led me into the small antechamber and left me alone to bludgeon myself about the brain with my blunt ignorance for the next half hour. I didn't feel I could just leave straight away, that would have looked pretty odd for a big fan of Wanhawhatever. I didn't want to offend her – or the wax dummy for that matter. I had to look keen. So I stared at the screen till my corneas separated from my pupils, wondering if this was what Matt meant by a jolted focus?

By the time I got out of the gallery I knew there was no way I was up for this art business. For a start I didn't have a big enough cheque guarantee card. I needed an excitement boost like I needed my vital organs, so I winged it over to Hamleys for an Action Man fix.

It's an addiction I try and hide – but I have got a serious Action Man obsession that I'm still getting round to owning up to my therapist about. I hadn't 'got over it in time', as Gran had predicted.

As I scuttled down Piccadilly, I took a few furtive glances behind me, expecting to catch sight of my stalker but it seemed as if my foray into art had been too boring even for a hardened stalker on uppers. Oh I get it, I thought, after a week of ducking and diving, side street chicanery and dangerous dashes through traffic, I had finally bored my stalker away with contemporary art.

I celebrated with a reckless purchase of the Action Man deep-sea-diving tank and splurged further with a cab ride back to Clerkenwell. It was a bit naughty really as I'd made a New Moon resolution not to take cab journeys that were likely to cost more than five pounds. I had even boasted this fact to my builders when they asked when they could expect to see some money. I thought that if I explained how much *I* was suffering they would take pity on me. Like hell. Paddy the bastard laughed at my disciplinary regime.

'You want to be getting a licence then, don't you, Miss Evelyn?'

'I most certainly do not.'

The cheek of it, I fumed. I hadn't just spent three times what I earn to buy a loft a hundred yards from my chambers, to waste time driving a car. When I get a car it is going to come complete with one of those drop-dead-gorgeous chauffeurs that double up as poolside slaves. 'Besides, Paddy, if I can't pay you, how can I afford a car?'

But Paddy was indefatigable in his aim to see me behind a wheel. A few days ago he had turned up with an old Volvo.

'You can learn with this, Miss Evvy. It was my wife's, bless her soul.' His wife had walked out on him a month ago and lately Paddy had started bringing some of the gear she'd left behind over, just in case, as he put it, 'You could make use of it, Miss Evelyn.'

'Someone may as well be getting some use from it. And what

with you wanting to save money and all, I thought you could be learning to drive.'

It was still there. Like a nemesis squatting outside my state-of-the-art loft development. Clamped and ticketed and hellishly permanent-looking. Paddy and I were hurtling towards confrontation, I thought darkly, as I paid the driver and asked for a receipt.

CHAPTER SEVEN

the ultimate in dyke madonna.

Sam was waiting on my doorstep holding Johnny. He was one heck of an enormous child – only nine months old and already half the size of Sam. She looked exhausted standing there in her habitual ripped jeans and obscenely knotted T-shirt, amongst all the bags and paraphernalia that go with motherhood. That was one of the main factors that put me off this generation of kids actually – they are like *the* consummate consumers.

'Oh, Evvy, where the fuck have you been?' she whined. 'We've been here for ages. What were you doing anyway?' Tiny and defenceless, holding that monstrous child, she looked like the ultimate in dyke Madonna.

'I'm sorry,' I pleaded, as I fumbled with the key. Johnny started crying – kids and I do that to one another, it's a symbiotic relationship. I think they sense that I'm not yearning for them to throw up on me.

'Look, hon, I know this is short notice but humour me will you? Charles and I are having a hard time at the moment. She's like mega stressed and I just thought I should take her away somewhere . . . to like – well, we need some time basically. So I bought us tickets to Nice.'

'And?'

'Well, I was hoping you could more or less, well, take Johnny for us?'

'What about the nanny? Can't she look after him?' I asked,

pretty sure that when she said 'more or less' she meant *more*. As in 'more than I could take'.

'Well, that's the problem see. Only now Bruce tells us she's booked in for some luxury spa thing in the country with a bloke she met at Trade. So I sort of thought you wouldn't mind. I know it's short notice but I mean you are always saying how cute he is and stuff.'

'What's this world coming to that even Norland Nannies are having sex lives? Sack her!'

'Lighten up will you. Weren't you ever twenty-four years old?'

This is what liberated women – women who have saving plans for face-lifts, call a kick to the clit. I was twenty-four years old just a few years back as it happened and I'm still getting over the hangover.

'You're getting old and bitter. You should get out more – live a little,' she continued.

'Thanks for the advice.' Sam was always telling me to live a little – right after she destroyed my confidence usually. By the time I had shoved the key into the lock and turned it, I was feeling defeated but still definitely pissed off. This was a warning to all childless single women – never, never admit to finding your girlfriend's kid 'cute'.

I reminded her that I had never had unprotected sex – the reason being I didn't want to end up like her. Knee-deep in nappies and extracted breast milk.

She slapped me on the back and told me to get over it.

'How the hell am I supposed to get over anything if I'm carrying around a thirty kilo sumo midget with no bowel or bladder control?' I asked her as she started handing over the gear.

'You can't be serious, Sam? I can't even change a nappy – I haven't got a kitchen or a proper bathroom and I've got that stalker out there. It can't be safe. You can't do that to little Johnny!' I reasoned, tweaking him under one of his double chins. He howled mercilessly. This loft share theme his mother was on clearly wasn't an idea that met with his approval either.

'He loves you, Evvy. He's practically your love child!'

I balked. Sam's grip on rational thought, like most bond traders, is woefully slim. Gamblers have to learn to give up logic – just like breast-feeders have to give up A-cups.

'My love child?' I spluttered. 'One night of misspent passion with a man who shaved his chest does not a love child make, Sam. I merely gave you the condoms. Johnny's got more to thank the turkey baster for than me!'

Johnny's howls were deafening by now. He had perfected the atonal wail down to an art form – if Sam was to tell me she'd had him trained up for the Wailing Wall, I would have believed her. Something was seriously the matter with this kid.

I told her.

'Don't be absurd. Its called childhood – no one likes it. How would you like to be incoherent with the muscle tone of a jellied eel and incontinent? It must be foul. Why do you think no one can remember being nine months? It's no party – that's what he's trying to tell us.'

Somehow Sam had managed to hand him over to me during this touching little speech and, as my vertebrae shuddered under the strain, I realised she was backing out the door, barking instructions about extracted breast milk, dill water, colic and allergic reactions to wheat.

I felt a wet stream of something warm running down my Armani jeans. This was not what the designer meant by casual lifestyle. But I didn't have time to brood – the phone was ringing. Ah yes but where was it? I still hadn't had Telecom in to wire the place so I was reliant on my mobile which, true to name, travelled the flat with a free will of its own.

I knew it was somewhere within this cavernous space. But even a void can take time to search when you've got a puking, shitting baby on your hip. This kid was on orifice detox. He thought I was his colonic irrigation nurse. 'You've spent too long in Notting Hill,' I chided, hoping that the human voice would soothe him. 'You're picking up jet-setting illnesses. Dysentery hasn't taken off in Clerkenwell yet – our plumbing isn't up to it.'

He looked at me like most people do when you discuss their emotional problems – like I should mind my own business. Then he went back to being inconsolable. By now every orifice on his face was running.

I found the phone. 'Hello, Evelyn speaking,' I yelled into the mouthpiece.

'All right you can have the stereo.'

'What? I can't hear you.'

'You may as well, I never listen to it.'

'Giles?'

'Maybe I was just being petty.'

Johnny got the precise angle on my eardrum guaranteed to render me deaf.

'Well, what are you going to do? I thought you could come over here . . .'

'Forget it, Giles, I can't afford the cab fare and I've got Johnny for the weekend.'

He started suggesting other alternatives and shouted something about bringing it around but my eardrum had given up the fight.

As if in triumph Johnny went quiet and smiled when I shut the phone. I was covered in baby pooh. Gran was right, kids ruin your life. This DNA shit has got a lot to answer for. Forget liposuction, when I get the money I'm going to have my DNA surgically removed.

Over the next hour, as I changed and rechanged nappies, my resolve to remain barren strengthened. My hands were blue from the disposable gloves I wore to swab him down with. This nappy change thing was a kind of surgery in its way – requiring vast quantities of disposable rubber gloves, disinfectant and a face mask. I mean it was a highly skilled operation requiring the assistance of trained nurses and it seemed incredible to me at that moment that this was once recommended as a fulfilling but unpaid career for women. My loft started to resemble a makeshift operating theatre in a war zone.

Sam had left me a mound of disposable gloves and nappies which had looked formidable at first glance but as I whittled them down during the hour, I calculated that there were probably three hours' worth left, max. It almost seemed pointless changing him. The waste mound was hellishly toxic like something better suited to the *X Files*.

I stuck Johnny in this mechanical swing thing Sam had left and was attempting to sort out the damage to my jeans when the doorbell rang. Brilliant I thought, Sam and Charles have changed their mind. I ran to the door like a like a disaster victim to an aid-drop but it was my builder Paddy.

'Hello. I, er, thought I might just bring you these round.' He was holding out a pair of green plastic shower sandal looking things with inch long metal spikes on the soles.

'Um, thanks,' I replied, stunned.

'Only I thought they might be useful for the roof garden. The wife left them, bless her soul.'

The roof garden was a patch of clay and clumps of turf that I had entertained great hopes for when I first bought this place. That was before I realised that my stilettos sunk in it everytime I walked outside.

'What are they?' I asked, holding them up for inspection – they looked like golf goes techno. Actually they looked conceptual – like an installation. Maybe I could put them on a glass plinth and impress Matt. Give that Wichiwanahato a run for his money.

'Aerator lawn sandals,' he explained without irony. 'You put them on like normal shoes and walk your way to a healthier lawn, or some such shite.'

'Oh!' I would have laughed if I wasn't so hot and pissed off and covered in shit.

'I don't want to keep you or nuttin,' he added, shuffling about. He looked sadly at his own dusty steel-capped work boots. He had bright red hair, a paunch and a ginger moustache that made him look mournful. I mellowed and invited him in for a cup of tea – after all he had been pretty good about my lack of funds.

Paddy wandered over to the swing which was jerking back and forth in sudden movements that made Johnny throw his arms out in shock. The combination of shitty nappies and the look on Johnny's face made me feel like I'd been sprung for child abuse. His little sticky face wore an expression of absolute disbelief for each split second before the swing swung back on its axis. Then he'd chortle gaily before the next jerk scared the 'bejesus out of him' as Paddy put it.

I put the shoes over on the pile by the loo, along with all the other stuff he'd brought round since his wife – bless her soul – did her runner. I could tell I was going to have to have a serious chat with Paddy about all this gear he kept giving me.

CHAPTER EIGHT

he was hardly the sort of bloke to understand the contemporary lineage of a loaded condom and a turkey baster.

We played happy families with Johnny for the next hour while Paddy drank tea from a pot he'd brought over the week before. It was one of those awful home-made pottery affairs his wife had made at evening class. I wondered if this woman had taken *anything* with her when she left.

Watching Paddy sink comfortably back in a vulva with Johnny on his knee, I could see he was a natural with kids. He managed with that ginger moustache what I couldn't achieve with Action Man in all his guises. In fact Action Man – The Red Beret had finally lost his face in the battle to entertain Johnny, his paratrooper boots were sticking obscenely out of the other red velvet vulva, where Johnny had turfed him like a rejected dildo. Kids these days are so demanding. Even at the height of my petulant adolescence that doll had been enough to wipe the most persistent scowl from my face.

Somewhere along the line, Paddy had asked me who the father was and when I told him about my miserable one night with the gay solicitor whose sperm I had donated to Sam and Charles, Paddy put two and two together and came up with Pythagoras' theorem. After that he kept saying things like, 'If you don't mind me saying, miss, you've done the right thing' and 'you can't turn your back on a little fellow like this.' Comments which gave me the distinct impression that he thought my responsibility for Johnny ran deeper than it actually did.

Once I realised this, it was too late to explain the far more technical truth of Johnny's parentage. Let's get real for a minute, Paddy was hardly the sort of bloke to understand the contemporary lineage of a couple of lesbians, their hetero friend, a loaded condom and a turkey baster. So I took his misconceptions on the chin and let it go. The idea that anyone could mistake me for a mother was so laughable, I couldn't help but enjoy the joke.

After tea we put Johnny back in the swing where he eventually drifted into an uneasy dreamland with his little chubby hands jerking out in shock when the swing hurtled forth. I didn't want to contemplate how I was going to get him out of the diabolical contraption so I left him there.

Paddy struggled out of his vulva and made noises about getting back home. 'Not that I've got anything to go back to now, like.'

Well, that was because he'd dumped it all on me – but I was too polite to point this out. Anyway, he had started lecturing me about my stalker.

'Now I hope you don't think me interfering, Miss Evelyn, but I noticed there's a bloke out there looking up at your place strange, like. A stocky fellow he is, scurried away like a little mole when I shouted out at him.'

Basically, Paddy was the one person I didn't want to take my stalker seriously. I didn't want him thinking that I was about to be murdered by a weird kook before settling my bill. Fear that he wasn't going to get paid might make him abandon work on my place before he'd installed the kitchen. I had to play this one down.

'Oh that's my stalker,' I breezed, as if explaining away a quirky accessory of the *beau monde*. 'He's always out there.

Totally harmless, doesn't do anything. Just stalks away,' I laughed insouciantly. I thought of suggesting he came from a stalker employment training scheme catalogue but I restrained myself. 'He doesn't scare me,' I assured him.

Paddy didn't seem convinced. 'Well, if you don't mind my saying, you'd be right to be scared. A young girl like you with a baby to look after. I've been around a bit, girl, and any man who stalks a woman like that is not right in the head, if you know what I mean. Now, I know you're of an independent streak, Miss Hornton, and I respect you for that. The lads and I, we all respect you, but, well, I've got a brother. Well he's me wife's brother actually, God love her.' He blessed himself. 'He's lived in New York for a while now – done a bit of private detective work and such like for society ladies over there and he's over for a bit, trying to track down my missus. We've not seen hide nor hair of her since she walked out and she didn't take nuttin with her either. I don't like to think it, Miss Hornton, but I think she might a come to harm or sometin'.'

My heart went out to him. I felt like a heel having teased him for all the gear he kept bringing over. 'Sit down, Paddy. If there is anything I can do . . .' I offered.

'Oh don't go troubling yourself, miss. You've got the little one here to think of now and that's as it should be.'

'Well, Johnny's not really mine, Paddy.'

'Hush now, miss. Don't talk like that. Main thing is we sort out yer man out there. Now if I have a word to young Rory he'll see the fellow off—'

'Paddy, I'm sure it's a very kind offer but I've got enough trouble paying *your* bill without the added burden of society ladies' private detectives.'

'If you don't mind my saying so, I don't think it's a matter of money, Miss Evelyn. You've got the baby to think of. Now, I know I'm not family or anything and I wouldn't want to poke my nose in your personal affairs, but yer man the stalker out there can't be right in the head. I'll have a word to Rory. I mean it,

Miss Evelyn, I wouldn't want to see any harm come to you or the baby there. I'll send him over.'

'Paddy, you've got enough on your hands. Really, I'm sure this stalker's nothing, he's just a bit mad as you say. In the end he'll get bored or go back to his hostel. I feel sorry for him really,' I lied.

'Up to you, miss, but keep it in mind.'

After seeing Paddy off I collapsed, exhausted, into a chair. The swing was still clanking away but I didn't dare turn it off. Best to let sleeping babies swing. Besides, I was still covered in shit and ravenously hungry. Not only did I have no washing machine, but I had no food in the refrigerator. I mean get real – me cook? With this manicure? I'm a single modern girl – I don't cook. 'Have a life – not a kitchen' was my motto. But now I was in the mood to trade in this so-called life of mine for a kitchen, a proper bathroom and a washing machine.

I went for a shower – well, it was called a shower but without a pump it was more like a leaking toilet. Nonetheless I was doing my best to luxuriate in the feeble spittle of water when Johnny started squawking again. And it hit me – oh God, the extracted breast milk. I was going have to deal with extracted breast milk.

This was not a concept I was equipped for – and I hadn't even started contemplating the wheat allergy and diminishing nappy situation. With all the scientific know-how and state-of-the-art equipment required to keep a baby alive, I began to wonder if I had the necessary qualifications to deal with this. If the future of my species was relying on me it was in trouble.

I decided to phone for a Norland Nanny to come and face the nappy/ breast-milk drama. Would they, I asked, consider an hour-long stint just to feed the baby a bottle of extracted breast milk and change a nappy? 'No' was their blunt reply. Even when I explained the severity of my ineptitude they were intransigent. But I was undeterred. London is a city of millions

I reasoned, someone must be prepared to handle an emergency nappy change and breast-milk administration. I picked up the Yellow Pages and allowed my fingers to do the walking.

Nothing.

'I mean give me a break,' I said to the odd-job man who had promised the earth in his ad, 'it must be worth something to you?'

'Look, luv, I'm not the man for the job,' he told me.

'Are you insinuating that I am?' I asked aghast. 'Just because I've got a womb? It doesn't automatically equip me for babbies, you know!'

'Well, he's your kid.'

Why did everyone keep saying that? In the end he suggested I try Great Ormond Street Hospital.

They were less than unsympathetic. Obdurate, in fact. Rude. They more or less treated me like a lunatic – even after I offered the nurse on the phone my Harvey Nichols' store card to do with as she liked. 'You're mad,' she told me.

'Oh right, and sane people are just lining up for this chore, aren't they? Come on,' I reasoned. 'It's only an hour-long stint. I'm prepared to pay you double what Naomi Campbell makes in a minute? Just to feed a baby extracted breast milk and change a nappy?'

'I don't have to listen to this. Why can't you do it?' she asked me. 'Women have been changing nappies and feeding babies for bloody thousands of years!'

Which was more or less my point. Time for a well-earned break I reckoned.

By now Johnny had woken up and I had him on my lap. 'OK, Johnny, the Norland Nanny confederacy et al say "no go". They're not interested in taking on a case like yours short-term and I mean we're talking professionals here – highly trained experts in the art of keeping guys like you clean, dry and fed. And frankly, mate, I don't blame them. You've got to up your game a bit, if you know what I mean.'

He screamed at me until his double chin slapped around his forehead. This kid was moving into the R-rated zone of violent expression. Even though I knew I was the ultimate failure, I was becoming afraid of him. Seriously, he was scary. I wasn't up for this so I changed him one more time, wrapped him up in a swaddling robe and took him out.

CHAPTER NINE

so much for being part of one big happy, genetically linked, new-age family!

Toby Lamb's was on St John Street which was practically within walking distance. I liked St John Street, not because it was the coolest street in the coolest city with the highest density of tripods but because if there was a photo shoot going on, and there nearly always was, the night was transformed from darkness into a blaze of light. And I was studiously avoiding darkness now I had a stalker.

Lugging Johnny, Action Man (in several guises), extracted breast milk, infinite nappy changes and several spare outfits, we set out with my faithful stalker slinking along behind me like he was in a black-and-white spy film.

I decided on Toby's because I was a regular – I'd been tipping them on top of the service charge for weeks. That must earn me a nappy change or at least a warmed breast milk, I figured. It has bright, modern minimalism, relying on its customers for decoration, but the best thing was the toilet graffiti which read like a who's fucked who of London glitterati.

The photo shoot going on that night must have involved someone really famous because the star stalkers were banked up outside the restaurant. A few cameramen looked less than thrilled when I arrived with Johnny and the equipment necessary to survive an hour with a kid in this town.

'That's not her,' someone said bitterly as I pushed through and knocked them flying. 'She's just a pleb.'

Even though I came here a few nights a week, it wasn't the sort of place where they condescended to remember your face. They were too cool for that. In fact I always got the feeling I had interrupted a special moment in staff-bonding history when I turned up and asked to be seated.

Tonight a bloke with a snail trail of studs along his eyebrow took one look at Johnny and showed me to a table as close as possible to being inside the men's toilets without actually breaking enough health regulations to be closed down.

I demanded to be given a table by the fish. 'Johnny likes fish,' I explained.

His silver eyebrow studs glinted with menace. 'Sorry, that's the only table I can offer you,' he snapped curtly, as if he were an inquisitor showing me my thumb screws. I got the impression that from his point of view I should be humbly grateful that he hadn't hit me with the butt of his rifle.

I scanned the empty table by the fish for a reserved sign. There wasn't one and I started to get suspicious. I handed him the extracted breast milk and asked him to do what needed to be done to make it fit for infant consumption.

'And be careful. That's straight from a human mammary.' Sizing him up though, I got the distinct impression that he wouldn't know a human mammary if he fell over one. Basically, I deduced that I was dealing with a bloke who didn't know his way around the female anatomy too well. You might say there was a glass ceiling between our sexes.

'Oh here, you take the baby, I'll speak to the chef,' I told him, passing Johnny over. He was sprouting another chin which meant he was working himself up for another screaming session. Better Stud-face than me.

'Um, I'll have to ask if we accept children first,' he mumbled, refusing to take Johnny who was now screwing up his face and holding his knees up into his belly the way sumo wrestlers do before they throw their body weight on top of someone.

'What do you mean, accept them? He's not a bad cheque, for God's sake. He's a sentient being.'

'Yes, I'm sure,' he replied dubiously. 'But our diners might find a child off-putting while they are trying to eat.'

'Hello? They might find the future of the species off-putting? Excuse me?' I asked him to extrapolate on this point.

He shrugged. 'A lot of people who eat here just don't *do* kids,' he told me as he looked at his nails. 'You know the saying – "Just say NO!"'

I looked at Johnny, who was giving the cutest, sweetest, most heart-melting smile ever to have graced a human visage. 'This kid is going to be paying for your geriatric care some day, Stud-face, so do yourself a favour and make friends,' I warned him.

All the other media-literate Clerkenwell diners lost interest in their meals and watched us. Some people cleared their throats. Looking around at their irritated faces, I was starting to get the gist of what Sam meant by child persecution.

Up until now I thought I was the one being persecuted, but the scales were falling rapidly from my eyes. Anyway you looked at it, Johnny was facing the same prejudice that women have faced for years. Us girls were getting over the worst of it now, but only after a long and bloody battle. What I wanted to know was who was going to burn their diapers and throw themselves in front of horses at the Derby for this little bloke? I didn't wait for any more backchat, I just plonked Johnny into Stud-face's arms and legged it.

He started yelling straight away.

A sultry woman with a tight bun stopped me at the entrance to the kitchen.

'Can I help you?' she sneered, as if I was light years beyond her assistance.

'Sure, table for two and breast milk to be heated,' I explained authoritatively.

'Hello?' she asked, giving me the same blank look Stud-face had given me moments before – the look that said, 'You are not our type.'

'Here it is,' I barked, thrusting the bottle into her hand. 'Pure A-grade mammary extraction. Heat it and bring it to the noisy table over by the fish. Oh and don't open it, it's sterilised. Oh and make sure it's body temp. Johnny gets pretty obstreperous when it's not thirty-six degrees on the nose.'

Despite her look of disbelief, she took the bottle and moved towards the kitchen with purpose. I went back to Johnny, who was screaming blue murder by now. Stud-face was holding him out in front of him like he was a wet dog. So much for being part of one big happy genetically linked New-Age family, I thought.

The thing that was really starting to get to me was the way everyone was staring at me, as if I'd set Johnny up to it or something. 'Hey, he's got the same chromosomal structure as you shit-heads,' I told them.

This mother thing was proving to be a lot harder than I'd imagined.

'I think he's done something,' Stud-face told me, handing me Johnny, who was now purple-faced with yelling.

'Something?'

'A shit or something,' he hazarded.

Considering how many shits and somethings Johnny had done in the last couple of hours, I thought this theory was beyond the realm of physical possibility and told him so.

'Well something's gone off.'

'Probably your hormonal time bomb,' I suggested.

'Very droll aren't we?' he sneered.

'I haven't even got into my stride, Stud-face,' I told him.

'Well, anyway, we don't have a mother's changing room so you'll have to leave, I'm sorry.' He shrugged and turned to go.

'People like you should stick to McDonald's – they don't mind your sort there.'

That was when I decided that I wasn't going to be made a victim because I had a kid. I was holding the salvation of the gene pool for God's sake. This kid was a DNA fingerprint of my generation. Without guys like Johnny, we as a species couldn't go on. And I was his matriarchal figure – for the moment anyway. So where were my accolades? I should be revered. Given the respect of mankind, worship even – adulation – maybe even the odd human sacrifice to honour my sacred state! Otherwise I was going to resign.

'What are you talking about, a mother's changing room? Do I look as if I want to change into a mother?' I put it to him. 'I've got a nappy in my bag – here – you do it.' I passed him the Hermes bag Sam used as a baby holdall. I mean, this bloke was on his knees pleading for it. I started to fantasise about how he would look staked out on an altar to female fertility.

'You're not serious,' he snarled.

I passed him a disposable. 'I'm giving *you* the nappy. You deal with Johnny while I gaze at the menu.'

'I'm sorry but we are a restaurant, not a crèche,' he scoffed, getting sniffier by the second. His pompous forbearance didn't sit well on his studded eyebrows and so I told him.

'Is someone going to shut that kid up?' an American smoking a cigar called out from a few tables away. Other people muttered their support for this idea. He repeated his request again, this time standing up for the benefit of the crowd. A camera lens peeked in from the entrance and a bright flash went off – just in case.

'Is this a restaurant or a crèche?' he asked for the benefit of his audience, who made appreciative rumblings like peers do in the House of Lords when they wake up. 'I thought this place was meant to be one of London's more sophisticated eateries?' he reflected, well into his stride now. A few people clapped.

I wanted to give him a nicotine suppository on the spot but

I wasn't the one with the support of the crowd – he was. Divide and rule, Gran always said, so I took Johnny over to Cigar-man and blamed the waiter for the noise. I pointed at the nasty Stud-face and explained that he had hurt my baby's feelings. Johnny gave credence to my claim by chortling contentedly and wobbling a few of his chins at Cigar-man. Putting his cigar out he seemed to soften. He tweaked Johnny on the cheek and looked at the waiter as if to say, 'You know that big tip you were hoping for on top of the twelve per cent service charge? Forget it!'

I took a peek down Johnny's nappy but it was completely empty. 'He accused little Johnny of soiling his nappy.'

My American looked scandalised. 'Did he slander you, fella? You wanna sue,' he gooed. 'Cute little chap isn't he?'

'Well he really seems to like you.' I smiled my encouragement.

'Hey, fella, you having trouble with the hired help, are ya?'

Johnny indicated with a little dove-like sigh that he was.

This was my opening. 'I wonder if you would mind, er, watching him while I sort out his bottle?'

His girlfriend, until now content to tap her talons on the white linen, pulled her lips in tightly together and squawked, 'We came here for a meal not to act as your nursemaid.'

Cigar-man turned to her and grinned. 'Gee, honey, he's a cute little guy, isn't he?' But she ignored him, giving me one of those looks that men never give to one another, leaving me in no doubt that my family line had just been cursed with infectious diseases and painful childbirth from here to the next coming.

If a bloke gave that look to another bloke there would be pistols at dawn or at least broken beer glasses in the face by closing time. But Johnny and the American were blowing raspberries at each other, so I held my tongue and went and spent my penny. A luxury I hadn't enjoyed since Johnny's arrival.

By the time I got back, the American had bonded so well he asked if he could feed Johnny his extracted breast milk.

'Gee you sure?'

'Hell yes – he's happy. We're getting on just fine aren't we, buddy? We'd finished hadn't we, honey?' he asked his girlfriend.

His girlfriend was looking through her bag for a broken glass or something sharp enough to go through my pupil. We weren't hiding anything from one another anymore. I allowed my top lip to curl.

'I hope you realise *your* baby has ruined our evening,' she snarled.

I ignored her. Some things don't need to be said between sisters.

CHAPTER TEN

my subliminal maternal instincts lurched into gear.

As we were leaving, the American gave Johnny his cigarette lighter as a present. It was a gold Dunhill and I felt a bit unsure at first – I mean about allowing Johnny to accept such an expensive gift on first meeting and also about letting him play with lighter fluid. Basically I knew I was going to have a screaming row with him when I got home, but the American was so insistent and he'd been so kind, it seemed churlish to refuse. As well as that, I knew how much it would upset his girlfriend.

I could sense the stalker was following us down St John Street. Well, I could see him basically – like I said, discretion wasn't on the curriculum at his stalker training course. The photo shoots were over and the streets were dark. My analyst is always telling me that all my problems relate to perception, so despite the fact that I was shaking with fear, I tried to perceive my stalker as a benign personal bodyguard with my best interests at heart. Yeah right – as if anyone with my best interests at heart would wear that coat!

I tried to take those broad assertive steps my self-defence tutor had taught me but it wasn't easy trying to look assertive lumping around this kid that weighed more than me – let alone the gadgetry that went everywhere with him. I kept dropping stuff and having to go back for it and then I'd catch 'yer man the stalker' ducking into a doorway to take a piss. Great, so now I had a stalker with poor bladder control.

All the same, I wasn't going to hire any Manhattan society dame's private eye. I was humming that old song from the seventies, 'I Am Woman Hear Me Roar', as I made my way down Clerkenwell Road. At one point I thought the stalker was even humming it with me – it must have been Johnny's colic on the march again. It was useless though, I couldn't shake off the grip of my paranoia.

By the time I got into my building, my pulse rate was going faster than the Eurostar. I was coming to terms with the reality that, latest accessory or not, this stalker was spooking the wits out of me.

Johnny, clutching his lighter in his sleep, was sweetly oblivious to my troubles. I gave his head a little kiss as I double-locked the door and put on the chain. Paddy was right on one thing at least – having Johnny around had given me a new-found sense of my own vulnerability. After I'd tucked him up on my futon and prised the Dunhill from him, I stacked the vulva chairs on top of one another against the door.

Given that my stalker had never tried to confront me or sent me letters, or miniature coffins, or plagued me with phone calls like the more dangerous stalkers I'd been reading about in the news, I was probably overreacting just a little, but when you've got an incontinent bloke with a bad case of constipation and a short fuse that could blow any minute following you around, it pays to be cautious.

I was feeling exhausted myself so I joined Johnny on the futon. It had been a heavy day and pretty soon I fell asleep, with his legs thrown over my belly, my arm under his head and my face burrowed in a pillow. Sleeping with the male of the species is a contortionist's training ground whatever their age bracket.

I became aware of an ever increasing numbness running up my arm as I was woken by a *sludge, sludge, sludge* sound above me, as if someone was up on the roof, walking around in those studded lawn sandals Paddy had given me. Johnny, true to his gender stereotype, slept on, snoring and passing wind while I excavated my arm from under his head to listen more carefully.

A cold worm of panic slithered up my spine. What if it was my stalker?

Paddy's wise words of warning came back to me. I had been wrong to treat my stalker with such insouciance. I should have hired a private eye long ago. Get real, I should have hired some 'muscle' and had him removed. Christ, I don't even put up with my own body hair when it's not wanted – what on earth possessed me to put up with a stalker?

When I was doing criminal cases down the Bailey I was always being offered 'muscle' by my grateful clients. 'If yer ever need any "muscle", girl, I'll see you right.' At first I thought they were offering their services as my personal trainer. Oh for my callow youth.

Sitting in the half-light of the room, I went over in my head the likelihood of my stalker getting inside my loft. Given that the only way on and off the roof was via the stairs inside the building, my stalker – if it was him up there – must have already made it inside my building. So why bang about on the roof wasting time – why not just knock down the door and waste me?

To scare the shit out of me that's why.

By now I had the taste of adrenaline in my mouth and my heart was throwing itself against the walls of my chest. Little Johnny continued to snore contentedly beside me while scenes from *The Texas Chainsaw Massacre* played in my head. I waited in terror, listening to my breathing like a disembodied spectator, but nothing happened, the noise had stopped again. I waited for it to start up once more and when it didn't I tried to do a yoga destressing exercise to get back to sleep but I must have got my Vedic paths confused because I ended up rebirthing myself. I came to, thrashing about in a lather of foetal regression and duvet.

After that the banging started up again – louder now as if someone was jumping up and down like King Kong. My body heat was plummeting. It was a sultry summer evening but my extremities felt like they were frostbitten. I remember watching a movie about the 1976 Israeli hostage drama when the Israeli commander is killed after a great act of selfless bravery. He complained to his buddies about being cold and about everything being dark. 'Don't worry, it's a dark night,' they told him as he died in their arms.

A siren went off in the distance. Darkness and cold signify death – this was my ersatz death – the real one was on the roof, so close there probably wasn't even going to be time for a selfless act of bravery.

I knew then that it was time to call the police – maybe even a little bit on the latish side, thinking about it. What could I say to the emergency services to strike the right note of panic? If death was upon me, I wanted something more extreme than a couple of Constable Plods with notebooks turning up to witness it. I wanted a swat team, tear gas, sniffer dogs, and automatic weapons aimed by experienced marksmen, basically. If I was able to make a request, I think I'd put in for a rocket launcher or two. I was fairly sure if the IRA was mentioned, Special Branch would go into rapid-attack mode. Maybe I should disguise my accent – tell them that 'yer man' the terrorist was on the roof threatening to murder innocent women and children.

I fumbled under the futon for the telephone battery recharger and prayed to God I'd remembered to set it up. More to the point, where was my mobile? My temperature dropped still further and I castigated my lack of foresight for not having signed up for one of the self-immolation terrorism classes I'd seen advertised in a telephone booth. Regret is the luxury of the doomed, Gran used to say, but I finally found the mobile and stuck in the battery.

Now the sound on the roof had changed to a scraping, as if whoever it was up there was endeavouring to claw their way in! Punching in my pin number, I practised what I was going to say to the switchboard operator to hit precisely the right note of urgency.

'Whatever you do, Evelyn, don't ever admit to being menstrual or pregnant!' That was the sort of advice we were given in self-defence classes in Sydney. As if some Westy, gay-bashing misogynist would give a damn about your fertility status while he was beating the crap out of you.

I dialled 666 and other apocalyptic combinations before hitting on 112, the emergency number for mobiles. 'If you're ever raped,' the instructor had warned, 'always yell FIRE! Remember, girls, no one wants to know if you're getting the shit buggered out of you by some bloke with a knife.' She was an explicit woman my tutor – with a vivid imagination. Not that she had anything on me now – my imagination was morphing between Kafka, Orwell and Punch & Judy.

By the time I got through, the flat had gone uncomfortably silent and still. Even Johnny had given up on his snoring. The woman on the switchboard asked for my details and I ticked her off for calling me 'madam'.

'For Christ's sake, woman,' I told her. 'You don't "madam" people when they're about to be sodomised and killed.' It was while I was waiting for her long-drawn-out sigh of irritation to come to an end, that I first began to have doubts.

What if it had just been a hailstorm, or something being blown around on the roof? Something innocent and not in the least bit life threatening – to put it simply, what if I had overreacted? It wouldn't be the first time. The last thing Johnny needed was a swat team to come charging in when he was trying to sleep. Sam would flip. A car stereo blasting out Spice Girls singing 'Wannabe' tipped the balance. One thing I didn't wannabe was ticked off by Sam for bringing in rocket launchers and swat teams to wake up her kid. I told Emergency Services that I wouldn't require MI5 after all.

Was I brain dead? I'd no sooner put the mobile down than someone started pounding on the door. I resorted to the primal scream – opening up my diaphragm so far I thought it was going to need stitches – and yelled the yell of the damned. I must have been heard from Bow Bells to the King's Road. This was the inner voice inside me that had been trapped since birth, flowing forth in one spine-rattling bellow.

People in Chelsea pay good money to get themselves a primal scream like that. I saw a poster once for a 'psychic healer' promising people with high disposable incomes that releasing their primal scream could free them from the emotional baggage of past, present and future.

As well as howling, I was running frantically around the flat in circles, biting back tears, scrambling through the darkness, cold, perspiring with fear. I had the mobile clenched in my hand but I was beyond speech. I tried to scream again for good measure, hoping someone would call the police, but by that stage I'd already coughed up my voice box.

The stalker was throwing everything he had against that door – I even thought I heard the burr of a chainsaw starting up. Despite everything, Johnny was still sleeping peacefully – his little hands curled around his bunny rug. It almost seemed a crime to wake him really – although nothing compared to what could befall him if the bloke throwing himself against the door with the chainsaw got to work on him. The hinges of the door were groaning.

My subliminal maternal instincts lurched into gear as I scooped Johnny up into my arms, swaddling clothes and all – and I ran. I didn't know where I was going to run to but I ran. Adrenaline coursed through my veins – I was compelled by inner strength. I was like some berserk exercise fanatic – like a lab rat on speed.

Even when taken from a positive perspective, my circumstances were grim – there was no back exit, no windows low enough to reach and the only possible hiding spot was the screen around the toilet – woefully inadequate due to the thirty-centimetre gap at the bottom. Tears streamed down my face as my profound inadequacy hit me. I was meant to be looking after this little child – well maybe not so little, I conceded as I struggled with him from one end of the vast space to another, like a demented refugee fleeing a genocide with her wounded husband in a pouch.

Sam had trusted me to feed him extracted breast milk, to tend to his colic with dill water and to preserve him from wheat. I saw the door bow. There was a muffled yelling on the other side like a dog in pain. Oh poor innocent deluded Sam. Wheat allergies were the last thing you should have feared.

The top vulva chair crashed to the floor and bounced.

It was a sign. We were doomed! I prayed for the martyrs. Hold me a seat, I told them, I'll be there soon. But where there is life there is hope, Gran always said. You've got to pull yourself together Evelyn, stay strong! Remember, Sam's relying on you. You must be the brave one. You are a woman with an infant in your care. Remember Kipling . . . If you can keep your nerve when all around you are losing theirs . . . It's not as if you're completely helpless, I reminded myself. You *are* a black-belt after all.

I hid Johnny – still blissfully sleeping – behind the toilet screen. With a bit of luck, I thought, even if the stalker quenched his lust for blood by massacring me, he might not discover Johnny. Such a selfless act should at least earn me some time off in Purgatory. I kissed his darling little head before I positioned myself by the failing door and prayed to God to give me the advantage. I planned to kick our intruder in the side of the head as soon as he got inside.

That moment was less than seconds away and there was I in a pair of baby-doll pyjamas and not so much as a pair of stilettos or a can of Mace to defend myself with. The door gave way with an almighty crash.

There was a lot of dust and noise but I caught sight of a shadowy form which I lunged at with everything I had. It was a triumphant moment to see the hulking shape of my intimidator fall so conclusively at the first blow. He grunted like a wounded beast – hey, what can I say, I've got a pretty significant left kick.

Johnny was awake now and threatening to bring in a swat team of his own. God that kid had lungs. No asthma in *his* genetic line-up then!

I turned the lights on to get a better look at my prey but there, in a puddle of blond curls and broken glasses, lay not my stalker but my ex – Giles.

It was the return of the superbastard.

CHAPTER ELEVEN

she took to the idea like a spermatozoon to an egg.

'What the fuck were you thinking of?' I demanded to know. Whacking him about the head with the ice pack, I roundly criticised everything about him – from his blood group to the way his molecular structure was arranged. Talk about severely pissed off. This bloke and his bloody insteps were that close to going on my hit list, it was scary. Not only had he woken my baby but he had broken down my door, which was going to hoik my builder's bill up even further.

'What was *I* thinking of?' he repeated over and over *ad infinitum*.

'Oh shut up, Giles, you demented parrot.'

'But you were the one who wanted the fucking stereo,' he yelled back. He must have been extremely cross himself because he was starting sentences with a conjunction – his equivalent to losing grip entirely. 'You said bring it round tonight!'

The vague memory of a phone call taken while Johnny broke the decibel range in my ear came back to me. 'I didn't tell you to break the door down in the process though, did I?' I had Johnny cradled in my arms, sucking happily on his extracted mother's milk. All my maternal instincts were alive and kicking now. Did I say I don't like babies? Pah! This little kid gave me a warm, safe, comfortable feeling – this little bloke was depending on me. He trusted me and I was going to come through for him. I felt a rush of power go to my womb.

'I heard you screaming. I thought you were being murdered.'

'Of course you heard me screaming. Any sane person on less than an overdose of temazepam would scream. I think those insteps you wear are affecting your judgement,' I suggested, amazed at my own ability to stay cool. I mean, I'd had my share of high-octane anxiety tonight too, but my lexicon was doing splendidly.

'Oh I don't believe this,' Giles groaned, holding the ice pack to his head.

'That makes three of us. You just terrorised a mother and child and rammed down my door. That's harassment and breaking and entering.' Just looking at him, sitting there like the pathetic victim that he was, made me squirm. How had I ever longed for this man's touch? His whole being just about summed up everything I hated about his sex – and then some.

I needed a man like Matt, a man with wisdom and charm – a man who knew his way around an art gallery. You wouldn't catch a bloke like Matt within a mile of an instep, I thought ruefully. 'Anyway, what were you doing stomping round on my roof for half the night? No wonder I screamed.'

'I haven't been near your roof.'

'Of course you were on the roof. Do you think I'm in the habit of screaming every time someone knocks on my door?'

'Well, you said you had this stalker, so when I heard you scream I thought something had happened. I never went near the roof.'

'You're telling the truth, aren't you? You really weren't on my roof?' I hadn't decided yet whether this was a good thing or not.

'I've got vertigo, remember?'

I slapped my head as if trying to get my brain back in place. Of course he had vertigo. This bloke was the archetypal wimp – just like most of the blokes I have ever been attracted to. He had asthma, claustrophobia, photophobia, arachnaphobia, xenophobia and a fear of meeting men in tight jeans in pubs. 'Well if you weren't on the roof who was?'

'I don't know. I didn't see anyone, but the door to the stairs was open. All I know is that when I spoke to you on the phone today about bringing the stereo round, I said I'd drop over around ten o'clock and, true to my word here I am. Why does everything always end up in ABH with you, Evelyn, tell me that?'

'The door to the stairs was open?'

'Well yes, but it was open when I arrived.'

'But that's always locked and it's a fireproof door – not the sort of door you can jemmy open.' I went back to being entirely stressed. Which was stressful in itself because stress always makes me retain fluid. In fact I could already feel my thighs swelling, which was causing me to stress even more.

Why had I ever decided to move to EC1? Things like this never happened to me when I was living in W11. Back at Ladbroke Square I considered missing out on truffles at the deli high drama. Oh how my friends had warned me: 'Oh, Evvy, we'll never see you again. You can't move to the East End, it's too dangerous. People get shot there.'

Rubbish I told them. Take a look at *Newsweek*, London is the hip city and Clerkenwell is its epicentre. Charles pooh-poohed the idea as a mad Yank fancy. 'The only thing that Clerkenwell is the epicentre of is the meat market. You'll smell animal carcasses every time you open your window,' she had warned me. 'Where will you do your shopping?' she pressed. Shops? I told her – who needs shops when there are martinis to drink and photo labs on every corner.

God what a fool I'd been. I should have bought a little ten-foot box in Notting Hill and thrown away my mad dreams of space. What did I need space for? My lifestyle was compact, practically nonexistent if you thought about it. My life could fit in a shoe box if it had to and, besides, no amount of square footage was worth this kind of aggravation.

'Evelyn, you really should come back to live with me.'

'You're like a stuck record, Giles. I left you because I couldn't stand living with you. I'm hardly about to move back now that I've gone into debt to buy this place, am I? But listen, is it really only ten o'clock?' I asked, slightly mortified to think that I had actually turned in before one a.m. Then I remembered the stereo. I went outside and, sure enough, beyond the rubble of my doorway there it was – speakers, CDs and all.

I set up the speakers and put on 'Dance Classics'. Johnny kicked his thick legs rhythmically just like his mother always did as the bass came pumping out like a jack-hammer. I was about to share this comparison with Giles, but knowing the way he felt about 'the girls' made me think better of it and, anyway, half an hour later Sam and Charles burst in.

Sam was at the helm, charging over the door like a one-woman swat team arriving ten minutes late on a genocide scene. 'What the hell happened here? Oh Johnny! Oh look, Charles. Oh no! I knew we shouldn't have left him on this side of town.'

Charles stood back to survey the scene and said in that W1 drawl that makes men's toes curl, 'Oh excuse us, Evelyn, you've got company.' Turning to Giles she purred, 'Oh it's you, Giles. I'm sorry I didn't recognise you in your new insteps.'

He just sat there going purple, like one of those druids that's been hitting the Belladonna too hard. He'd never really gone for my friends, in fact he was always making dark-age remarks about their 'bad influence on me'.

Hello, Giles! Tune into the nineties boyo! What about eyeball knifers on the tube? What about some of the blokes I represent in my legal capacity for that matter? What about active participants in assault with a deadly weapon for a bad influence, hey? I had clients who told me all the ins and outs of every crime from cheating the tax man to causing serious injury to internal organs without visible bruising. I was offered drugs most weeks – a few weeks back the learned counsel for the prosecution had offered me genuine MDMA. Hell I was for ever telling Giles I was getting bad ideas from all quarters! Bad influences positively threw themselves at a girl in this town. A couple of dykes with a kid were hardly going to push me over the edge.

'Fuck, Evelyn, it looks like the Vandals and the Huns have been through here. What the fuck is going on?' Sam demanded with her hands on the hips of an indecent hipster skirt that revealed muscular brown knees exactly like Johnny's.

'What about you? You were meant to be off on some exotic dirty weekend,' I reminded her.

Charles went red and turned away.

'Yeah, well we had an argument and went shopping instead – so what? Doesn't mean we want you to put our kid through a practice Armageddon. Like the skirt?' she asked, doing a little spin. 'Chanel. And I bought a car.'

'Don't ask,' sighed Charles, brushing her arm against her forehead in mock drama.

'A Ferrari,' Sam explained. 'Black naturally with all the "look at my big dick" trimmings.'

'Black?' I squealed. Johnny stopped sucking. This was gob-smacking stuff. Black Ferrari's had hitherto been Sam's symbol for everything she loathed about the city. 'Not a, not a, not a . . . Testosterone?' I mean, I could remember a time when she couldn't say that word without a spasm. Like last month.

'Naturally!' she purred, pulling out a nail file and filing an errant nail down to the quick. She seemed remarkably relaxed for a mother who has just discovered that her baby was being looked after in a loft which had obviously been the scene of catastrophic violence. But then, like I say, shopping is a kind of sedative. Heroin without the kidney damage. When *Trainspotting* came out Sam had observed that if the characters in it could have afforded to shop, they wouldn't have bothered with smack.

'It took like for ever, Evvy, and we don't get it for a month. They've got to build a baby seat into it,' Charles explained.

'Gees, you should've heard the salesman,' Sam butted in, mimicking him. 'But it is a Ferrari convertible. It's not meant to be a family car. You can't put a baby in a Ferrari. It is a convertible.'

'So Sam told him to convert it!' Charles laughed.

They always did that – butt in on one another's sentences. I recognised it as a sign of true love. Giles always said it was hostile. And this time, as Charles interrupted, Sam did give her a pretty hostile look. If I didn't know better I might have got the impression that there was a serpent in their garden of Eden.

Giles was still sitting quietly by the door with his ice pack, opening and closing his mouth and gasping like fish do before they give birth or die, when Sam started to remove her Gucci rib top – exposing two big round breasts with nipples like bull's-eyes on them. 'All right, pass him over. Come on, kiddo, time for the real stuff.'

Shortly after that, he left. Breast-feeding was probably another one of the myriad things he had a phobia of. Alone with the girls, I was finally able to let out my worst fears. I needed a plan of action more than I needed sex at that moment was which saying something, considering the dry patch I'd been experiencing recently.

We talked into the early hours about my stalker and my options. Charles didn't think the 'muscle' idea was a good one. 'Sure they might move him on for a bit but these stalker guys are true creeps. Who's to say what a nutcase like that might sneak back and do to you?'

Mulling this over, we listened to PJ Harvey and drank El Vino's white wine. Charles and I eventually managed to get the door to hang back on the hinges although it looked almost as drunk as us. I doubted its ability to hold its own against an intruder. I would have to get Paddy to sort it.

'Better pray Giles doesn't come to visit too often,' Charles teased.

As the dawn was breaking, we went up onto the roof and tried to work out what the noise had been. Even though Giles had fiercely denied going up there, we took turns parading around in the lawn sandals and mimicking his pompous mannerisms.

'It's great up here, look at this view. You've got to have a party, Evv. Seriously, what's the point of having all this space if you don't throw a party? You haven't even had a house warming yet.'

'Yaah, that's what this place needs – a party,' Charles agreed. 'To Clerkenwell, the IT party area!' she called across the rooftops, tossing the last of her martini to the rising sun.

'Hear that, Mr Stalker?' Sam yelled. 'You're in the IT area now!'

We were quite drunk and for the first time in the last month I was feeling relaxed. It just shows how therapeutic friendship and martinis can be. No analyst in the world can give you the feel-good factor of a real friend.

'It's because of blokes like him that this area has gone up in tone,' Sam theorised. 'I mean, I bet they don't get stalkers in Wandsworth or Clapham and definitely not in boring old Putney,' she snorted. 'No, think about it,' she insisted, clearly warming to a well-thought-out theme. 'Stalkers follow gorgeous babes, right? Then the press get hold of the story and the general property buying public think, "Yeah I'll have some of that" and wham bam you're looking at a des res. Prices go through the roof.'

This specious argument scuppered my short-lived sense of calm. 'So basically you're implying that stalker density bears a direct correlation to real-estate values?'

'Yeah. More or less.'

'Actually all things considered, Sam, I could almost fancy a stalker-free zone. Besides, I don't think I've got the right emotional make-up to deal with an obsessed bloke in a macintosh – whatever the property price advantage.'

'Absolutely!' Charles agreed. 'I mean how insensitive. This bloke could be out there now planning how to chop our best friend into tiny pieces. We don't have any idea what kind of sickoid maniac he is. I mean he could just be biding his time before bursting in here and cooking Evv up in a cassoulet or something.'

I gulped. I hadn't thought of that. I mean a bit of straight-out slaying and bludgeoning, yeah, OK I could just about take that on the chin so to speak – but being turned into a human stew created an entirely new fear zone in my subconscious.

Sam picked up on my squeamishness. 'Oh yeah, and like she really wants to hear that. It's you that's being insensitive. At least I was keeping it light. Do you think you're the only one incisive enough to recognise the danger she's in? I just read in the newspaper about this animal who eventually abducted this woman he was stalking for months and tortured her for six weeks in a caravan in Cornwall. Her life must be total excrement now . . .'

In an effort to nip this line of gruesome one-upwomanship in the bud, I told them about Paddy's suggestion that I hire his brother-in-law, the private detective.

Sam took to the idea like a spermatozoon to an egg. 'Your very own private detective? Wow! That would be soooooo brilliant! Is that the same as a private eye?'

'Yeah I think.'

'A private eye? Wow! Come on, Evv, you've got to do it. You just have to! A private eye? That's unreal – that's like *the* latest "must have" accessory. Even cooler than a stalker in fact. Think about it – it's just mind boggling.'

'Yeah you've got to do it, Evv, you've just got to! I've always fancied having my own private eye,' Charles agreed.

'I'm not a complete fashion victim you know!' I told them. But they just looked at me and nodded the way the sales staff do at Versace when I start fingering price tags.

CHAPTER TWELVE

the ultimate
fashion accessory.

That Monday I shuffled home from work, hot and sticky and not a bit in the mood for meeting private detectives. London wasn't made for the heat and nor was the judicial pomp of horsehair wigs. I'd bungled a submission and Candida was furious – she told me, not for the first or the last time, that she would never *lead* me again. Promises, promises.

Walking home I'd bumped into Orlando, who had asked with genuine concern about my stalker. 'It must be like really phenomenally cool to have your own stalker,' he gooed. I threw my hands around his throat and attempted a crime of passion. This was getting scary – people were actually beginning to worry about the welfare of this bloke now.

Back at the apartment my nemesis, the Volvo, was shining brightly in the heat, clamped, ticketed and sinister. Paddy's private eye was due in about half an hour. Strangely, I hadn't seen the stalker all day. Although Paddy had informed me that 'yer man the stalker' was there when he'd arrived that morning, he was nowhere in sight on the way home. I prayed that he was catching up on a bit of sleep, and I hoped he would wake up calm and refreshed with a much longer fuse.

I showered and dressed and undressed and dressed again and again and again. Paddy had said that this private eye had done some work for society ladies in New York, which brought about a slightly competitive streak in my nature. Did I go for a youthful, contemporary, slightly eccentric chic – say Gucci? Or a sublime sophistication – say Selina Blow or Amanda Wakely? I went for both and the Anna Sui and the Lacroix and the Donna Karan and the Liza Bruce and the Isaac Mizrahi and most of the rest of my wardrobe as half an hour late extended to an hour, then to two and finally to three. I had to face it I'd been jilted and these little Isaac Mizrahi dresses are not the sort of outfit you wear to a jilting.

So, changing back into the Gucci I had started with, I abandoned my wardrobe and wandered the loft. I was hungry. Where the bloody hell was this cove? How dare he. I bet he didn't treat his New York society broads like this!

I thought about calling Paddy but I didn't want to appear desperate – I mean knowing Paddy he might insist on coming over himself, with another remnant of his wife's dowry. The walk-your-way-to-a-healthy-lawn sandals lay on the top of the heap by the loo. I mean this pile of mad junk was something a private eye could really get his teeth into. Maybe I should test Rory's investigative talents by asking him to give me a profile of this woman? But then I remembered he was another one of her legacies – her brother.

Out of sheer boredom I sat cross-legged beside the pile and began to riffle through. There was a workman's hat that had a place to put a drink in. Paddy had said I might find it handy as there was no table in my loft! I put it on my head and attached the Velcro strap. Even without a mirror nearby I knew I must look like a complete and utter ovary.

There was also over eighty foot of indoor washing line. A Seat Saver still in its packet – promising 'firmness like it used to be'. Twelve rolls of Gripper Tape, 'In case you'd be wanting to put down some nice rugs, Miss Evelyn.' A bit cheeky considering I'd paid him two thousand pounds to polish the floorboards.

Strapping on the lawn sandals it occurred to me that maybe Paddy was right, I should walk my way to a healthier lawn. A herbaceous roof garden was probably just what I needed – I could become the Donald Trump of Clerkenwell. And looking down at my feet I had to concede that with their chrome buckles these lawn sandals had a certain street-cred appeal. No one would want to get in the way on the tube if I was wearing these mothers.

The next item I unearthed was a portable TV-dinner table – adjustable for arthritic limbs – electric tartan slippers with matching tartan card table (still in its wrapper). There was a broken teas-maid and a lady's satin patchwork puffa jacket. As I was pulling it on, I discovered a proverb embroidered into the sleeve – testifying to the bird in the hand being worth two in the bush theory. This was real consumer fetish gear.

Talk about driven by despair, and all because she couldn't have a baby. Wearing the sandals and the jacket I guess I was trying to get inside her head – to imagine her motivation. It was as if I was stuck in a *Desperately Seeking Susan* plot, only minus the trendy gorgeous blokes. Maybe in the end she had left Paddy to flee all this shit. Maybe she had flown the coop as an ultimate form of consumer remorse. I stood up to get a look at myself in the new mirror Paddy had put up for me by the door, but as I clomped over in the lawn sandals, I realised I was sinking into my newly reclaimed floorboards – leaving deep symmetrical holes. Basically I had just destroyed my feature parquetry floor.

When my estate agent showed me the place he had told me he lived for floors like this. 'Floors like this make my job worthwhile, Miss Hornton!' The poor bloke would commit suicide if he saw it now.

To say that I was unfocused when the long-awaited knock at the door finally came is to take euphemism into lexicon hyperspace. I fell to the floor, struggling with the wretched straps on the sandals – the chrome clips were stuck. I panicked, the rapping on the door increased. Just what I needed – an impatient private eye.

'All right. I'm coming!' I shouted as I attempted to wrench the bloody things off.

'Are you OK in there?' an American voice called out. Then he started rapping again.

'Can you give me a minute?' I pleaded. The door was still pretty rickety from Saturday night and it wouldn't take more than a shove to unhinge it. He waited like two seconds and then started bashing at the door again.

'What was that – a Manhattan minute?' I yelled – but ultimately there was nothing for it. I was going to lose my door or let him in so I stood up and punctured my way over.

A tall, rugged, well-built man with collar-length hair, an unbuttoned shirt and a Costa del Sol tan, grabbed his stomach and fell to his knees with laughter.

'I'm sorry but you . . .'

I drew myself up to my full six-feet-something in lawn sandals and cast my frostiest look over him. And believe me I've learnt some pretty chilly looks from Candida over the years. I took in a very toned and tanned body – basically most of it was on display through the strategically ripped jeans and sleeveless unbuttoned shirt.

'Can I help you?' I asked regally.

'The name's Rory,' he managed to explain before falling about in paroxysms of hilarity again.

I tried to sound as stiffly English as I could as I introduced myself. 'You must be Paddy's brother-in-law. I didn't think you would sound American. How nice to meet you at last. I've heard such a lot about you. Do come in.'

He had a lot of trouble gaining his composure. 'Sorry, doll, but . . .' He pointed. 'That hat! Those shoes! That jacket. Paddy didn't give me a clue. You're really something aren't you?' He collapsed again into an obscene belly gurgle.

'Something'? I really didn't like this man. '*Something* is a name you give to things you find at the bottom of the fridge, or down plugholes.' I imparted my distaste for his remark with another cold look. But my cool demeanour was wasted. He was snorting in and out, trying to muffle his laughter – I mean his nose was actually vibrating. I thought it was going to explode. I was also pretty aware of the way he was gripping his groin as if he was about to wet himself.

'If you would care to come inside,' I suggested in a tone my aunt often used when she was blind drunk. I led the way – piercing my two-thousand-pound floor with every step I took. But there was no way I was going to back down now. Oh no! With each imperious sinking step my stately manner grew.

He was stunned. Gran would have been proud. 'You'll have to excuse me but I am studding my floor,' I told him. 'It's a designer look you see and not one readily available. One does what one must for fashion.' I laughed lightly as I turned to him and bathed him in the sort of avant-garde look Simone de Beauvoir might have given Sartre when he caught her without her teeth in.

Then I took the jacket off and tossed it casually to the floor. It's times like this that a girl's glad she studied deportment under the glare of Sister Conchilio.

'Whatever you say,' he replied in a tone that suggested he was really awed or maybe just verbally challenged by the insanity of it all. Either way, I was fairly confident I had him on the hop. That was until I remembered I was still wearing the hat.

'You've come about the stalker I believe,' I continued fridgidly. 'Can I offer you a drink, Rory? I normally carry one in my hat, but I'm a bit disorganised at the moment – I've only recently moved in. If you could help yourself from the fridge.'

How was I ever going to carry this off?

Rory seemed to pull himself together at the mention of what he was there for. 'Yeah, this stalker. I've been doing a bit of checking up and it seems it's not *your* man the stalker after all, in fact I think it may have been a case of mistaken identity.' He then took the liberty of sitting down on one of my vulvas and stuck his battered cowboy-booted foot over his knee. I felt like I'd been violated.

I looked back and surveyed my damaged floor sadly. Why had I let this Yankee brat into my life. A fashion accessory? He was worse than a thousand stalkers. Good-looking or not, his jeans looked greasy, his hair was unkempt and I could smell his body odour – and it wasn't Armani Pour Homme. It wasn't an unpleasant smell but it was intolerable just by virtue of being there.

'What do you mean by not *my* man the stalker? Of course he's *my* man. Are you suggesting he's stalking someone else in his spare time? Because I assure you he's been stalking me relentlessly, day and night. Apart from a cat nap here and there, I really don't see how he would have enough free time to be attaching himself to someone else as well!'

I must have lost total grip to be feeling so suddenly defensive and protective of my stalker, but the very idea that this jumped up Iro/American was trying to take away his exclusivity made me boil.

'All right, hold on to your panty elastic, I'll explain it all in a minute,' he said, waving me to relax. 'But without seeming out of order, Evie, I wish Paddy had given me more of an idea about what I was going to be dealing with. I have to tell you, you're not what I expected, I mean you've got to admit you're really something.' He cocked one eyebrow and grinned.

I gave him the hard stare I reserved for the most truculent witnesses in court. I wanted this man out of my life. He had called me Evie! She of the first sin, she who had driven the genetic line of *Homo sapiens* into dark despair. 'How dare you stroll in here and suggest that I'm some sort of a deviation from the norm. That you should need prior warning before meeting "something" like me. The impudence! I have never been so seriously humiliated and outraged in all my life.'

He laughed. 'You should get out more.'

I wanted to rip this bloody hat off and throw these lawn sandals in his face. They were his wretched sister's anyway!

'You're one hell of a loopy lady that's for sure. I hope you don't mind me saying.'

'Well I do mind actually,' I shrieked. I was that close to not holding it together it wasn't funny. My frosty looks were all used up. I felt tears stinging at the back of my eyes. 'How dare you insinuate that I attracted *my* stalker (note the possessive pronoun) through irregular dress or behaviour. You, you stinking bastard.'

'Oooh the doll's got a temper.' Leaning back on the chair with his hands behind his neck he reminded me of a teenager teasing a kid sister – even though he must have been thirty-something on a generous day. He looked so relaxed, so careless, so, so, well, wanton basically. Everything about him unnerved me, from his cruisy New York accent to his washboard stomach. 'I like a woman who's hot-headed as well as gorgeous!'

For even the most servile little woman in Iran, this sort of taunt meant war. I lifted my hand to slap him, but he put his hand on my forehead the way my brothers did when I was young, making me feel impotent and patronised – not a bit like a woman with a custom-made diaphragm and the right to say 'no' should feel. Plus I still had this bloody hat you can put your drink in, strapped to my head.

'Just forget it will you. I don't want you on the case. That is it. You are not going to come in here and sit on my vulva, and manhandle me, and patronise me, and take my money. I'm a professional woman with Internet access and a can of Mace. I can look after myself,' I told him. 'And my stalker!' I finally broke the strap and wrenched the hat off.

'Your *vulva*?' he asked, laughing.

I didn't appreciate the way he was treating me like a joke, so I replied with a superior sneering sound, which didn't quite come off given the way things had gone between us. 'My chair. I call it my vulva. Well not *my* vulva obviously but it looks like a vulva. See you can see the . . . Just forget it will you. The point is, I don't want you here and there's nothing more to discuss.'

Rory stood up and walked around the chair, chuckling to himself.

'And you can stop your insinuating bloody laugh as well,' I added. I was ready to kick him out – literally. My feet were itching to go except they were stuck six inches down in my floor.

'Sure, doll. I've got the message. I'm meant to be on holiday anyway. It wasn't as if I was planning on getting involved in something as sleazy as this.' He was stroking the chair now. 'It's nice. The chair I mean – I like the design.'

'I'm surprised you know the meaning of the word,' I scoffed, giving him one of those sarcastic looks the bitch at Toby Lamb's had given me on Saturday night.

'Oh yeah? Philip Johnson and me are like this.' He crossed his fingers to demonstrate. And then, while I was still scraping my jaw off the ground, he strode resolutely to the door and let himself out without a backward glance.

How dare he! Just walk out like that without a fight. I flopped on the chair where he'd been sitting. He'd been here for less than five minutes and had managed to strip me of every vestige of dignity my parents had spent their lives and incomes trying to instil in me. I was submerged in that state of utter degradation that always makes my thighs feel like cellulite-ridden slabs of blubber. I threw myself on my futon, stuck my hand under my bed, pulled out my Belgian chocolate stash and proceeded to stuff my face.

CHAPTER THIRTEEN

his groin looked
very gyratable.

The next day I was in court acting in my capacity as Candida's
dogsbody and wondering if law was the right career choice after
all. I was having one of those 'was I called to the Bar or was I
shoved?' kind of days. Unusually, it was one of my own sex who
turned the tide on me this time – Mrs Justice Gallen, the sexiest
woman to sit on the bench. Put it this way, if I was going to be
a lesbian, I'd start with her.

There's already something sexual about all the judicial
pomp and ceremony – the wigs, the robes, the garters and
the veneration – but add to that Dame Mary Gallen's sharp
blue eyes piercing into you from above and, well, it's like being
undressed in court more or less. But not today – well not in
that sense. She'd sent a note to my clerk complaining about
the buttons on my shirt actually.

Lee was beside himself with laughter when I returned to
chambers.

'I'm sorry, Miss Hornton, but you've got to admit it's pretty
funny,' he argued, flashing the handwritten note under my nose.
'Old Sex-On-Legs Gallen, ticking you off about you bursting
out of your—'

I interrupted his flow with a withering look. Snatching the
note, I pushed it into my case. 'Naturally, Lee, I take your
counsel in all things – including humour.' I always think sarcasm
works better than a direct hit to the groin with co-workers.

Lee was a man who knew when I had the better of him – he turned back to DOOM 2 as if nothing had passed between us. But my burning humiliation was not about to be alleviated by a semi-successful ego tussle with my clerk. So when Orlando passed me in the corridor and asked me how my stalker was getting along, I engaged him in energetic conversation and even went so far as to invite him to lunch. Hell, I needed cheering up.

He looked at me like a rabbit caught in a car's headlights. Normally you see, I give Orlando a wide berth. Let's face it – it's more than my life's worth to chum around with Candida's enemy number one. But this note had temporarily destabilised me.

When we got to St John's, I passed it over to him, hoping for some reassuring words of comfort about my buttons. His reaction was similar to Lee's. 'Wow, how outrageous,' he giggled. 'How inexorably cool. I guess her umbrage was based on the way the buttons are sort of straining against the fabric of your blouse?' he suggested as he ogled my bust. 'Is that orange flash a bra by any chance? Or is it one of those lacy camisole things that—'

I snatched the note back and waved at the waiter to take our order. I opted for the rocket salad and pig's-head terrine while Orlando went for the more obvious bone marrow and sheep gullet. When he next redirected his interest to my stalker, I set the record straight and explained to him that I found the whole stalker business very alarming. I peppered my descriptions of life with a stalker with emotive imagery of dark shadowy forms leaping out of doorways at lone vulnerable women. I tried to describe the unmitigated horror of noises in the night when you are a woman living on your own. I even outlined the precedents for stalkers who eventually do their stalkees harm.

But Orlando insisted on treating my stalker like it was a hip drug that he wished he was taking himself. Orlando takes a lot of drugs. He doesn't see a conflict of interest between drugs and his career. Not that he'd go to court on E like I did once – although I want to make it clear that it was a complete accident, a one-off and, anyway, I won the case. Orlando thinks that drugs heighten his intelligence. But the evidence was increasingly stacking up against his theory. They were definitely wrecking his judgement over this stalker thing.

I decided to change the subject by telling him about my plan to hire a genuine Manhattan private eye to get the goods on this stalker cove. Orlando agreed with the girls in declaring a private eye to be an even groovier accessory than a stalker. I told him what had happened when Rory came over. I left out the bit about the drink hat, but admitted to the walk-your-way-to-a-healthier-lawn sandals.

'Like spiked Vivienne Westwood's you mean? I say, how frightfully cool.'

So I gave up going for the sympathy vote and tried to make Orlando see that Rory was a boring little tic. He was always referring to men far more powerful and successful than himself as boring or sad little tics. Almost any man actually. Orlando was pretty arrogant when you got down to it. In fact I think he thought he was a bit gorgeous. Like I said, drugs were eroding his judgement. Just the same, he stuck by Rory like Caesar to his horse, going on and on about what a brilliant life Rory must have, watching over the lives of New York society matrons. This was definitely not lifting my mood. Who was paying for this lunch anyway?

Our food arrived with Guinness. Orlando tucked his napkin into his collar and proceeded to suck out his bone marrow and gobble up his sheep gullet like a collie dog. He kept snuffling and wiping his nose on his sleeve. At one point I asked if he was on cocaine. He laughed and said, 'How inexorably outrageous!'

I twirled the rocket salad around my plate and tried to look careworn in the hope of soliciting a bit of comfort. But my artifices were wasted on Orlando who slurped and snuffled his meal heedlessly, until he eventually spilled his third Guinness all over both of us and laughed and laughed.

'That's fine, Orlando – laugh away, it's not the slightest bit of an inconvenience for me to go back to face Mrs Justice Gallen reeking of liquor.' But my sarcasm was lost on Orlando who was laughing so hard that snot came out his nose.

In spite of myself I couldn't be angry with him though. He was altogether just too off the wall. A different set of standards have to be applied to the Orlandos of this world. Besides, Candida made his life hell enough.

Back at chambers she was lying in wait for us in reception, gossiping with our new receptionist Mrs Keeney like a couple of hungry Venus flytraps. We had taken on Mrs Keeney – an old bat with bright pink make-up – after Candida had finally managed to have Gabby removed. Yes, she of the famous pierced navel had been sacked last month over an incident of a lost brief, but that is another story. I didn't like the unctuous Mrs Keeney, who could manage to be both obsequious and condescending at the same time. She had a fake nasal accent that made me want to punch her.

My fears as I faced Candida were real and fully justified – when she gunned for someone she was a one-woman execution line-up of crack marksmen. The full enormity of what I'd done, cavorting with Orlando – her idea of the devil's manservant – hit me like a hangover.

'Evelyn.' She said my name with honey dripping from every syllable. 'I was wondering when you'd decide to grace chambers with your presence again.'

'We just went out for a bit of, er, lunch,' I explained, like a schoolgirl explaining a truancy.

'So I smell.'

'That's my fault,' Orlando admitted bravely.

'Oh, Orlando, I didn't see you there,' she meowed, as in, 'You little insect, if I had I would have trodden on you.'

'We were drinking Guinness . . . and—'

'I'm sure you were,' she cut in.

Out of a misjudged sense of compassion I gave Orlando a get-out-while-you-still-can look. Even Mrs Keeney had seen the sense in leaving, which suggested she knew what was coming and would prefer to listen to it on the intercom.

I remembered the time I had caught Candida being fucked by our head clerk on her desk and how even that was used by Candida to her own advantage. I knew, from experience, there was no winning with this woman.

'I hear you received a note from Mrs Justice Gallen!' she started, but my imminent dressing down was brought to an abrupt halt when Rory walked in. He was wearing his obscenely torn jeans covered in grease and he wasn't wearing a shirt – it was tucked into the waist of his jeans. My feeling is that this particular sartorial flourish should remain the exclusive preserve of petrol-pump boys in Coke ads. As I looked from Rory to Candida, I felt like Indiana Jones in the *Temple of Doom* when he's going from trap to trap.

His pectorals were standing out like breasts – completely hairless. He looked like one of those Chippendale blokes and even I had to concede that his groin looked very gyratable, but I managed to brush this comparison from my mind.

'Doll!' he called out as if we were in a crowded bar. As he planted a kiss on my cheek, I contemplated denying him thrice or even once as in, 'Who the hell are you, sir?'. Believe me, if I'd had a wooden crucifix I would have waved it about like mad.

'Back on the Guinness, I smell.'

Candida and Orlando looked on like Lucrezia Borgia and Gumby as he explained that he was fixing up the Volvo and asked me for the keys. I was speechless. I swallowed my tongue and wondered how long it would take for me to choke to death.

Rory took advantage of this pause to introduce himself to Candida and Orlando. He grabbed Candida's hand first and shook it warmly with both of his.

'Good to meet you, Candy,' he said.

Candida's top teeth started pushing through her lower lip. She looked at her hand when he'd finished shaking it like it was a dismembered entity. It was covered in grease, so Rory grabbed it back and rubbed it off with a corner of his shirt – after he'd spat on it first. 'Forgive me.'

I briefly toyed with the idea of fainting, but the fear of coming to stopped me.

Rory gave Orlando a nod and a wink. 'Better keep your hands behind your back with me around,' he laughed. I prayed Orlando wouldn't say, 'how cool'.

But he did.

I gained a semblance of composure and girded my loins for a scene. 'Firstly I don't know what you are doing here and secondly, no I don't have the keys – perhaps you'd like to ask Paddy. Why don't you take the car back to your sister anyway, I don't want it.'

'I just might do that if I can find her,' he said to me, before turning to the others. 'Hey, but she's fabulous in anger, isn't she?' Rory asked, leaning over to jab Candida in the ribs. I don't think Candida knew what had happened. Her head sort of shuddered and her eyes rolled lifelessly back in their sockets. No one, but no one, has ever jabbed Candida's ribs.

'Don't worry about it, doll,' he said to me with a suggestive wink. 'I'll jemmy the lock.' Then he turned to Candida and said cheerfully, 'Takes more than locks and bolts to keep me out, hey Candy!' And he winked at her too.

Candida did that thing with her teeth and lower lip again. I'd never seen her like this before – speechless. No doubt she was mentally preparing my obituary.

Orlando was dribbling hypnotically. 'How outrageous, how outrageous . . .'

'Outrageous? If you want outrageous you should have seen this doll here last night!' Rory told him. 'She's really something.' Then he slapped me on the back so hard that I fell forward into

Candida's chest and left a disgusting greasy, garlic-scented, olive-oil smear on her silk shirt. He didn't appear to notice though because by then he was bent over, doubled up with laughter like he was about to be sick. I deeply regretted not taking the fainting option while I'd still had the chance.

'She had on this hat with a place to slot a drink on top. And a pair of golf sandals. What a doll,' he choked. 'I'm telling you it was the best night I've had in years. Seeing is believing,' he promised them. Tears were now streaming from his eyes so he probably couldn't see how furious Candida was and how violent I was about to be.

'How phenomenally cool,' murmured Orlando over and over like some drug-fucked cult follower.

It was another few minutes before Rory managed to gather himself together. 'Anyway, can't hang around philosophising with you lot all day. Man's gotta work,' he sighed, slugging me on the back again. 'See ya, doll. And go easy on the liquid lunches, will ya? I don't want you coming home legless tonight. And some chow around six'd be great. I'll be hungry by then.' He tweaked my chin.

Then he nudged Candida in the ribs again while she was still wiping the grease mark off her no doubt priceless designer silk shirt. 'And take a bit of advice from someone who knows, Candy,' he told her earnestly. 'Drop the Candida business. Your folks probably didn't get around enough to know, but take it from a guy who's seen it all. Candida's a cheesy disease. Now don't take it personally but the guys you meet will be worrying they'll catch it.'

He gave Orlando an enthusiastically reciprocated 'five' and left.

CHAPTER FOURTEEN

why do men always think their dicks are a panacea for the world's problems?

Suddenly, being cooked up by my stalker didn't seem half as bad as the evil revenge Candida would no doubt inflict on me. At least death at the hands of a stalker would give me a certain tragic dignity. My clerk would sell my story to *News of The World* and some sicko Glaswegian scriptwriter would probably be inspired to make a fortune out of recounting my misfortune as a stage drama.

Far more terrifying was the long-term horrors that awaited me at the hands of Candida. We were a team – like Fred Astaire and Ginger – we might hate one another but the audience loved us. So we would stick it out together and I would allow her to torment me like a cat with a squirrel. Year in year out, I would suffer the slings and arrows of her jibes, all because some pumped-up muscle-bound Iro Yank got it into his head to fix my Volvo. I was no inexperienced fool where this woman's predilection for humiliation was concerned. I knew my punishment for Rory's visit would stretch way into my next lifetime.

When I bought this loft thing I'd consulted an astrologer who'd predicted a year of successful enterprise and luck in love. So what went wrong? I felt like I'd been caught up on the spin cycle of another religion. Maybe the Hindus had claimed me due to some bureaucratic error on the astral plane and I was being visited by karmic justice meant for a sadistic murderer or something.

With these gentle Eastern faiths, if you do the dirty in this lifetime, you pay with your soul. That's why I've always preferred Catholicism – you make a mistake, you front up to the priest, make your reconciliation with God and Bob's your uncle. We love a prodigal son or daughter. Whereas this karma idea would see a girl belted from one incarnation to the next for stepping on an ant. Maybe the Karma Collection Agency had the wrong woman – some sicko sadist was probably walking around thinking she'd got off scott free for the serial killings of a past life while meanwhile I was taking her rap. Good luck to you whatever your name is, you are well out of it.

On my return from court, I sneaked past the clerk's room and ignored the squeals of laughter. I dropped in to see Orlando to give him back his bands. It was his idea that I should wear his bands underneath and slightly lower than mine as a button concealer but judging from Mrs Justice Gallen's withering glare it was a non-starter.

'How'd it go?' he asked as I slunk into his room.

'Don't ask. Let's just say I'm thinking of getting my face remodelled and forging a new identity. I think I'm suffering under the tyranny of someone else's karma.'

'I had a client once who had his whole face reconstructed, new identity papers, the whole thing – cost him millions and he still ended up in Wormwood Scrubs.'

I slumped into a chair.

'That bad?' he asked. I noticed that his face now disclosed the sympathy I had been yearning for earlier. 'Look, Evelyn, I know this probably won't help, but I just wanted to say I feel really bad about spilling the Guinness on you. What can I say, I'm a clumsy idiot. I'm more ashamed than I can ever express. I take full responsibility for the whole debacle with Candida. Anyway look, here's something by way of comfort.' He passed over a condom.

'Comfort?' I looked at him, I looked at the condom. I was mortified. Why was this day happening to me? 'Orlando!' I squealed, dropping the prophylactic like it was a used one.

Orlando picked it up and looked at me. I could tell he was hurt. 'Sorry, Evelyn, I didn't think you'd react like that. It's really good quality, I can promise you that.'

The man was deranged. 'The quality of the thing isn't really the issue here, Orlando,' I explained. 'It's not AIDS that I'm worried about, it's you getting your wires crossed. The last thing in the world I want is sex.'

He looked crestfallen. 'I just thought you needed cheering up.'

Why do men always think that their bloody dicks are a panacea for all the world's problems? I wondered, not for the first time. But because Orlando looked so dejected, I started to feel slightly guilty. It's a fact that the male ego is as fragile as tissue paper in matters of the groin. He was a sweet guy and I didn't really want to hurt his feelings. Perhaps I should have held onto the condom a bit longer and pretended to reflect on his offer carefully. Maybe it was a bit ungracious of me to throw an out and out rejection at him without due consideration. I suppose it was a pretty insensitive way of saying, not on your life, buster. He had gone very pale.

I attempted to resuscitate his ego. 'It was a sweet offer, Orlando, it really was. I shouldn't have reacted like that – it's just that, well, basically, sex is the last thing I feel like after everything that's happened today. Don't take it personally. Hell, Hugh Grant couldn't have budged my libido today. Not if he came at me on his knees, naked. No, Orlando, you just hit me on a rough day. Why with your looks, your personality, I'm flattered – definitely flattered. If anything you're too good for me.'

He was still looking pretty glum, so I stepped up my panegyric. 'I know a lot of women around the Inns of Court have got their eye on you. Any why not? You're an absolutely great bloke – dream division and I . . . well, quite honestly, Orlando, you're better off without me. What with all my problems and neurosis, my stalker and Rory, you'd best forget me and offer yourself to someone more, well, appreciative basically.'

God this was hard. During my little ego massage his eyes had become quite bloodshot. I had hurt him deeply. In fact he looked like he might burst into tears. Obviously he had taken my rejection bitterly. It's not uncommon after all for junior barristers to fall in love with their female superiors. Not uncommon at all. Why the poor boy was probably love sick and I, like a Boadicea in Blahniks, had walked all over the fragile bloom of his heart.

'I'm offering you cocaine, not myself,' he snapped.

Now I felt like I'd been struck. I reeled back.

'No offence, Evelyn, you're a brilliant advocate but – how can I put this delicately – you are *far* too old for me.'

God, he wasn't bothering to let *me* down kindly was he? I wished now that I'd held back on that bit about him being first on my libido list. What did he mean by too old? I was twenty-seven for heaven's sake. Only last month on my birthday my mother had sent me a card stating that 'the best was yet to come'! Don't tell me it had been and gone and I'd missed it?

By then Orlando had started undoing the condom with his teeth. 'Look see,' he insisted, aggressively thrusting the thing under my nose. I looked at the powder concealed in its prophylactic disguise. Then I looked at the door, expecting to see Mark Sidcup QC or Candida looking over my shoulder. Barristers' chambers are a bit like rabbit warrens – no one bothers to knock. But we were alone.

'God! I can't believe you thought that I actually wanted to sleep with you,' he repeated. 'How absolutely appalling.'

'Steady up,' I said. '*Appalling* is gilding the lily a bit.' OK so I got it wrong, but I think a little chivalry was called for here. After all I had had the compassion to cushion his rejection with a few sweeteners. Hadn't I just told him he was a great bloke, more or less promising my body to him next time I had the urge?

'Look, you've got to believe me,' he ranted, his spots lighting up like fairy lights. 'You are the last woman on earth I would harbour feelings of an amorous nature for.'

'All right, I believe you. Can we just drop it now? I admit I had the wrong end of the stick and I agree I was mad to misread you. I was way, way, way out of line. End of story!'

But Orlando wasn't going to drop the bone that easily. He threw his arms in the air as if summoning the angels in heaven to come to his aid. 'I mean that is just *so* far from the truth . . . How utterly appalling.' He repeated the words 'utterly appalling' like a chant I was expected to join in on.

'Utterly, utterly appalling,' I agreed.

'I mean it's monstrous,' he declared, slapping his palm against his forehead and shaking his head. He still looked like he was about to cry and I was torn between wanting to wrap him in a maternal embrace and slap a gagging writ on him.

'Can we just forget this ever happened? I think I've got the picture now, Orlando. Fucking me is the absolute last thing you'd be caught dead doing if your life depended on it. You pitied me. You wanted to give me drugs and I stupidly misread the scenario. I'll put an apology in the next issue of *Time Out* if you insist.'

He started to laugh. 'You're utterly outrageous you know that?'

Five seconds later we were inhaling the contents of his condom through a fifty pound note when Lee came in.

He stood at the doorway and coughed. Topping stuff – I had just been caught taking class-A drugs by my clerk. Excellent. What a splendid way to round off my day.

'Yes, Lee?' Orlando barked curtly.

'Yes, er, um, excuse me, Mr Porter-Meade. Sorry, Mr Porter-Meade. I was just bringing in a brief for you – it's the new Mossad case.'

'Very good, Lee, on my desk please. If you'd care to leave us now. We were in the middle of a meeting.'

Lee backed out red-faced and whimpering apologies.

I was speechless. What was that scene I had just witnessed?

Was that the same self-opinionated, stuck-up clerk that had giggled without pause over my troubles with buttons and Mrs Justice Gallens? Orlando had white powder rimming his bloody nostrils for Christ's sake. We had been caught with the proverbial red nose!

'How did you manage that,' I gasped in undisguised awe.

'What? You mean Lee? I hope you don't think I would take any shit from that sorry little tic of a man.'

CHAPTER FIFTEEN

i was getting my ethics mixed up with my men.

When I saw Matt outside the Wren church on Holborn Circus as I was walking home from chambers, I realised I had fallen inexorably in love. No not lust, love. Get this, he was putting down the bonnet of his yellow Merc, and he must have jammed it on his finger because I saw him mouth 'ow' and shake his hand a few times. Wasn't that adorable? Ow. Not shit, or fuck, just a simple childlike ow. I felt my nipples grow erect.

I watched him as he wiped a hair from his face and left a grease mark and I thought of Rory. How could two men be such diametric opposites, I wondered as he took his jacket off, swung it over his shoulder and started to walk away.

I called out to him, running through the peak-hour traffic like one of those Japanese suicide-mission pilots. But the lugubrious heavy flow and the brain-dead drivers were too heat-fucked to effect a direct hit. He smiled at my approach and took off his sunglasses.

'Ms Hornton, what a surprise.' He smiled.

I was his. He could take me now, in the traffic or grab me and drag me down to a portico in the churchyard and snog me senseless. I immediately affected the most unfeminist eye-dropping pose. 'Hi, Matt and please it's Evelyn. I'm Australian too, remember. Let's drop the titles. Besides, it's miss,' I simpered. Oh sad, sad creature, a voice inside me said.

'Of course you're Australian, I always forget that. You've

got to admit you're just too awesomely sophisticated for the down-under stereotype I'm used to.'

I blushed. From anyone else that little speech might have sounded patronising but Matt was different. I smiled appreciatively at the slur on my homeland – I may have even shuffled. I felt a bit giddy, like I'd inhaled too much carbon monoxide, but maybe it was the coke still working. My fears of a karmic mistake were clearly unfounded. If this was sadist's karma, count me in at the Marquis de Sade's next banquet, I said to Shiva, or whoever it is who takes care of these things. I was prepared to change religions for this man. Hell, I was prepared to change into a cow if it meant sleeping with Matt.

'Are you, um, having car, er, um, whatchamacallit?' I stammered. (God that must have sounded about as awesomely sophisticated as a Vegemite sandwich.)

'Flat battery I think.' He wiped his hands on a rag that he'd fished out from under the dash. 'I'm ashamed to say that despite being a Darlo Bar dropout, I don't know the first thing about cars.'

I gave one of those little tinkly 1930s' laughs – as opposed to my usual foghorn hoot. 'Don't apologise, I'm a bit of a Darlo Bar dropout too,' I said meaningfully. Even then I couldn't believe I had actually said that. It was a manifest lie, obviously. Girls from the banks of the Harbour don't do the Darlo Bar, but we were talking seduction here – and the truth was about as sexy as class privilege to a self-made man like Matt.

Even thinking about the Darlo Bar made me feel shaky. Just off Kings Cross in Sydney, it was a shark pit of corruption, drugs and skulduggery that I had never had the bravado to enter. It was the sort of place girls hardly ever went to unless they were scoring drugs and their boyfriends had DTs. It was the sort of place you went to play pool and get pissed before getting a tattoo. It was the place to hear live bands and get the grapevine lowdown on squats. Whatever it was, it was not the place where North Shore girls who were planning to study law went.

Matt had come a long way – the boy done good. I, on the other hand, had barely done anything. Say no to class privilege, I was going to tell my daughters – get ye to a Darlo Bar. While he put the bonnet down, I couldn't help imagining what it would have been like sauntering into the Darlo Bar now and seeing Matt's ponytailed head bent over the smoke and smog of the pool table.

'I was about to phone the AA but I can't get a signal here,' he explained, interrupting my daydream just at the point where I was going to sashay up to him and his tough mates and offer to take him to heaven with my lips. 'Can I invite you for a drink while I wait the inevitable hour or so it will take them to arrive?' he asked. 'Or would that be unprofessional? You barristers have an ethical code don't you?'

'That's doctors actually. We don't let ethics get in the way of a good case.' God I thought, don't tell me he's looking for ethics! I knew I had to knock that illusion on the head right away if I was going to get anywhere on this seduction campaign. 'Tell you what, I live just near here. Why don't you phone them from my place and we'll have a drink there.'

As we wound our way through the massive refrigerated lorries, past the meat market where cool characters and wannabes spilled from bars and cafés across the streets, I knew I wasn't the riveting raconteur I longed to be, distracted as I was by a range of unnerving fantasies about tearing his Calvin Klein knickers off with my teeth. In fact I was having to jiggle from one leg to the other to stop my clitoris dive bombing through my knickers.

He meanwhile carried on a really suave conversation about the latest art happening he'd attended. As we turned into St John Street he explained that there had been a latex wall with which viewers were invited to interact. I responded with answers about as cool and sophisticated as fried halibut.

Now was my chance to jolt his focus with my newly discovered art-speak, to tell him how I loved the Mitchie Fuckawanoo or whatever his name was, but the grunts and silly simpers and tinkly giggles kept on coming. At one point, as we trudged past a new art space on St John Street, where the flotsam and jetsam of the art world were congregating like an influx of nineteenth-century refugees, I started to mention my visit to the Saatchi gallery. Talk about bad luck – just as I was warming to my theme, a charge of press and art-world familiars rushed into our path. A new crate of Beck's was unloaded.

'That new space must be opening,' he explained. 'Do you know Jibby Beane?'

I made an ambiguous noise as we cut across the street to avoid the frantic convergence on the Becks. The truth was I didn't know anyone. Even if I knew all the Jibbys and the Bowies and the Mitchie's in the world, how could I show him I was a gutsy, hip, contemporary, art-literate Aussie girl with attitude and sex appeal, when my bloody libido rendered me inane? I couldn't remember when I'd last felt this way but I had a strange hunch it was when I fell for that gay solicitor. Some women have a built-in radar where the wrong sort of blokes are concerned. I've got a satellite dish with the arsehole-detection range of a NASA tracking station.

Anyway, by the time we reached my place it didn't much matter what I said because, once we got inside, there he was – Rory O'Reilly, large as life, still shirtless and demanding his tea.

'Doll! At last. Where have you been, woman? I was scared shitless wondering what had happened to you. Couldn't you have phoned or something? I was about to mount a search party.'

I noticed Matt's focus was jolting about like crazy now, but before he could run, Rory had grasped his hands with two of his and introduced himself.

'What the fuck are you doing, Rory? How did you get in?' I asked as calmly as I could. Even though my brain was practically liquid with rage, I could see the sense in not using my jillaroo tone in front of Matt this early in the relationship.

Rory slapped Matt on the back. 'Isn't she a treat when she's aroused?'

'Don't manhandle my guest!' I told him. 'Answer my question – how did you get in?' I turned to Matt and gave him a reassuring eyeball roll of mock irritation.

'I thought the least you could do was fix me some tea,' he said, as Matt went over to a quiet corner to make his call. 'Anyway who's your new friend with the ponytail?' he asked with an aggression I hoped would land him a smack in the mouth from Matt. I looked over to give him the thumbs up but he was already on his mobile, on hold to the AA.

'This is *space* invasion,' I told him, taking him aside. 'And how dare you insult my guest. Matt happens to be a very important client.'

'Very important client,' he mocked.

'I don't know why I'm bothering to explain anything to you but as it happens he's got car problems so I invited him in to wait for the AA.'

'Doll, doll, doll! Why didn't you say?' he asked, suddenly all concern. Next minute he was snatching Matt's mobile off him and leading him out the door. 'You'll never get them out at this time of day! If I can fix that Volvo I can fix anything. Let's go take a look at this car of yours. Fix me some tea while I'm gone will you, doll?'

And with that they left.

CHAPTER SIXTEEN

upper-east-side women were falling over their bloomingdale's bags to catch their husbands in flagrante.

Talk about depressed. One minute I was about to have the object of my desire alone with me in an enclosed space and the next I was saddled with Rory and his iniquitous brand of foot-in-the-mouth Iro/Yank charm. How on earth had I arrived in this ridiculous situation with a private eye I didn't want – I mean I hadn't even engaged his services. Nor did I have any intention of doing so. For a start I hadn't even seen the stalker all day. Who knows, maybe he'd packed it in and found a new girl to torment?

As it was I'd rather have a thousand stalkers on my case than this hood. If this was what New York society dames were looking for in a man they could have him. He was more intrusive than the most proficient stalker in London. I mean at least my stalker never called me 'doll', never mocked me, never marched uninvited into chambers or slapped Candida on the back. At least my stalker knew his place – outside skulking in the shadows at a respectful distance. In fact, this jumped-up private eye could learn a thing or two from my stalker.

I had decided that it was time for a confrontation so I stuck a suitably *up* CD into the stereo and sharpened my heels. I didn't have to wait long. Rory was back before I'd even chosen my weapon, wiping his hands on something that looked suspiciously like one of my DKNY T-shirts. 'Flat battery, nothing more. He said to say goodbye.'

I looked at him with studied indifference. I had reapplied my blood-red lipstick and had run through all the seminal points drummed into us in the assertiveness-training class. The first thing was not to let him get comfortable, so I'd taken the initiative and perched myself rather splendidly on one of the vulvas – just the same I was feeling less and less formidable as the seconds ticked by.

He was grinning at me like I was some kind of entertainment he'd rung up for earlier, which didn't help my concentration. He slouched against the door as if waiting for the stand-up comic to do her stuff. While I was rehearsing my script in my head, formulating the right phrase with which to bring his ego to its knees, he said, 'What a wanker!'

'Excuse me?' This wasn't how my assertiveness-counselling tutor had said it should go. Rory had put *me* on the defensive. I gripped the sides of the vulva as I struggled to gain control.

'Matt, who else? What a pretentious bozo. How'd you get mixed up with a jerk like that anyway?'

'He is not a jerk. He's a client – a very important client – and I'm not mixed up with him. He happens to be a very successful businessman with scads of class which no doubt went way over your head.'

He shrugged. 'Well, whatever. He's still a prize wanker and into some heavy shit if you ask me.'

'Aha! But that is the point isn't it?' I remarked, crossing my legs and swinging a stud-heeled Manolo Blahnik menacingly back and forth. Now was my chance to demonstrate my superior combative skills. 'I didn't ask you for your opinion, did I? Just like I didn't ask you to fix my car, or invade my chambers. In fact, you seem to have gone way beyond your remit on all counts.'

106

He shrugged again in that maddening way. His arms, as smooth and brown as a worn chesterfield, were folded high on his chest.

'Sure, anything you say, doll. So I take it you're not offering tea then?' The knee poking through the hole in his jeans seemed to mock my anger, his whole aura cried out 'mother me' and, like the anti-evolutionist victim I was, I heard a voice I recognised as my own asking, 'Oh all right then, what do you want?'

Somehow I ended up making him boiled eggs with soldiers and tomatoes on the side. Pretty much a first I realised later – me cooking for a man! I didn't have an egg cup so he ate them whole in the most disgusting way I could believe. I don't know how or why I held my tongue but I did. At one point egg yolk ran down his chin and he wiped the toast across it, laughing when I grimaced. 'Waste not!'

The manic grin was perpetual and the pre-suffragette comments were endless, but nonetheless I had to admit the evening wasn't that bad – surprisingly intriguing actually. He told me about his last six years in New York and how it had all started with a woman he'd met at the Grosvenor one night. He was telling me how he'd gone there with a friend 'for the craic'.

I thought he meant the drug. 'Oh,' I sighed. 'That explains a lot.' I was there thinking I'd finally unlocked the secret of his erratic antisocial behaviour. The poor deprived boy from Kerry had got tangled up with drugs, and not just any drug – crack I mean, I almost felt sympathetic.

'Explains a lot of what?' he laughed, opening up the second bottle of red. His muscles flexed as he screwed the waiter's friend into the cork. In the candlelight his tanned skin was unsettling, shiny – effulgent even. I looked at my own thin pasty limbs. Drugs hadn't ruined his complexion then.

'Well, I mean crack is meant to be a pretty dangerous drug. I defended this bloke in Brixton once and—'

But I didn't get to finish my liberal little speech. He leaned back, cackling so hard I could see the scars from his tonsillectomy. 'Gees, doll, you never let up on a bloke do you? What do they teach you about the Irish down under? I mean it's bad enough being taken for an IRA henchman, let alone a crack addict.'

'But I thought you said —' I started.

'The craic, doll, the craic!' he repeated, dragging out his vowels like a piece of chewing gum, and I couldn't help finding his New York accent kind of attractive despite myself. Then again we were into our second bottle of red which tends to make me love my fellow man – a throw-back from Communion I guess.

'It's like a lark, mucking about. You mean you actually took me for a crack-head? With this body?' he teased as he performed some body builders' moves.

'I thought . . . well, I just . . .' I blathered.

'Don't worry – it's nothing. But it's down on your permanent record,' he chided.

'Get on with the story, then.'

'OK, so Darcy and I were at the Grosvenor getting a bit worse for wear. We'd been at a charity do, for leukaemia I think it was. One of those black-tie jobs. His old lady's on all those charity committees and she'd roped me and Darcy in. We were at uni together see.'

'You went to university?' I screeched in disbelief.

'That's enough from you. You've accused me of being a crack-head, don't start on about me illiteracy now,' he warned. I coloured in shame, even though he winked at me. 'So I left Darcy with the auction and went for a wander looking for the craic and this doll was up at the bar knocking back the G&Ts like there was no tomorrow.'

At this point he had paused to roll a cigarette. I wanted to tell him not to smoke but I was too interested in what he was saying. I'd never met anyone like him before, and his wrong-side-of-the-tracks anti-charm held a curious fascination – at least after a few glasses of red. By now I had thrown common sense to the wind in my desperation to know all about him. He offered me the tobacco.

'I don't smoke.'

'Why not? Asthma is it?' he asked, clicking his tongue as if only a severe disability could keep a sane woman parted from something that was a known cause of heart disease, blindness and cancer. I shook my head.

'No, I don't smoke either,' he told me as he licked the roll-up closed and took a box of matches from his pocket. 'Just if I drink and that.'

'So go on,' I urged, well and truly hooked.

'Where was I? Oh yeah! Not bad-looking – old, around forty plus but in good shape. I didn't fancy her at first but, well, one thing led to another if you get my drift? She had a style I liked. Anyway she sat at the bar with us and we all got pissed. She told Darcy and me about how her husband was having an affair. Well she suspected he was, so she wanted him followed. She offered me five grand, expenses and a trip on Concorde to New York with her.'

I raised my eyebrows. It seemed a bit far-fetched.

'What?' he asked, as if hurt by my doubt.

'Well, you've got to admit it's a bit much for a rich society dame to hire a boy from Dublin on the strength of a few drinks at the Grosvenor.'

'A bog Irish, illiterate crack-head of a boy you mean? Na. She fancied me didn't she?'

He was stretched out on the floor at my feet so I could gain the full benefit of his animal magnetism. OK, so after one and a half bottles of wine he didn't seem half as hateful as he had two hours ago. Neanderthal comments to one side, he was the sort of person it was hard not to feel relaxed with.

I wondered how old he was. Thirty-something – ageless really. Basically this bloke didn't know the meaning of limitations. He was painting a picture of a life lived with a startling lack of complexity, a world where anything could happen –

and I was being seduced into believing him despite my better judgement. All right, so I decided to buy the first-class tickets to New York – at least for the sake of the story.

'So you went?' I prompted.

'Next day we flew into JFK and I was set up in the Algonquin with a new set of hot clothes and a dossier on her man. You should have seen the room, the gifts and the fuckin' perfumes she bought me. Man, I hate . . .' He paused to drag on his cigarette.

'Hurry up . . .'

'Sure, so anyway she was right. That bloke was putting it about like Don Juan. Not only that – he had a mistress set up on the Lower East in an apartment a bit like this.'

I bridled at this comparison. He laughed and pointed a taunting finger at me. 'Woah but this doll's got a temper!'

I settled back into my seat. I was gripped, heedless of an innate urge to hand him his exit pass.

'No, it was nice work. Very satisfying actually, stitching that bastard up with photos and sworn statements. It was a seriously good feeling. The sex wasn't bad either.'

I felt the colour rise to my cheeks. His body stretched out on the floor seemed almost heckling in its languor. 'So tell me the details,' I asked a little more brusquely than was necessary.

He smiled teasingly. 'The details? My, what a prurient doll we have here. Well if you really want to know . . .'

I scowled. 'The case, Don Juan. The case!'

'Ease up, doll, just jiv'n you. Once I'd got her all the evidence she needed, see, my job was finished. She got herself a hotshot lawyer and took him for everything he had. The sex sort of petered out and one day I got back to the Algonquin to find my stuff in the porter's room and a note waiting at reception with a thank-you cheque attached. Not that I minded. Upper-East-side women were falling over their Bloomingdale bags to have their husbands caught in flagrante.'

'That's a big word!'

'I am a big boy,' he joked, doing this smouldering trick with his eyes.

'I think I'm out of my innuendo depth here,' I told him. 'Tell me why you're back then – I mean if you were as in demand there as you say you were.'

'Now you wouldn't be doubting an honest Catholic boy like me would you, doll?' he chided turning on the Gaelic accent.

I shook my head.

'Let's say a little bird told me there was a damsel in distress in need of my services over here.'

I curled my feet around the legs of my chair. All the bonhomie of the evening disintegrated with that one sneering remark. How dare he refer to me in such a patronising way. How dare he, when I had never asked him to get involved. A damsel indeed. I was a kick-boxing black-belt with a map to my own G-spot. A rapturous look of smugness came over me. Now was the time to put Mister Rory Too-Big-For-His-Boots O'Reilly in his place. And I was going to play this moment for every kick to the ego it was worth. 'Well I'm sorry you've been brought all this way for nothing,' I sneered. 'But as you can see I'm not in distress any more than I'm a damsel. You really should stop listening to birds, you know – you'll get a reputation.'

He smiled sweetly, stood up and stretched. As his arms went up so did his shirt, revealing a stomach that gave me a complete X-ray of his torso. 'Sorry, doll, didn't mean to mislead you. You do a mean egg but you're not my damsel. She's well . . . let's say it's a personal matter. Another story and the wine's gone.'

I looked up. He was smiling down on me like big brothers smile at kid sisters. 'Mind if I kip in the Volvo tonight? I'm too knackered to get back home now.'

I was so numb with embarrassment, I nodded.

'I'll grab a shower in the morning too if that's OK? Thanks for the tea. You know you're not a bad cook when you try.'

I don't know why I should have felt so stupidly inept and rejected when the man was so clearly an oaf. But I did. I was also irritatingly keen to know what it was he had studied at university.

CHAPTER SEVENTEEN

a pair of blahniks and a girl can vanquish anything.

I woke up the next morning with a hangover. Pulling on my kimono and wrapping agnés-b sunnies around my eyes, I walked tentatively out to the kitchen and made a Descartian effort to pretend that the detritus of last night's meal wasn't really happening. I have read the French philosophers and I can recognise existential despair when it's hitting me with the force of a red-wine hangover.

I piled the coffee grains into the espresso machine and looked out the window. The streets were quiet and empty – not even the odd hungover bummaree from Smithfield meat market stumbling home broke the emptiness, there wasn't a stalker for miles. I had to face facts, he hadn't just nipped off for a nap, this bloke was gone for good.

I don't know why that should have niggled so much, I should have been dancing in the streets, but it just came at me like another rejection slip that morning. I looked at the calendar – it was three months since I'd last had sex and three hours since I'd last had a chocolate. The feel-good factor wasn't working for me.

Maybe Orlando was right, I was too old. I was becoming one of those sad spinsters that no one, not even stalkers, or drug-crazed junior barristers wanted to bother with. Locked in these thoughts I didn't hear Rory's approach.

'Hiya, doll!'

I spun around so hard my brain collapsed in on itself. He was standing inches away from me with his wet hair slicked back over his skull, water trickling from his nose, a tattoo of Raphael's angel on his left pectoral and my best towel wrapped around his washboard stomach.

'That's my towel.'

'Mmm, that quaffee smells good, any chance of one, doll?' he asked, pronouncing the word coffee like a native Brooklyner.

I didn't want to go into the theories of Kristeva on the servitude of women, so I shoved a hellishly strong espresso into his hand and waited for him to spit it out, all the easy companionship of the night before was gone. The bloke was in my towel for starters – that was a class-A violation. There'd be no U-turn down the road of friendship now. I wanted this man out of my towel, my life and my loft for ever.

He gulped it down.

'Good coffee. Tell you what, doll, if you fail at law you could always work in a coffee bar,' he called out to me as I stormed off to the shower.

My colon was sick with a mixture of red wine, chocolate and anger that wasn't alleviated when the trickle of hot water I was expecting turned out to be a surge of cold that made my heart stop. Deciding to generously offer up my suffering for the souls in purgatory, I reached out for the shampoo but it wasn't on the hook. I looked down at the drain and watched as the last of its precious contents disappeared. I was cursing the Celtic race as I bent down to pick it up.

'Nice ass!' Rory whistled behind me.

I shot round to swipe him but he was gone.

'Just bringing back the towel,' he yelled from behind the cubicle.

'Right that's it! That's the bloody limit,' I screamed.

I turned off the shower and grabbed the towel. It was sodden! Bugger! I used my kimono and made a dash for my bed, acutely aware of my lack of walls. This man was going to feel my wrath in his balls. I lay down low so I couldn't be seen above the futon and pulled on the remnants of clothing lying about the floor. Yesterday's stockings and no knickers. How could one man make me feel so consistently inept?

Well the worm was going to turn now, I affirmed as I pulled a black linen skirt out from my duvet cover. It was crushed – last year's look I knew but that was going to have to suffice. I rescued a Nicole Farhi black stretch cardigan from under the futon. Then I donned my war paint – a colour going by the name of 'plague' – and psyched myself up to do damage to the most jumped-up Irishman this side of the Atlantic. A pair of nail-heel Blahniks can put a woman in a position to vanquish anything she sets her heart on. These shoes were lethal.

I strode through the loft, pulling the comb through my wet bob, bellowing, 'Right, you bastard. Enough is enough. Either you get out of my place in the next micro-second or I'm calling the police and having you for harassment, trespass and anything else I can think up while I clean my teeth.'

As I walked into the kitchen, Paddy stood before me, stricken. 'Sorry, Miss Evelyn, only you said eight o'clock would be OK. I'll get my gear out right now though.' His moustache was all roughed up from where he'd slept on it and his complexion matched my mood – red.

I tried to smile. It was hard in this lipstick shade to carry off calm and charm but I gave it my best shot. 'Er sorry, Paddy. I was talking to someone else,' I reassured him, deciding it would be prudent not to mention that Rory had spent the night. We both looked around the empty loft. The bewildered Paddy started to back away.

'Of course I was, er, um, expecting you. I was just, er, just, um . . . Just go right ahead, Paddy.'

I'm sure the only thing that made him stay was the money I owed him because he looked like a man suddenly in the mood for a cross-channel swim. 'You all right, Miss Evelyn? You look a bit shaken. Has Rory not seen to yer man the stalker? Here, I'll call 'im on mi mobile right away.'

'No, Paddy. I'd rather you didn't. I've, um, seen Rory as it happens and the stalker situation is in hand. He seems to have, well, gone in fact. So you see I won't be needing Rory again. Perhaps you can tell him that from me, thank him for his help.'

'Well if you don't mind me saying so, miss, you seem a bit troubled by something. Only I don't like to think of you here all alone with the little baby.'

'The baby?'

'Little Johnny.'

'Oh, er, yes, well, you see the baby's gone, Paddy.'

He took his hat off and came over towards me. 'Gone? How's that?' His moustache had visibly drooped.

'Yes, I, er, gave little Johnny back,' I stammered.

Paddy let out a heartfelt sigh and looked me in the eye. 'Oh, Miss Evelyn. What do you mean you gave him back? I thought he was yours. I thought, well, I thought it was more permanent.' For a minute I thought he was going to cry.

I could see this conversation was becoming too delicate to handle without intravenous coffee for both of us. I remembered how I had stupidly let Paddy believe that Johnny was mine.'

'Well, Paddy, you see I more or less misled you basically,' I tried to explain, while inwardly bemoaning how complicated my life had become. 'He wasn't really mine, I was just looking after him for friends, you see.'

'Oh? You never said anything about friends. I got the impression . . .'

'Well that's because I, er, you caught me at a bad time you see, Paddy. I was rather stressed about, er, this and that. It was this stalker business actually. That was it – I was delusional. That time of the month I guess. Ha, ha.'

I could tell by the way he said, 'Oh well then,' and backed

away that he was one of those blokes that live their life in fear of women's hormonal fluctuations.

'I'm sorry,' I said. 'It was just that I honestly wished he was mine but it wasn't true. I was just looking after him. I'm sorry I let you think he was mine, Paddy. I feel quite ashamed about it all.'

We looked at one another for what seemed like for ever – the Irish builder and his hormonal, financially challenged employer. He was probably calculating how he should hit me over the head with a brick before he rang the Care in the Community Hot Line.

I must have awoken something inside him though because next thing I knew he had grabbed me to his chest and his big rough freckled hands were stroking my wet hair. He smelled of Weetabix and toast. I think it was probably incumbent on me to sob, but I just didn't have the stomach for it. In fact if someone had said the word 'egg' at that moment I would have been ill.

'Hush! Don't say a word, Miss Evelyn. I know how hard it is for a woman. My Rosy had needs. She wanted a baby more than anything, more than anything in the world. She bought all that stuff I gave you over there to compensate. That's what the doctor said. Truth was I gave it to you because I couldn't face it after she left. My poor Rosy, where has she gone? Where has she gone?' He was sobbing now, clutching me to him and crying his heart out. I patted him lamely.

'It's not the same for a man,' he went on. 'I tried to understand, but it's not the same for a man. Oh why did she leave me, Miss Evelyn? Where's my lovely Rosy gone?'

I made a muffled sound into the polyester of his jumper and felt my temperature. As I suspected it was feverish.

CHAPTER EIGHTEEN

clothes maketh the man.

Candida was meowing like a cat on heat when I arrived in chambers the next morning. 'Quick, grab your cleavage, Evelyn! We're off to the Royal Courts of Justice – a chambers hearing with Judge Threep-Smith. Quick, quick! No time to lose. Hitch up that skirt and redden those lips. You can borrow my Chanel compact. Quickly, quickly! Matt's depending on us for this one. The length of your skirt could be the difference between tea at the Ritz and a ham sandwich from a transport café for our dear boy.'

I did as bid. Judge T-S was our favourite of all favourites, known around the Inns for enjoying a good sherry, but to Candida and me he was a cleavage connoisseur extraordinaire, so I held my D-cups to my chest and tore off after her up to the Strand – hair flying. Barristers loitering around the Temple gave us quizzical looks as they stood aside to let us pass. Some of them knew our reputation as the chanteuses of the RCJ. Some of them just thought we were joke people escaped from a *Carry On* film set.

I couldn't run as fast as Candida in my nail-heel Blahniks and pencil skirt so Candida was having to run back and entreat me. 'Run, run, blast you, we don't want to be late as well as perspiring!'

I conceded her point, basically I was hobbling rather than moving. These might be just the shoes for getting your own way, but alas they weren't the best footwear for getting from A to B. Basically, I don't think Manolo had cobbles in mind when he dreamt up these heels.

I stopped and handed over my pilot's case and files to a lost-looking pinstriped man under an archway while I leant against a wall and removed my shoes and pulled off my tights. My man started to mutter something about the PC police and did I know chivalry was supposed to be dead. 'Like who cares?' I told him. 'So's Elvis. Do you think that put an end to Gracelands?' Before he got onto my sex as a metaphor for turbulence, I was grabbing my gear back and tearing off, barefoot, over the cold cobbles of the Temple.

We arrived with minutes to spare, bursting through the doors, panting like wolves back from a night of heavy prowling. The plaintiff's counsel was already there reading his *Telegraph*. He had a white bandage over one eye and wore a dusty brown, pinstripe suit of the sort worn by Eastern Europeans fleeing genocides.

He eyed us out of the corner of his good eye as if sizing up his chances and then, clearly deciding they were good, he let out a satisfied grunt and slumped back in his chair like a dead mule. If he knew what was good for him he would start meditating on those wise words from Shakespeare – 'clothes maketh the man'. Candida and I communicated with a wink.

All in all, our prospects were conservatively hopeful. My skirt needed a bit of a going over with an iron and my legs were bare but my lips were rouged, my top buttons were undone – in other words all our cannons were loaded and aimed.

Just the same, even given the most dazzled judge in the world, we couldn't realistically have the injunction set aside. All in all, things didn't really look as good for Matt as we'd told him but you don't hire a counsel like Candida to tell you she's charging you for your own doom. At this point our modest goal was to seduce the bench into varying the terms, thereby giving Matt more reasonable living expenses than the pathetic five hundred pounds a week set. I mean, what's five hundred pounds between friends staying at a suite in The Grosvenor?

The case was being heard 'in chambers' which meant we

didn't need to wear our wig and bands, but Brown-suit was clearly one of those blokes you get at the Bar who can't resist an opportunity for a full fancy dress. He wore his battered wig like a crown, with his patched gown draped lazily over his hunched shoulders like an ermine stole.

Candida and I did our last minute facial repair jobs while we waited for the judge to arrive. Brown-suit licked his finger loudly and turned the pages of the *Telegraph*. I teased my bob up into a bouffant as instructed by Candida and allowed her to starch my chest with Poison. The sacrifices a girl has to make for the Bar!

Judge Threep-Smith walked in wearing a nicely cut navy herringbone from Gieves & Hawkes and a flourish of pink handkerchief in his breast pocket. He eyed the brown suit with a distaste that increased as counsel for the plaintiff waffled on and on about the age in which we lived until Judge T-S finally blew his nose to silence him. Candida had passed me a little note earlier which I had had plenty of time to memorise by the time our turn came. She nudged me to speak – claiming laryngitis to the judge.

I used my sweetest little-girl-lost voice. 'If my lord will give me leave to address the bench when I am so inappropriately dressed? Only we had thought, my lord, that this application was to be heard "in chambers".'

An ominous silence collapsed on the room as I smiled sadly at the judge, letting my lower lip droop in a really subtle look – combining miserable wretchedness while still retaining my tough-as-testicles professional-woman demeanour. 'Only, judging from my learned friend's apparel, I can only deduce that I made an error.' I pretended to look ashamed as I wiped my hand over my pile of white books.

Judge T-S smiled reassuringly back. 'You did no such thing, my dear. Any error of judgement is being worn by counsel for the plaintiff,' he soothed, before turning to my learned friend and booming. 'Look at yourself, you fool! Remove that wig and gown. Why, the impertinence! What do you think this is?'

Brown-suit's good eye practically shot across the room.

'At once!' His Lordship bellowed.

Brown-suit bowed his head and began the miserable task of divesting himself of his dignity. Victory was mine. My bosom heaved in triumph, exonerated after that humiliation at the hands of Mrs Justice Gallen. I felt like I had a bottle of amyl nitrate up my nose. It was all I could do to stop myself slam dancing into the judicial mosh-pit. Casting a last withering look at the vanquished, I turned the full force of my cleavage back on Judge T-S. I wished Matt could have seen me, but neither he nor Mitzy were in attendance. Wigless and gownless and bandless, her representative scowled from under his bandage while I requested an allowance of five thousand pounds a week for my client.

Judge T-S was nodding solemnly at our cleavages, in fact he was practically whimpering with desire. He freely admitted he would be entirely delighted to please us in any way the law would allow.

'Let's make it ten shall we? After all we are not here today to clip Mr Barton's wings.' He tapped Matt's sworn affidavit which testified to his outlandishly expensive lifestyle.

There were more snorts from the plaintiff's counsel. But Judge T-S was undeterred by nasal interruptions, his mind was made up and that was that. Afterwards he sent his clerk out to invite us to his private chambers for a drink. Candida hooted as she read his hastily scrawled note out loud.

'Damn improper!' Brown-suit muttered darkly as he was leaving the building. Candida gave his back a squirt with her Poison atomiser. The few lawyers who saw pretended they didn't.

'Sherry, ladies?' Judge T-S enquired once we were ensconced on his big soft chesterfield.

Candida flirted mercilessly, all memory of the laryngitis which had rendered her mute in court now gone. She was batting her eyelashes so hard I thought she was going to knock herself unconscious. 'Absolutely, Judge, the quality of your sherry is famous.'

'Good of you to say so, my dear, though I hardly ever imbibe myself,' he winked. 'But I like to give pleasure where I can.'

'How good you are, Judge,' Candida cooed, geisha-like over her lashes. She had her flaws but she knew how to treat a judge.

'One does one's bit, my dear.' He waved the decanter at me. 'And you, Miss Hornton, sherry? I know its not a popular tipple with young people these days – so my son tells me.'

'Thank you, Judge, just a small one.'

'That a girl. A remembrance of things lost, eh?' He smiled benevolently as I sipped on the sickly sweet nectar and sank back in the leather of the chesterfield and tried to relax. For some reason though all I could think of was Rory's arms.

CHAPTER NINETEEN

ec1 ennui, i.e. – martinis, cellulite & lime-green lycra.

There was a note from Telecom pinned to my front door reminding me that I had missed another opportunity to have a phone line installed. Basically, this meant that I was still dependent on a mobile phone I could never find and a battery charger that had more mood swings than I did. I poured myself a martini – three inches of gin and the mention of the word 'vermouth'. Then I curled up on my vulva and toyed with the idea of alcoholism as a lifestyle.

The evidence was irrefutable – there was a hole in my life that even a toxic blood-alcohol level wasn't going to fill. I was depressed and lacking in self-esteem and it hadn't helped that my stalker had apparently given up on my case. It was the old Catholic guilt thing again. I felt I had failed him. Maybe I didn't fulfil all the criteria he had been banking on? Maybe he was really hopeful that stalking a young female barrister would take him on to all sorts of inspirational destinations and situations.

I looked forlornly at the neglected invitations stacking up around my door – things like the Temple Ball, theatre performances in Temple Gardens, El Vino's wine tastings at the City of London Club, Bond Street sale invites – promising an added ten per cent off – and the new spate of invites to art openings that had been arriving since my foray into the art world. A whole host of cultural events which I hadn't bothered to attend.

125

Maybe that was the sort of stuff my stalker was into though? I mean barristers do have a sort of rampant, boozy, sex-mad image that I didn't really live up to. He was probably expecting leather parties and naked cavorts through the Inns of Court when he took on my case. Some chance!

Speaking of cases, Rory hadn't reappeared either – which should have been cause for champagne, I know, but as far as I was concerned three-quarters of the way through my next martini, it felt like another rejection on my dance card. Added to all this, Matt hadn't called to congratulate me on having the Mareva Injunction varied – giving him a hefty great ten grand a week pocket money, thank you very much. There wasn't even the light relief of Paddy dropping in with a new pair of lawn sandals. Face it, I had been dropped by my social world – such as it was.

I was struck with an overwhelming sense of ennui. I was twenty-seven years old, for Christ's sake – I was too young for ennui. I should be painting the town red with a list of suitors longer than my American Express bill. So where were they?

When the gin ran out I decided to throw off my ennui and the bulk weight of chocolate I'd been consuming lately by doing dance aerobics in the lime-green lycra catsuit I'd bought during a previous bout of ennui. I stuck on a Spice Girl's CD I'd bought for just such an occasion and started doing star jumps in the mirror, but I got all wheezy and hot after ten minutes and the lime lycra stuck to me.

Half an hour later, when I'd exhausted my exercise repertoire, I looked like something that had been spat out of the *X Files*. I collapsed on a vulva and tried leafing through a year's worth of back issues from *Vogue*, *Tatler* and *Harpers*. But all that did was give me an acute awareness of impending cellulite. I started jogging around the flat.

The phone rang just as I realised that Paddy's main progress today was to render my erstwhile inadequate kitchen facilities i.e., microwave and sink, totally useless. A really funky designer might call it deconstructed, I told myself, looking hopefully at the hole in the floor where my sink used to be and the tangle of copper pipe and wires that looked like one of the chippies had left their intestines behind.

'Evvy!'

'Charles?'

'I know it's short notice but, er . . .'

'Can I baby-sit?'

'Oh would you, Evv, that would be so good?'

'When?'

'Well now actually, we're downstairs on the mobile. Johnny's due for a feed. I'll bring him up so you can get started shall I?'

Hell it wasn't as if I had anything else on, so I said sure. But as I put the phone down something even worse than ennui struck me. Despair. Face it, a voice inside me said, you're going to end up a maiden aunt, eternally baby-sitting your lesbian girlfriend's kid. This was ominous. I, Evelyn Hornton apple of her gran's eye with a first from Oxford and a D-cup chest was going to end up with a reputation as a sad old homebody.

You'll get SKY TV and bore people with the plots of all your favourite shows, a voice inside me warned. People will ring you up and ask you to video things just to make you feel needed. You'll be one of those thirty-year-old spinsters who make crafty things like home-made candles and marmalade – or worse, tapestry covers for cushions. Your social life will deteriorate into underwear parties and fat friends with relationship problems.

'Evvy, what's the matter?' Sam asked as soon as she walked in. That's Sam, ever the sensitive one. Like not!

'Oh I'm just a bit down,' I owned up. 'My stalker's gone and now even Rory's given up on me. I guess I'm starting to feel old and—'

'Bugger that – what about your kitchen? I can't leave you to heat up Johnny's breast milk in there,' she pointed out, with all the compassion of a serial humiliator.

'Well I wasn't exactly expecting you!' I reminded her – sticking a good measure of asperity in my voice.

'You are his godmother, Evv. It's your duty to be on hand for your little godson.'

'I do have a life of my own you know!' I informed her, without much conviction.

Sam raised her eyebrows as she gave my green-slime skin the once over. Charles stood stiffly silent beside her, looking at her feet nervously like a murder trial witness who has been threatened.

'Anyway, I'm not his godmother. He isn't even christened. You can't go awarding godmother status like Maltese Crosses,' I explained.

'Oh don't be so technical, Evv. Chill out,' she told me, tickling little Johnny under one of his half-dozen chins. 'Isn't Aunt Evvy a neurotic, Johnny?'

'Well, can't I heat it in the toilet sink?' I suggested.

Sam and Charles gathered Johnny to their bosom in a sort of Fascist-realist pose. 'The toilet?' they shrieked in one voice. 'Have you heard of E-coli?'

'All right, all right so forget the loo idea.' I was starting to feel like a failure even on the maiden aunt front by this point. 'Actually, I think there might be something for heating babies' milk in that junk by the shower cubicle. The stuff Paddy's wife left behind!'

CHAPTER TWENTY

a crucially excellent catastrophe!

Johnny had decided not to sleep that night – it was in his
horoscope or something that this was his big night for making social breakthroughs. His bright, eager eyes were leaping
around in his head the way mine do when I've been greedy
with the strawberry daiquiris.

As predicted, Paddy's wife had a great device – the Perma
Content, a plug-in wonder for keeping babies' milk on twelve-
hour hold. Not that this little kid was going to let his mother's
brew sit around gathering dust or anything. As I plugged it in,
the sadness of this device cut me to the core. My concern for
Paddy's wife's sanity had never been greater. This was the sort
of stuff bored women get into when they're like really depressed
and Valium is no longer enough. This was throwing your money
into a black pit of consumerism. It was bloody mad, that's
what it was!

Sympathy aside, I was going to have to put my foot down
with Paddy. After all, one of the major incentives for buying this
place was the space, much of which was rapidly disappearing
under his wife's junk. I was going to have to confront him
once I got our relationship back on a more employer/employee
footing.

I began to gather all the shit into the middle of the room and
divide it into Johnny safe and Johnny danger. He was at the
stage where he was starting to pull himself onto his knees, doing

this rocking back and forth thing like he was about to take off or something. At this point he wasn't actually getting anywhere but I didn't want him committing suicide on the lawn sandals when he did. I talked Johnny through all my major decisions holding things up for his opinion. He chortled with delight and rocked back and forth even more, building up a momentum for the big takeoff – there was no escaping the fact that this kid was seriously cute.

We were getting along splendidly, right up until the point that he began to exude abattoir smells and I saw my affection slip into disgust. I wasn't cut out for kids. Love him as I did, his nappy left me cold. Sam had provided me with a jumbo box of disposable rubber gloves but there was a knock at the door as I was trying to get them on and I got such a fright I stuck a nail through one. In my struggle to pull it off I'd ended up with a prehensile hand that, juxtaposed to my lizard-like outfit, might have frightened off a lesser human.

As it was, Orlando was wearing five-inch Vivienne Westwood platform slippers and bondage trousers that buckled his legs together tightly at the knee. 'Hi! Hope you don't mind? I was in the area,' he explained – shyly passing me a bottle of Veuve Clicquot.

'Right, well hardly surprising really, Orlando – you live here!' I reminded him. Not a hundred yards away as it happened, in a basement flat with no windows whatsoever because he was paranoid about ultraviolet light ruining his complexion. Orlando was paranoid about all the wrong things actually.

I invited him in. 'Oh wow, love the gloves – how cool,' he enthused, struggling to stay upright. I stepped aside and watched this spectacle from a Japanese humiliation game show fight the conjointly attacking forces of gravity and bondage all the way over to Johnny's little rug.

'Oh wow, excellent. I didn't know you had a kid. You are truly incredible, totally outrageous.'

'Well actually, Orlando, he's not really—'

'Love all the gear. Love your outfit too!' he announced, fingering the hat with the drink cup in it. He held it up. 'This stuff is sublime, what is it all?'

'Nothing, Orlando, just, er, some artist's sculptures.' I wasn't going to get into a big discussion about Paddy and his marital problems and why he had dropped the residue on me.

'Cool!'

I got to the kitchen – or rather where my kitchen used to be and sized up the pit Paddy had left there. It looked like an IRA practice site. 'Orlando, we'll have to drink it from the bottle I'm afraid,' I called out. 'My kitchen has been demolished basically. I can't even get in there to get a glass and I don't think you should try in those shoes.'

I returned to find him with the hat that holds a drink on his head and I could tell I was losing it because instead of laughing, I just stood there and stared. This bloke made even me feel sane.

'This is phenomenally outrageous, Evelyn. Truly inexorable! Superb. Hey, do you think I could borrow this for clubbing sometimes?' he pleaded, making the sort of eager face my doctor makes when prescribing a particularly nasty antibiotic he's agreed to try out for Roche.

'Sure,' I said. 'Keep it.' Like Paddy, my generosity knew no bounds where this gear was concerned.

His lips wriggled around in a comic grin of gratitude. 'Outrageous!'

'So you don't mind drinking vintage champagne out of the bottle?' I checked. Orlando could be funny about things like that. Despite appearances he was a stickler for form. It was as if all the drugs he took eroded every other area of his brain except the bit where he stored the etiquette cells.

'Sure, how extraordinary,' he replied, pulling a rubbery face for Johnny. He was struggling to crouch on his haunches (while his knees were braced tightly together to his trousers) beside Johnny who was lying with his nappy off, kicking the shit all over his play rug and up his body. Orlando pressed his little button nose which made Johnny chortle delightedly.

'Do you know anything about kids, Orlando?' I enquired hopefully, impressed with his skills thus far.

'Such as?'

'Well, changing nappies and stuff.'

'Nappies?' he asked, pronouncing the word like an Egyptian at his first English class. His eyes were shining as if I might be about to inject him with a new psychedelic drug.

I pointed.

He squealed. 'Oh I say, how frightfully outrageous!'

'You can wear some of these,' I offered, holding my gloved hands out and wiggling my latex fingers temptingly.

That seemed to sell him. He nodded solemnly, as if accepting costs in a hearing. 'OK, deal. I do the nappy, you open the champagne.' His eyes flicked excitedly around in his head.

Deep down I suspected that it was the lure of the gloves rather than the genetically programmed father in him. As he dug excitedly into the box and pulled a pair on with the practised skill of a surgeon, his brow creased in a look of grim determination. That was when I started to feel a bit iffy about the whole plan. I mean getting excited about rubber gloves and baby pooh? Hang on a minute, was I inviting a fetishist to change my baby's nappy here?

After the champagne cork flew out, I wrapped my mouth around the ejaculation of bubbles which shot up my brain like a bottle of poppers. I started spitting and choking. By the time I regained my breath, Orlando was rubbing Johnny's legs, feet and bum vigorously with the baby wipes and, what's more, appeared to be doing a fairly thorough job. Johnny wasn't screaming and the pooh seemed to be coming off well. I began to concede that, despite my initial misgivings, this bloke was a bit of a hero in the shitty-nappy war.

I offered him the bottle, which he signalled I should hold to his lips while he worked. As I did so, his nose practically exploded with bubbles. He collapsed on the floor in a spasmodic coughing fit like a trussed turkey.

I fell on him like the experienced paramedic I wasn't and asked if he was all right but he was in no position to answer. Buckled together by the strap still, his legs were thrashing about so much I was thrown off. I tried to undo it but I couldn't get in close enough. He was like a surfer being attacked from all sides by sharks in a feeding frenzy. I was helpless. Plus he was still in that stupid hat with the tricky Velcro strap and I was more worried he'd choke – well he *was* choking actually.

I ran over to my bag hoping against hope that I would find my mobile. I was watching a man in the throes of death and for some reason it struck me that even now his testicles were producing sperm in quantities capable of impregnating China. Focus, Evelyn, focus!

More than anything I was terrified by what my clerk would say, which probably sounds really selfish but it's hard to keep a grip on the subconscious when faced with death. I wasn't myself and it was certain that Lee would flip if he knew I'd been instrumental in bringing about the untimely demise of one of his barristers – and for all his eccentricity Orlando was a damn good lawyer. Come to think of it this could even be manslaughter – and I was measuring his sperm count?

I made another attempt to unbuckle his legs as his jerkings decreased. He had started to go blue now. How would I ever explain the deplorable circumstances of my colleague's death at the inquest? 'Well Coroner, it was like this – we were changing a baby's nappy – you know those cute little chubby things that cry a lot? Seriously dangerous stuff my good man.'

But maybe there was still a chance to save him. After all I did have one of those first-aid certificate thingamies. I tried to think of what one was supposed to do in such circumstances but my mind was a blank. That summer I'd spent getting the St John's Ambulance certificate evaporated into a mist of heavy petting with Joseph Mendez.

I jumped on his chest and threw his arms about but all it did was bring me out in a sweat – my sense of doom increased with every shade of purple Orlando's face discovered in its fight for air. Within seconds he was looking like one of those anthropological morphs that sickhead med students put on the Internet for a laugh. I mean, talk about the evening degenerating.

It was such an incredible back flip of fate that Matt should have turned up then. If I hadn't loved him before I was prepared to have his babies when I opened the door. Johnny was howling and Orlando was looking like he might explode any minute.

'Quick, help! My friend's choking,' I spluttered as Matt started to pass me more of the lethal-vintage Veuve Clicquot stuff. They must have been chucking the stuff at passersby to get rid of it or something.

It wasn't long before I realised that Matt was proficiency incarnate. Boy, had I fallen for the right bloke. He took in the accident scene pretty much immediately which required a progressive moral code for starters. A lot of people might have balked. Or run away even. Face it:-

One man in platform slippers, rubber gloves and bondage trousers in death throes
Oh, and let's not forget the hat.
One half-naked child covered in excreta, yelling its head off.
One woman in slime-coloured second skin and rubber gloves.

Get real, a lot of people would have required an explanation, a signed affidavit, guaranteed anonymity and danger money even. But not Matt. I suppose they get stuff like this in the Darlo Bar every second day, I mused, as without so much as an expletive or a request for a stiff drink, he gathered Orlando into his arms and pulled him to a standing position. 'Get some water,' he shouted to me.

Ah! What to do? I ran in the direction of the kitchen where

the tangled pipes spewed out in a blockade. Then I ran to the bathroom and realised I had no available vessel. So using the good old Loreto-girl improvisational flair, I cupped my hands under the tap and ran back to the emergency scene where I offered my sad attempt at innovation to Orlando. He was flailing about in Matt's arms like a jelly but he licked at my soggy hand like a rabid dog!

'Don't you have any glasses?' Matt asked obviously enough.

'I couldn't get into the kitchen. My builder's torn it apart,' I explained, doped to my eyeballs on a mad cocktail of shame and panic. Johnny's howling wasn't helping.

'In the hat,' he ordered. 'In the fucking hat!'

I seized the hat cup and ran back to the loo. But by the time I returned, Orlando was in definite recovery, slumped in a vulva sucking on a Ventolin inhaler. Matt looked into my eyes and smiled. God! It felt as though he was boring into my soul.

'Why, Miss Hornton, what an exciting creature you turn out to be,' he announced.

'Crucial,' Orlando rejoined over Johnny's howls as I passed him the water.

'So what have we got here?' he asked, looking about the room and rolling up his sleeves. 'One screaming infant, one enormous amount of shit and two absolutely hopeless adults, eh? Come on, mate,' he said to Johnny, probably the only one of us he credited with any brain cells. 'Give it here. Let's get this mess cleaned up.'

Johnny gazed up at Matt lovingly – the way I wanted to.

'Spiffing!' said Orlando.

CHAPTER TWENTY-ONE

it was written all over his penis.

By midnight we had drunk all the champagne and Johnny was fast asleep, having crashed out in Orlando's arms while he was dancing around in the drink hat. Matt and I managed to flirt despite his unabating interjections of 'how inexorable' and 'how outrageous'.

After he'd put Johnny down on my futon, Orlando explored the pile of toys Paddy's wife had left behind, which were now in the two sorted heaps by the door. One of the things he'd unearthed was a blow-up man.

I'd never worked out what it was in its deflated state – it just looked like a deflated tyre ring. In fact I had even put it on the Johnny-safe pile. But as Orlando blew it up, it became 'Brad, your very own Negro lover'. It was written in pink print on his penis.

Matt and Orlando were overwhelmed for different reasons.

'It's not mine!' I hastened to explain, as Brad reached his full majesty, but Orlando was already suffused with giggles and Matt's eyeballs were orbital.

'It belongs to my builder's wife. Rosy I think her name is, she, er, she wanted kids but, er, well, she kind of lost it and bought all this stuff to compensate and Paddy was kind of distressed by it all and so he, er, brought it all around here and er, er . . .'

But all explanations were ignored – even in silence Brad said it all.

'Inexorable! Can I take it clubbing with me tonight?'
Orlando pleaded.

'No!' I snapped – perhaps a little too harshly. It was just that
I didn't want Brad's origins (my flat) to get around.

'What if I put a G-string on him?'

'Absolutely not.'

'How outrageous – do you use him?' Orlando enquired, as
the finishing touches of air puffed Brad's penis to a whopping
great twelve inches.

'I've never seem him before in my life!'

But Orlando wasn't listening. 'Oh look, he's got a back
opening too,' he remarked. Bending Brad over to observe it
more closely, he inserted one whole latex-gloved hand. 'Seriously
excellent.'

I began to have an out-of-body experience.

'You're incredible, you know that? You never cease to amaze
me,' Matt said, pulling me to him and I decided that it was almost
worth the embarrassment of Brad to have the body contact with
Matt. My astral body returned to enjoy the physical thrill. Things
were most definitely looking up.

'I think maybe we are coming to a point where three's company
and four's a crowd,' Orlando announced a little later, by which
time the atmosphere was charged with the electricity of my desire
to tear Matt's trousers off him.

As soon as we were alone Matt fell on me, pressing me
up against the wall as he kissed me long, hard and slow. In
hindsight it was the basic cliché swoon-making first kiss made
spectacular by the taste of bubbles and cigarettes and beaches
and sun and barbecues and harbourside views. I hadn't kissed
an Aussie in years. He was one of those kissers that make it all
happen with the lips rather than the tongue. I hate those tongue
kissers – they always leave me with an acute awareness of my
plaque situation. No, Matt definitely had a kissing technique
worth lingering over but we both felt as if we were being

watched by Brad, who was eyeing us lustily with an almost sinister desire.

'Right, big boy, time for you to hit the hay,' I told Brad as I stuck him under my arm and stuffed him behind my futon. Johnny was still sleeping beautifully.

I could hear my mobile ringing in the distance somewhere but I ignored it as I walked back in to Matt and reconnected myself to his mouth socket. He ran his arm over the lime-green leotard that I'd put on for aerobics. It was one of those peel-down, pull off jobbies – about as tight as a sausage skin. While we were both wordlessly debating how to get it off someone started ramming down the door and woke Johnny up. Matt went off to get him while I undid the new locking system I'd had Paddy install.

'What a bloody shitty evening,' Sam cursed as she barged in.

'They gave us the wrong tickets,' Charles explained as we embraced. 'We couldn't see the stage.'

'Whose fault was that?' Sam sneered, and I could see they had chosen my flat as the ideal battleground in which to burn off their disappointment. Matt walked out with Johnny who was waving a nappy flag-like over his head. I smiled at him, thinking how sweet they looked together. Face it, kids are the designer accessory for men in the nineties.

Sam obviously didn't think so though. 'Thank you I'll take him,' she snapped, grabbing Johnny who protested with a howl. She turned around and glared at me like she'd just caught me selling her kid into slavery.

'This is Matt,' I told her. 'A client of mine. Matt, this is Sam and Charles, my best friends.'

Sam, rocking Johnny on her hip, scowled. 'I'm very fussy who I let touch my baby,' she said flatly, eyeing Matt up as if trying to remember his face from a paedophile register. 'Even if they are Evelyn's *clients*!'

I bridled at the way she put the edge on this last word. 'Matt is a natural with Johnny,' I assured her. 'It was very lucky he turned up when he did actually,' I said, hoping to soften her mood. 'God, Orlando was here choking and Johnny was covered in shit. You should have seen the mess. It was outrageous.'

'How very encouraging,' she sniped sarcastically as she flounced off with Johnny.

'Maybe I'd better be going,' Matt suggested.

I told him he didn't have to leave and gave Sam a cold glare. But Charles gave him a shove towards the door. 'Yes, it is getting late. You mustn't miss the last train.'

'Train?' Matt repeated, like it was a word he wasn't familiar with. Face it, it was equivalent to telling a homeless person to go back to their penthouse. The atmosphere was ugly.

'Sam's a bit overwrought,' Charles offered by way of justification as Matt took the hint and opened the door to leave.

'I'll call you!' he shouted as the door was slammed on his face.

'Why do my friends do these things to me?' I asked God. 'Why don't they just take a gun and shoot my suitors for me? I mean it's all right for them to be joined at the hip but as soon as I look as if I'm about to do a bit of cohesive bonding with someone, out come the long knives.'

Before the heavens could respond though Sam came storming over with Brad tucked under her arm. 'And while I'm in the mood for murder would you mind telling me what the hell this is?' His erection seemed even more formidable juxtaposed to her tiny form. 'What the fuck has been going on here?'

She looked ready to hit me and for the first time in my life I knew how Garbo felt.

'Calm down, can't you?' Charles said, rubbing her temples.

'Calm down is it now? Oh that would be right. Talk about patronising. I've had it with you and your superior-bitch attitude!' she yelled.

'I can explain,' I offered, throwing myself between them, hoping to defuse the situation. I can't bear it when my friends argue in front of me.

Sam sat down and stuck Johnny to her left breast. 'Try me.'

There was a knock on the door but in my rush to answer it – hoping it was Matt coming back to invite me back to his place – I tripped on Brad and splattered indecorously on top of him in a sort of obscene sex pose which was how Rory found me when Charles stepped over me and opened the door.

Normally Rory would really go for something like that – me spread-eagled at his feet, compromising myself with a naked blow-up black man. I waited for the howls of mirth, but not a thing.

'I just saw that creep leaving,' he snarled. 'What was he doing up here?'

I climbed off Brad and stood up – trying to strike a woman-in-charge-of-her-own-destiny pose. 'What creep? Oh, you must mean Orlando,' I breezed knowing damn well he didn't.

'Not Orlando. *The creep* – Matt.' Then he pointed at Brad as if noticing him for the first time. 'I'd watch that guy at your feet if I were you, doll – he's looking up your lycra.'

'See, everyone thinks Matt is a creep!' Sam called over, switching Johnny to the other breast.

Rory threw her one of the sexiest wry smiles I'd seen. 'Hi, name's Rory, fashion accessory to the rich and gorgeous. Cute kid you got,' he grinned.

Sam blushed. 'I heard Evelyn was thinking of hiring a private eye but she didn't warn me how handsome you were.' For a second I thought she even batted her eyelashes.

'I don't see what his looks have got to do with it,' I told her. It sort of unnerved me the way she was turning on the sweetness and light for Rory.

'Good looks mean everything when you look as good as Rory – why he looks good enough to eat.'

My God! This was unbelievable, my dyke girlfriend was actually flirting with a new lad? Hello? Was I in orbit or what? Usually I have to struggle to get her to be civil – even to an

NASGS (a new-age-sensitive-gay-sexist). I tried to recall if I'd been knocking back the vanilla essence recently.

'So what sort of services do you offer?' she simpered away.

'Well, the client usually calls the shots,' he drawled. There was that word again – *client*. How come when he said it, it sounded so respectable, so clean and decent? 'Private eye's my game, but, hey, I'm flexible.'

'Erggh!' I choked – waiting for Sam's cliché alert to go off. Surely she was just giving him enough bullshit line to string himself up with? That was it. Once she had him dangling from his own personality bypass she'd go in for the kill.

I wanted to warn her that maybe she was leaving her lunge too late but she smiled at Rory earnestly and told him she might wish to engage his assistance with a matter of her own.

Hang on a minute. Why would a man-hater like Sam want to call a sexist Neanderthal like Rory? I was missing something, right? He passed her his card. I looked over to see what Charles was making of all of this. I think the customary thing to do when your partner starts hiring private eyes is to hit the roof and demand to know what the bloody hell for. But she was too preoccupied with Brad to pick up on any of Sam's weirdo dialogue. With that twelve inch erection and his face lit up with sexual anticipation, he was a dominating force – even for a lesbian.

'Who's your new man then? Aren't you going to introduce us?' Rory turned to me and quipped.

Sam sighed like a long-suffering martyr. 'I found him beside her bed when we got here – right beside Johnny! God knows what she was thinking of, Rory. Johnny's at a very formative age with his role models, as you can imagine. I blame that creep Matt she had in here, it wasn't here before he came around.' Then she pointed to me. '*She* was even letting the creep hold Johnny.'

They all stared at me in appalled silence as if I was some kind of lethal weapon about to discharge. Even Brad seemed disappointed in me.

I decided it was time for me to express a bit of righteous self-defence. 'Will you stop going on about Matt! I know him far better than you and even though he's being sued for fraud he happens to be an extremely charming and intelligent man. I think he's brilliant, sophisticated and honourable actually and for that matter so does Johnny.'

Johnny came off the breast and gurgled his agreement. I folded my arms and gave them all a smug look.

'You are seriously wrong there,' Rory insisted. 'Look, I know you're not keen on what I've got to say about this guy but I think you're going to have to listen when you see what I found in the glove compartment of his car that night I fixed it.' He reached for his groin. Charles, Sam and I all made instinctive terrified squawks.

'Careful, buster, we're all lesbians here,' Charles warned, holding Brad out in front of her as a shield. Her warning became irrelevant though when we saw what it was he was pulling out of his jeans.

'It's OK, it's not loaded,' he assured me as he passed it over.

I took the gun in my hand. It was warm which made me feel a bit squidgy – thinking about how it had got this warm. 'But this is a gun?' I announced, somewhat superfluously.

He grinned. 'No actually it's my detachable dick, I was just pleased to see you.'

I showed him he was beneath my contempt by handing him back the gun gingerly. I hoped he'd get the irony.

He stuck it back in his jeans. 'Too corny, huh?'

'Amongst other things,' I sneered. 'Anyway, what's this got to do with Matt?'

'I told you, I found it in his car when I gave him a hand to get it going.'

'Oh yeah? And like I really believe you!'

He shrugged. 'I just thought I should warn you. There were some hydroshock bullets with it too – as in maximum pain and damage ammo. This guy plans to do someone a lot of harm. Let's just hope it's not you. As you seem content in your delusions, I'll be on my way.' He nodded to the girls as he turned to leave.

'No, wait,' Sam called out. 'Shit, Evvy, this is heavy. Let's hear what he's got to say at least. I think he's right. You've got to agree, Matt does come across as distinctly cheesy.'

Charles agreed. 'God, Evvy he's been accused of a serious fraud, apart from anything else. Surely that dents his honourable standing to some degree, even in your lust-struck eyes.'

'What – you mean guilty till proven innocent? God, Charles, you're a barrister, how can you say that?'

She sighed. 'Evvy, get real.'

'So where there's smoke there's fire is that it? Just because some stupid bitch gets jilted she wants to blame Matt. It's not his fault that she chooses to trust strange Spaniards.'

Rory interrupted. 'Look, cheesy is putting it mildly. I happen to know of this creep through another source.'

I didn't like the way he kept referring to Matt as that creep and I told him so.

'You don't think that you're thinking with your clit here, girl?' Sam suggested.

'Fuck off!'

'For one thing it's not as if "Matt" is his real name,' Rory interrupted before things became dangerous between Sam and me. 'I can tell you this much for free. He's a con man. I've heard his name being tossed around New York and it wasn't in connection with the donations he gives to charity either. He preys on the sort of vulnerable women I work for.'

'Oh excuse me while I get the violins,' I sneered. 'I keep forgetting that you are the protector of women.'

'Seriously, Evvy, you're a nice woman. I just don't want to see you get hurt. This guy takes risks with other people's money – fact. The risk is that if it pays off he's laughing and if it doesn't they're destroyed. He doesn't give a shit, people are dispensable to creeps like him. He screws them, he moves on, simple as that. I don't know what stories he's fed you but my advice is steer clear. He's been jerking you around.'

'Oh yeah? Well I think I know who's jerking me around and it's not Matt.' There was no way I was prepared to believe that Matt was anything but wholesome and delicious – for one, the taste of his lips was still racing through my neurones.

'Trust me,' he grinned.

'As if,' I sneered.

'Evvy, shut up,' Charles snapped. 'I think you should take this seriously – investigate this. It's hardly ethical for you to get so involved with a client anyway. Pretty bloody unprofessional I would have thought.'

I turned on her like a banshee. 'Oh look who's talking! You're the one who told me to "go for it" remember? Who told me to seduce him with my knowledge of art, who said "wake up to the nineties, even judges are doing it" – or have you conveniently forgotten all that?' I had started to raise my voice without realising it. The first rule in an argument is not to show you care. If you show you care it can be used as evidence against you – to prove you're probably not thinking straight. 'Why should I trust *him* rather than Matt? Why should I trust you, you, you turncoat! I know Matt, you don't and neither does he. He says he's found a gun but how can he prove it? He's just doing this to get back at me because I didn't want to employ him. I don't know why you're so willing to believe Rory when he's such a sexist pig!'

Rory flicked Brad's member and smiled. 'Well, you're the one with the impeccable taste in men, Evvy, no one's in any doubt there.'

I didn't appreciate the way Sam and Charles laughed as if it was the funniest joke they'd ever heard.

'How can you be so sure Matt is up to no good as you put it? OK, so you've heard rumours but do you have anything more solid on him?' Charles asked him when she'd finished choking on her tonsils.

'Sorry. My word is my bond. You just have to trust me,' he replied, shrugging his bare shoulders.

'Oh puh-lease. "My word is my bond?" Get a life!'

'Well, think about this then – why would I lie?'

'Ha!' I said. 'Hardly a waterlight case.'

'Let me see that gun again,' Charles said. 'Who is it licensed to?'

He passed it over. 'It's American, Smith and Wesson .38 Special, five-shot revolver. I did a check on the licence number, obviously, but I can't give you those details.'

'Why not?'

'Because I can't. Look I agree, I'm not giving you a lot to go on. Keep the gun. Think about what I've said, I've got no reason to lie to you on this. Paddy told me to look after you and that's the only reason I'm here. No ulterior motives. No hidden agendas. I've got a life of my own and as for me being pissed at you for not giving me a job, that's a joke and you know it. If you can't even pay Paddy you can hardly afford my advice, let alone my services. I was doing you a favour.'

After he'd gone, Sam sat there staring down at his card. Charles had started to turn Brad into a contortionist – at that precise moment he was giving himself a blow job. I still had the gun in my hand. I needed a headache tablet, an aromatherapy massage and a month with a good analyst at one of those luxury health farms where they put liposuction on the list of leisure activities. Staring at the gun I wondered if I'd have the guts to use it on myself – at least it was a cheap way out of this mess.

CHAPTER TWENTY-TWO

giving good cliché.

I am not the sort of girl who'd normally be picked out of a line-up for sleeping with a gun under her pillow but, given that up until a few weeks ago I wasn't the sort of girl to have a stalker, a private eye or a gun, I decided to play it by the script.

The longer I lay there trying to get to sleep the more convinced I became that Rory was up to something. There were a lot of questions surrounding this mess, like how had this Iro/American hood even sleazed his way into my life? What did he want? I mean, it wasn't as if I was paying the guy even. Had he really found the gun in Matt's car? And then there was Sam – what did she need Rory for?

Face it, this bloke was turning *me* into an unpaid private eye!

My head throbbed as my normally sybaritic sleep pattern slipped further and further away. When I did get to sleep, I dreamed that Rory and Matt were in pitched battle – that Matt was the devil, that Rory was his advocate and that I was about to become a victim of both. Light was just starting to struggle through my closed blinds when the phone rang.

'Are you alone?' Sam hissed.

'Well, what did you think I was doing at five in the morning with a gun under my pillow – entertaining the vicar? Why are you whispering?'

'I don't want Charles to hear. I'm in Johnny's room.'

'What's going on, Sam?' I asked, sitting up and rubbing

sleep from my eyes. 'What the hell do you want with a private eye, for God's sake? Huh?'

There was a long silence and then a sob. 'I think she's having an affair.'

My stomach heaved. This was heavy shit. 'No, she can't be. What I mean is how do you know?' If the events of the night before had been distressing, this last piece of news was enough to destroy my faith in the future of the human race altogether. They'd been together for six years – proving that monogamy can work. Get this clear – Sam and Charles *were* the future – the good decent future of womankind. The ideal post-nuclear family, damn it they were the ultimate nuclear-warhead family. If they blew, we all went up in smoke, it was as simple as that.

'Oh, Evvy,' she sobbed.

The ground beneath my futon was seriously subsiding. Sam, the one-woman Panzer division of the City did not do tears! Sarcasm – yes. Aggressive irony – all the time. Bullying, sneering, cajoling, winding-up, tormenting people more vulnerable than herself – constantly. Tears – never. Things must be really bad. 'She's been so off lately, moody, always busy. She never wants to go anywhere,' she explained.

'Well, maybe she is busy, Sam,' I argued. I mean busy and moody does not an infidelity make in my book. I started to relax. Sam was just being menstrual after all.

'I caught her in Café Bohème with another woman,' she sobbed.

'Oh?' I said, in that voice parents use when their sixteen-year-old daughter tells them she is pregnant.

'They were holding hands.'

'Well . . . maybe she was just being, you know, well, kind of sisterly.'

'Charles doesn't do body contact, Evv, you know that.'

I did.

So I did my best to console her and reassure her, but I suspect my best wasn't good enough. This spinster act was really beginning to dig in. I didn't go back to sleep after that. This was all I needed in the turbulent sea that was becoming my life – my one possible life raft was about to sink. I had relied on Sam and Charles through the ups and downs and darkest descents of my menstrual cycles for the last four years. They were what girlfriends were all about – strong coffee, martinis, laughter and support. They were there when I went through my two-year 'all men are bastards' celibacy stint. They were there when Candida had tried to have me thrown out of chambers and they were there when I actually thought Giles was my white knight. Face it, I told myself, they were there when thousands would have moved to Crouch End to avoid you. They simply couldn't, wouldn't and mustn't be allowed to break up.

Dawn was lighting up my room like a nuclear flash and my head hurt from the champagne of the night before as I tried to think of what I could do to help. I looked at the gun but realised I wouldn't have a clue how to use it, or whom to use it on. I couldn't even fire my Mace spray accurately. The only time I'd attempted to use it, I had spent six hours at Moorfields eye hospital getting my eyes washed out. My mugger was incredulous. 'What the fuck did you spray yourself for?' he'd asked, almost hesitating before nicking the Mace as well as my purse.

Sam, who had presented me with the spray as a moving-in present, had to pick me up from Moorfields. She had torn strips off me in front of a roomful of people nursing various eye injuries. 'What kind of idiot bitch can't use a Mace spray?' she'd asked – in reply to which half the waiting room had raised tentative hands. With sisters like her a girl hardly needed bastard muggers.

To top off my feeling of inadequacy that morning, nothing worked. My electric toothbrush had a flat battery. My Chanel lipstick had melted into the compact and I didn't even have a kitchen to make a cup of coffee in anymore. And now I was being watched by Brad – leering at me like some kooky, dance-party dude who'd been snorting angel dust all night. In an effort to regain control of my life, I was just about to deflate him when Paddy arrived.

He looked at me, looked at Brad and began to back off. 'Sorry, Miss Evvy, didn't realise you had, er, company.'

I don't know why I allowed myself to feel so humiliated when Paddy was responsible for the wretched thing. 'Paddy, it's the blow-up doll you brought round, remember?' I pushed Brad into his arms.

Paddy threw Brad across the room like I'd just declared him to be herpes positive. His chippies coming in behind him sniggered. 'Who's yer man Paddy? Introduce us then.'

'I never did, Miss Evelyn. You've got the wrong end of the stick, girl. She's talking madness,' he told his men.

They sniggered louder. I started to feel sorry for him and shameful that I'd insinuated at his involvement with a sex toy. 'Well not intentionally, Paddy,' I reassured them all. 'But it came with a pile of stuff your wife left behind.' I knew as soon as I closed my mouth that I had just pushed my good and loyal builder into a ravine of perpetual humiliation. God knows what I was thinking of. The sniggering turned to outright hoots and howls of derision. 'Eh, Paddy, yer wife . . .'

'Shut up will yez! It's nutin to do wit me I'm tellin you,' Paddy shouted, his face now as red as his moustache. 'I've nothing to bleedin' do with this here . . . this . . . evil demon. Git yourselves in and start sorting this kitchen out,' he yelled, on the verge of tears.

I'd never seen him so angry and, as he shoved past me, wordlessly followed by his smirking men, my guilt knew no bounds.

In chambers I came upon Warren and Lee fussing over a massive display of ugly orange orchids like a couple of vicars at a fête. Candida was always receiving extravagant gifts from her mad, mad extravagant duke although, granted, more tasteful bouquets than this one.

'The eternal courtship' was how she referred to her relationship – because after a lot of Lacroix, holidays in Monaco, moored yachts and baby-seal fur coats there was still no ring. It was the one factor in her life where she exposed herself as vulnerable. Occasionally I even caught myself feeling sorry for her.

'Check it out, Miss Hornton. Who's the new man?' Lee asked.

'These came for you a moment ago,' Warren explained.

'For me? Who are they from?' I asked, peering through the foliage for a card, thinking how these flowers were something we would spray with dioxin in Australia.

'No card, Miss Hornton. The guy delivering them said it was weird.'

I wasn't surprised – after all who would want to admit to buying these virus-coloured blooms?

'Ooooh secret admirers, Miss Hornton,' Lee chuckled as I made a face.

I instructed him to take them to my room in my most imperious voice, hoping to emulate the commanding tone of Orlando.

'It's all right for some,' he muttered under his breath.

I went through the rest of the morning like a pre-programmed robot with the lurid orchids on my desk. As I wrote advice after advice I couldn't keep my mind off them. At the back of my mind I hoped they would be claimed by Matt, my supposed gun-wielding infatué but, given how hideous they were, I sort of hoped they weren't

I thought about the kiss of the night before – I simply couldn't believe that a man who could kiss like that would be a gunman let alone the sender of tasteless orange flowers. Matt was decent, Matt was funny, Matt would have an explanation. That was it – he was probably carrying the gun to protect himself from the mad Mitzy and the flowers were probably some kind of kitsch, bad-taste art statement. That was it, I decided, they are meant to be a sort of anti-art installation piece. I would have to remember to impress him with my understanding of anti-art statements. Despite the flimsiness of my evidence I was content, and it improved my mood noticeably. I gazed at the orchids wistfully. Besides, orange was meant to be this season's black according to the latest *Vogue*.

After lunch I received a strange phone call. 'You don't know me, Miss Hornton, but I know you.' I decided not to answer. This was freaky – you don't know me but I know you – it sounded like one of those daytime TV quiz questions. It was a woman's voice I couldn't place – harsh and rasping – it sounded muffled, as if it was coming from a very long distance or from behind a sock.

'I'm afraid I've caused you a few problems,' she continued, then there was a heartless grunt that sounded a bit like a sarcastic laugh but I couldn't be sure. I started to nibble on my nails.

'The flowers were by way of amens.'

'What?' I asked, panicked despite my resolution to let her do all the talking. What did she mean by amens? Was she getting liturgical or was she implying my time was up, as in Amen? Was this one of those coded IRA messages? Should I be taping this? 'What do you mean Amen?' I demanded, consuming another nail.

'You know amends? To make up for the . . .' The line went dead. Amends? What had she done to me? Or, even worse, what was she going to do to me?

'Miss Hornton, visitor for you in reception. Mr Barton,' Warren announced at my door.

'What?' I shouted, startled out of my dark imaginings of mauled corpses and Baader-Meinhoff assassins. That all this should come less than twelve hours after my private eye had presented me with a handgun and a warning!

'Mr Matt Barton. Are you OK, Miss Hornton?' he asked, looking at me warily. Warren was the sort of clerk who lay in constant hope that the female barristers in our chambers would go gaga and prove what he'd always hinted at – that women were simply not up to the job.

'Send him in. Er no, actually I'll come out. How many people are in reception just now, Warren?' I asked.

'Miss Hornton?'

'How many people are there in reception?' I repeated.

'Just myself and Mrs Keeney. Miss Hornton, are you OK?' He was staring at a space between my eyeballs, convinced this was his big moment. He was practically drooling.

I followed him out to reception, wondering what the chances were of Matt slaying me in cold blood in front of a sixty-five-year-old fanatical born-again Baptist and a seventy-year-old woman made up like the young Fred Astaire. Pretty damn high, thinking about it. I started flicking through the statistics for counsels being murdered by their clients *before* they'd lost the case.

But I was way off target with this bloke or rather Rory was. Sitting benignly in reception in a pale mint Paul Smith suit, his hair gelled back, sat a man about as dangerous as talcum powder. When Matt saw me his face lit up with a smile I'd often thought worth the twenty-four-hour flight back to Australia to see. This was a smile you can only really do if you've spent your childhood in perpetual sunlight, on a diet of mangoes and paw-paws, under the discipline of the surf.

Within minutes he had whisked me off in his car. Off to where all good white knights should take their damsels – Knightsbridge. Guns or no guns, this was a bloke who knew how to give SERIOUSLY good cliché!

CHAPTER TWENTY-THREE

an outrageous charge!

The London sales were on, which meant the traffic was doped to the eyeballs with lack of sleep. Get real, who can sleep when Gucci is slashing prices by up to forty per cent? The air was heavy with the sticky moisture of twelve million bodies metabolising and moving towards a Bond Street or Knightsbridge bargain in thirty-degree heat. Brilliantly though, Matt's car was air conditioned to the max.

Locked in there with his mellifluous vowels – well his nasal vowels actually, but they sounded bloody honeyed to me – I was lulled into forgetting that he was supposedly the type of bloke to keep a gun in his glove compartment. I had blanked out Rory and his warnings and the voice behind the sock that claimed to have sent the flowers. And lastly, but most heinously, I even stood guilty of forgetting that the rock-solid relationship of my girlfriends was crumbling away.

All I could think about in fact, was how much credit I had left on my cards.

Shopping is the best antidepressant there is. If they could bottle the effect of three hours' unrestrained spending and offer it intravenously, they could clean up! But first they would have to eradicate the harmful side effects of traffic, parking inspectors, tight shoes and Visa-card spending limits.

'I thought we might start at the bottom at perfume and work our way up to the top, to champagne,' he said, smiling at me over his thin gold Armani shades. 'I'm in the mood for a really big splurge.'

'I'm in the mood for a new set of cards,' I said, distractedly searching through the cavern of my Prada bag for a card that I hadn't cut up in one of my erratic and wholly unsuccessful budgeting drives. Eventually I found my Harvey Nichols card, but it was in eight pieces. I had even attempted to burn one of the eight pieces after receiving an especially hairy bill that spread onto four pages. Later on I had obviously had second thoughts and decided to put it in a little plastic bag, like it was forensic evidence or something. We are talking about the sort of bill people move house to avoid. Well I did move house basically.

'Forget it – charge it to me,' he said, putting his foot down as the lights at Hyde Park Corner changed to amber. 'Think of it as a thank you for doing so well with the Mareva Injunction.'

'Don't worry, you can thank me by paying the outrageous bill you'll eventually get.'

He placed his hand on my inner thigh and I thought about all the times I'd wanted him to touch my inner thigh when he hadn't. It was as though I had been slapped bang into the middle of an erotic fantasy. 'No I'm serious, Evelyn. Charge it to me.'

Despite having no intention of taking up his generous offer, I felt elated at the sense of freedom this phrase evoked. Two simple words that divide the free world from spending restriction. *Charge it!*

By the time we had parked the car – illegally – pushed our way through the marauding crowds and stepped into the cool polished marble and glass tabernacle of Harvey Nichols, we were looking for an immediate consumer fix. Breathing in the syrupy exotica of the cosmetic department, I decided – bugger my budget. This was the sanctum of the fashion faithful and I was damn well going to prostrate my bank overdraft and worship. Besides, I had finally found my American Express card – intact!

The first thing I did was convince myself that if I didn't buy Blonde, the latest scent by Donna Versace – like instantly – life

wouldn't be worth living. Come on, I cajoled my conscience as I
elbowed my way to the counter with a steely resolve, forty quid
isn't going to kill me.

'Charge it!' I declared wildly, thrusting my card towards
a gum-chewing assistant, willing her to gasp with awe at my
spending power. Her reaction was delayed. At first she just
stared at me blankly. I threw my head back and shook my mane
of hair the way I'd seen Nicky Clark do in commercials, but she
didn't look as conclusively awed as I would have liked. 'Wort?'
she sneered, holding her gum out between her teeth.

'Charge it, er, um,' I repeated, a little less assertively this time,
twirling a bit of hair nervously in my fingers.

'Wort's that then?' she asked belligerently, pressing her pink
tongue through the gum. Something told me this little role-play
of mine was dead before it had even got underway. I toyed briefly
with the concept that maybe I wouldn't become an utter kudos
void if I didn't buy Blonde. Hey, I had a hundred bottles of
perfume at home just sitting around gathering dust – like most
childless women my age I was still looking for my signature scent.
Face it, I was being exploited by these Yves, Calvin and Gianni
blokes. It was as if they had a read-out of my vulnerability zones
or something.

But I managed to shrug off my doubts and my inner voices
and passed my American Express card across the counter,
explaining the charge card concept in simple terms. 'I want
to pay for this perfume with my American Express card, see?'
This time I made direct and, I hoped, dominant eye contact
with her.

She curled her top lip into a pose of sheer contempt. 'Oh, I
fort you said something else,' she growled, snatching the card
from my hand. As she licked the gum back into her mouth I
caught a glimpse of a silver ring in her tongue.

While the assistant from hell grappled with my spending
ability, Matt had been buying Calvin Klein aftershave at a nearby
counter – he'd tried to get me inspired but Kate Moss didn't cut

the grass with me. Lank hair and kiddy attitude? Get a life – I wanted voluptuous curves and irresistible blonde sex appeal. I already had enough lank hair and kiddy attitude of my own – I sure as hell didn't want to smell like it though.

Watching him laughing flirtatiously with the girls on the CK counter, my heart missed a beat. I mean we were talking three gorgeous blonde Claudia Schiffer clones, plying my man with free moisturisers and samples like they were grapes.

I glanced over at my own sales attendant who gave me a look of scorn. I could tell she despised me by the way she slumped off despondently to whisper with her fellow attendant – a middle-aged woman of tank-like proportions. I turned back to Matt, even from behind this guy looked edible. It wasn't that he had a magnificent body, if anything he was probably a bit out of condition – seedy even. In fact Matt probably thought Gym was a bloke he'd met down at the Darlo Bar once. This thought made me giggle out loud.

'I'm sorry but American Express have asked me to cut up this card,' the tank woman announced in a voice which boomed throughout the store like an emergency announcement. Then she repeated her broadcast again for the benefit of anyone who might have missed it the first time.

'What?' I whispered, feeling my fate closing in on me like a tomb. In the last nanosecond a sizeable audience had gathered and they were all breathing on me. A Japanese man in a towelling hat took my photograph and said something in Japanese to his friend. They roared helplessly with laughter. For one insanely paranoid minute I imagined it was Mitchie Wannawhatever taking a shot for his 'Buyer Beware' series.

'I'm afraid they have asked me to cut your card in half,' she explained imperiously to her audience – in an accent somewhere between Chelsea borders and Slough. A few people made *tut-tutting* noises.

I couldn't believe this was happening. My face burned like it had the time I had OD'd on kahlua and vodka on Bondi Beach without sunblock. 'You're not serious,' I gasped, vainly trying to keep the volume down. Besides, I knew for a fact that I still had three hundred quid left on that card! More or less.

'Oh God, don't you just hate it when they cut your card?' an American drawl beside me commiserated.

But you don't understand, I wanted to scream. I am a barrister! A bastion of law and order and bill paying. OK, so I've got a handgun licensed to someone else in my bag – but it's unloaded and I can explain.

'She was talking weird when she came in,' the gum-chewing bitch explained. Tank woman nodded and turned to me severely. 'I have been instructed to cut up the card. You can make any objections you may have regarding this decision to American Express.'

'Let me speak to them,' I pleaded trying to push the crowd away so I could fall on bended knee. 'There must be a mistake.'

'They don't care to speak to *you*,' she said as if the pronoun alone was enough to make a civilised person call for the death penalty. 'At this point it is my duty to cut the card in half. Observe.'

'Observe?' I repeated hoarsely. The word was passed through the crowd like a marijuana joint. The commiserating American backed off, allowing the throng to move in closer. Always bay with the crowd, I remember Gran saying. When they start throwing Christians to the lions again, make sure you're in the stands, Evelyn. A bit rich considering she was a devout Roman Catholic. And pointless advice now – the lions were most definitely circling. I started on a novena – offering God a few plenary indulgences and promising to start attending mass again if he held back on martyring me for a bit.

It was while the scissors were doing their worst to my ego that I fainted. It wasn't a genuine faint, I'm too solidly hearty for fainting. I just allowed my legs to collapse from under me, cushioning my head with my Prada as I hit the floor. It seemed like the right thing to do at the time – maybe they would feel sorry for me, maybe they would clear the crowd, maybe Matt would leave me alone with my humiliation. Maybe I would die. Most of all I was hoping that an elegant store like Harvey Nichols would have a policy on the treatment of unconscious customers.

They did – a furry mouth with a hock of garlic rotting inside pelted Exocet-like towards my face. Halitosis – the latest security guard weapon. I started choking as he squeezed my nose and began to give me mouth to mouth garlic.

Matt took over – dealing with the situation in that laid-back, it's-no-big-deal voice. He pushed the guard aside and explained that I wasn't unconscious just drunk. He said that I must have forgotten that I'd blown my limit by buying Barbados tickets with my American Express. I was always doing things like that he told them – I was a mad alcoholic. It was an attention-seeking problem, he explained going into details about how I'd been seeing a psychiatrist for years. The prognosis was not good, he sighed. I was still regressive. (Thanks, Matt.) 'Hence the tablets that made her faint,' he said sadly.

That was when I saw my position for what it was – supine.

My skirt was up around my armpits and my legs akimbo. The only thing I had to thank God for right now was that this was one of my knicker days. I was an object of derision and pity. The store guards – all two dozen of them – made understanding grunting noises. Their leader – Garlic-mouth – retained his hovering position two inches from my nose hoping no doubt my breathing would fail. I was slipping into a fume-induced coma – this was odour assault.

Later, on the fifth floor after Matt had dosed me with a few stiff something or others, I started to grasp what had happened. My life was out of control, it was time to head for Spenders Anonymous – or maybe not so anonymous in my case. I had to face it, after today's little fiasco I had a reputation. Store guards were probably being issued with my photograph this very minute, courtesy of Mitchie what's-his-name in the towelling hat. Oh swallow me up, life.

CHAPTER TWENTY-FOUR

'outing' the consumerist.

I felt my stomach heave in disgust as I made the first incision into
the pink flesh of my cold poached salmon. We were in the Fifth
Floor restaurant – native habitat of sensationally stylish people,
people who could afford ego consultants and quality time.

My ego needed more than a consultant to get it back up on
the diving board of life, I was so crestfallen, the vertebrae in
my neck felt like they had dissolved. My shame was boundless
– I would never be able to look judge or jury in the eye again,
now that I had been so unceremoniously outed as a spendaholic.
I looked around the dining room hoping to spot someone more
shamefaced than me.

There were two types in evidence, the very stylish and
the very 'slung together rich'. Look around you sometime,
Charles told me when we first met as I deliberated over my
annual wardrobe clear-out. London does two things really
well, drop-dead-pick-your-eyeballs-up gorgeousness and shoot
yourself hideousness. Keep everything that makes you look
gorgeous and everything that makes you look shit and chuck
the rest, otherwise you'll look like you've come up for a day
trip from the Home Counties.

The waiters, forming a tight cluster by the bar with their
little menu computers stuck to their waists like sci-fi weapons,
gossiped, laughed and sipped on coffees, occasionally looking
resentfully at their patrons as if we were intruders at a private
party. No respite for my self-esteem there.

A jazz band was wiring up a stage in the corner and I got the feeling there was ill feeling in their group when one of them gave the other a live wire to hold. As he fell to the floor twitching, they all laughed good-naturedly as if it was all part of his act.

On one side of us a middle-aged Spanish woman, dressed head to foot in Ungaro, hid behind dark glasses and sipped languidly on a long drink like a James Bond bimbo on a mission. On the table opposite, a cabal of Russians with Armani jackets slung over their shoulders practised the body language of East End thugs, while Italian tourists laughed and chatted through dark glasses. Everyone pushed salad leaves around vast plates.

Part of being cool, it seemed, was based on your ability to avoid putting food on the other side of your lips – or if you did to make out like it really pained you. This was the year to clean up with a restaurant called 'Anorexia' – even the table of beefy Russians were sneering at their meal contemptuously, like they'd seen better in Siberia.

'So what was all that about your card?' Matt asked for the first time. I was still in awe of him for sticking by me when a lot of people might have frogmarched me out of their life after a scene like that.

'I guess my spending's got out of control lately,' I explained, staring fixedly at my fork as it dissected my salmon fillet into microchips.

'Hey, you're not embarrassed about having your card cut up are you?'

I wanted to fall on him and sob about my builder's bill, my overdraft and my credit problems and how chaos didn't even come close to the pace my life was running at. But I stopped myself just in the nick of time. Because, let's get real, what bloke wants to be seduced by a woman who's life is so manifestly out of control? I needed to buck up a little. Coquetry was what was required here.

'The public humiliation is part of the initiation of adult spending,' he assured me.

'Well, thanks so much for stepping in there, Matt. I don't know what I would have done without you. Garlic-mouth was about to take my skin off with his breath.'

'Well, you sure had me shocked. There was I thinking you were a little Miss Goody Two-Shoes and now I discover my barrister is in fact a . . .' The jazz band started up and the bloke who'd had the electric shock was getting his own back on his band by singing. Revenge works in mysterious ways. The Russians rose to leave. Ungaro-woman tortured her ice some more with her straw.

'Look, Matt, thanks for all your help but I'm really, really embarrassed. Could we just—'

'Drop it? Sorry. But, hey, listen. Don't be embarrassed, that woman who cut up your card was way out of line. If she'd been a man I would have hit her.'

I suddenly felt as far from hunger as the rest of my fellow diners. Who could eat salmon with a god like Matt staring at them with those cool green eyes? It was like I was experiencing laser surgery on my heart.

Ungaro-woman's food arrived. She stared at the enormous pudding bowl of rocket leaves and parmesan through her sunglasses as if it was krypton.

Our table was surrounded by six large Harvey Nichols bags concealing the expensive purchases Matt had made after we'd escaped Garlic-mouth. I had considered his spree a little insensitive at the time and pleaded with him to take me home. 'Nonsense,' he'd said. 'If we leave now you'll feel like you've done something wrong. Besides I came here to spend what money I have left to me. I need cheering up now I'm living on a budget. Humour me.'

And so, weak as I was, I had humoured him, all over the women's designer floors while he purchased shoes by Patrick Cox, underwear by Dior, a dress by YSL and a hat by Philip Treacy. All for someone else.

So this was it, the man I wanted to desire me more than

I had ever wanted anything, had his mind on buying another woman a frock I'd poison a kitten for. And I mean that with the greatest respect to the designer. You see I have always thought it the height of romantic sophistication for a man to buy a woman clothes. Most blokes wouldn't even entertain the idea – jewellery in a pinch but clothes, never!

After we had dressed 'her' we went down to menswear where we raided Dolce & Gabbana for his outfit – black to her white. I had to face it, they were going as a couple. It was all I could do to stop myself breaking down and weeping – actually it was fear that Garlic-mouth would have another go at me. The one bright point was when Matt held the purchases up to me and admitted that the object of his spree was a decade older than me, a dress size larger and a foot shorter. But even this normally encouraging info about another woman didn't cheer me up. I mean, think about it, I was prepared to eat razor blades for a man attracted to chubby, height-challenged, older women? Hello! What did that say about me?

He then went on to prattle away about her as if she was a latter day Madame De Staël, all the time ringing up till receipts that read like my tax demands. 'She's an incredible wit,' he assured me. 'She's had four novels published. Not that they sell of course. She's an intellectual, not a bodice ripper if you get my drift.'

I tried not to look interested but he was unstoppable. What was it with this man? What kind of hyperreality was he inhabiting? He had just spent close to four thousand pounds on another woman and he wanted my *understanding*? He'd be better off getting her twenty-four-hour surveillance. Read the colour of my eyes – I wanted the bitch dead.

All this subtlety was wasted on Matt though, who seemed to imagine that this woman's trousseau was as close to my heart as it was to his. He went on and on about her. 'She's a dead ringer for that American actress Ann-Margret,' he warbled. 'Know her?'

I explained, through gritted teeth, that I wasn't old enough to remember Ann-Margret. Later, as we wove a debit trail through men's designer jackets, I tried to get him excited about how good a Moschino jacket could look on me – as in I'm so tall I look good in men's suits.

'A real head turner,' he announced and for some idiotic reason I thought he was referring to me. No chance. 'I mean it,' he assured me. 'She's the real McCoy – a genuine eccentric. She refuses to use the phone, can you believe it – she survives courtesy of the Royal Mail. "If it was good enough for Byron it's good enough for me," she says.' He seemed to find her communication peculiarities the height of hilarity.

I laughed with him, making a mental note to get her address so I'd know where to send the letter bomb. 'You'd love her,' he assured me.

I gave a weak no-teeth smile, which anyone who knows me would have instantly recognised as sarcastic. I mean I'm as ready as the next girl in a Wonder Bra to put my hand up for sister solidarity, but at that moment I wanted to burn his 'very dear friend's' face with acid. I wanted to out myself as a jealous fundamentalist there and then. I contemplated bursting into tears and breaking down but somehow the martyr in me put on a brave face and said, 'I already love her like a sister.'

When our wine arrived he made a toast. 'I think some compliments are in order now, don't you?'

I swallowed hard as he put his hand to my throat and stroked my neck.

'Would you mind if I state the obvious?' he asked as he sunk his eyes into mine.

I nodded my assent. 'Please be my guest.'

'Apart from your brilliant legal advice, I hear you were a bloody knockout in court. Not that I'm surprised, you could make any man your plaything if you put your mind to it.' He took my hand in his and kissed it. By this stage I was fluttering my eyelashes so hard I was bruising my cheekbones. With a bit of luck we were moving into seduction realm, finally. He did love me after all. Gone were my jealous twinges of earlier, the woman he had bought all the clothes for was no doubt his mother.

It was all I could do to stop myself saying something stupid like – I've got my diaphragm in my bag. I took some deep breaths and tried to focus on my navel. I said a few prayers to the Virgin Mary to oversee my ravishment. His hands had started stroking his cigarettes when I first got an inkling, call it a gut feeling, that his dialogue had taken a turn for the worse.

'No, there's no doubt about it, she's going to love that hat,' he said, lighting his fag and blowing the smoke into my eyes. 'It was so handy that you've got exactly the same head size as her.'

The whole restaurant fell silent as my ego hit the floor with a thud. What I needed then was one of those do it yourself blood-pressure units. My uncle is obsessed, he never goes anywhere without one. He uses it to repress uncomfortable conversations at family gatherings. As soon as anyone pisses him off, or dares to mention his failed attempt as a talk-show host, out it comes – as if to say, 'You might have just pushed me over the edge with that last remark.'

We're talking about Catholics here, guilty, fraught, neurotic people with consciences fully booked into the next millennium. I was being pushed over the edge by this other woman and I didn't have so much as a thermometer to hang on to.

'Not as lucky as you getting to choose them though, to try them on, to watch them tucked up in the tissue paper. I always think the shopping is ten times as much fun as the wearing. Don't you?' he asked, gleefully tapping the ash into his empty glass with childish excitement.

It was a telling show of IQ. This is where the intellect-versus-looks debate was sorted. I certainly wasn't attracted by his mind, let's get that much clear. The man's brain must be smaller than his testes to come up with a line like that. I looked at Ungaro-woman rearranging her rocket leaves. With her ideas about food and his about shopping, maybe these two could get together and start a religion or something.

I gave him an encouraging smile, like my sister does when her kid misses the potty, while he stumped his butt vigorously into the carcass of his salmon.

'I can't wait to see her face. She's one of those people who loves surprises.'

'Great, remind me to put her on my letter-bomb mailing list – that should surprise the hell out of her,' I heard myself saying before I could get a grip.

Instead of standing up and walking out, he threw his head back in laughter. Ungaro-woman looked over the top of her glasses and accidentally swallowed a piece of lettuce.

'Don't tell me you're jealous?'

'Well, all right I am! So what?' I admitted, like the green-eyed monster that I was.

He brushed a stray hair away from my eyes. 'Well, I hate to ruin the mystery of the other woman but, as much as I love her, she's very much a married woman. And quite honestly she's not my type, well not in that sense.'

'Oh, well I guess I . . . er . . .'

'Don't you dare apologise – not when I'm so flattered.'

He reached into his jacket pocket and pulled out a packet. 'I bought you this the other day. Under the circs, I think it was an appropriate choice.'

I tore open the paper and exposed a pair of Versace sunglasses as wildly sequinned and as gaudy as only Versace can be and still get away with it and not look cheap.

'Subtle huh?' he laughed, putting on his own discreet Armani shades. 'They were meant to be a joke but, given the nature of your entrance, you might find them just the thing.'

CHAPTER TWENTY-FIVE

it was going to take more than a competent tongue to relax me!

Four hours later, we lay sated in a knot on my futon. OK, so it was like making love on granite but at that moment I considered it was worthy of a glass podium.

He swung his legs over the bed and looked down on me. 'God, you are beautiful. Do you know how beautiful you are?'

Well, what's a girl who's acutely aware of how long it's been since she last shaved her legs and checked her nose for blackheads to say? In lieu of anything startlingly witty, I moaned while he traced his tongue along my thigh. I was all orgasmed out. I would make a lousy insatiable porn star.

He had done with me as I never imagined I wanted to be done before. Best of all, he didn't ask that stupid question I've hated as long as I can remember – 'have you come yet?' Like waiters who bully me to order in restaurants – 'have you decided yet?' Matt just insisted I *come!*

'Come!' he yelled. 'Come!' And hey, I didn't want to get into an argument with a bloke who was practically swallowing my organs of reproduction – so I came.

I'd never known anything like it. My previous orgasm history – pretty light reading admittedly – had always been a simultaneous event. But this was the sort of sex you needed a crash helmet for. Not that I was complaining about Matt's style, it was just that for a girl familiar with the ins and outs of

a spermicidal gel tube and a map to her own G-spot, it seemed
a tad dictatorial.

But what was I bitching about – I must have accidentally
switched on to my pleasure destruct cycle. Wake up to yourself,
woman, I chided as Matt teased my nipples with his tongue.
This was sublime – this was sinful. If this was tyranny he could
oppress me any day.

'Um, I didn't get a chance to shave this morning,' I blurted,
when he got to my underarm.

'That's OK by me – I prefer my women unplucked.'

I blinked. 'Unplucked?' What was I, a chicken? Surely he
meant undepilated or hirsute even? Giles used to be livid if
I didn't shave – said I looked like an anthropological exhibit.
Either this bloke was dyslexic, a failed metaphorist or he could
say stuff like that and get away with it.

I tried to envisage Rory saying something along those lines.
Like sure. No, Matt was so cool he could talk at length on women
and plucking and still sound suave. Surely I was looking for
problems where there weren't any. He was experienced, that
was all – my problem was I was too used to immature men. I
was like the slave who feels agoraphobic out of shackles.

Later on he purred something about going out to make
coffee.

'That's very new man of you,' I teased. 'I thought you might
want to light up or roll over and go to sleep even.'

He patted my buttocks as he left. I spun around and checked
them for cellulite but they looked pretty clear for a woman who's
been keeping the Belgium export trade going single-handedly for
the last month. I snuggled under the sheet and luxuriated in the
smell of his scent and thought how I had definitely fallen on my
feet with this man – this sexual despot could put me under house
arrest any day. God, the bloke deserved a chapter in the *Ascent
Of Man*.

That was when I heard the voices. A woman's voice screaming and Matt's voice entreating. I lay still as a board and listened

hard, trying to work out what was going on. I heard something about, 'What are you doing to her?' And then I heard Matt saying, 'Don't be mad, it's just sex.' I missed the next exchange but the last thing the woman said was frighteningly clear. I was so still my leg went into cramp when I heard the words, 'If you (muffle, muffle), I'll blow the whistle.'

The whole exchange lasted about three minutes and then the door slammed. Matt came in looking desperately ashamed and threw himself into my arms. 'I didn't know she'd come here. You have to believe me! Please forgive me. I had no idea.' He was as white as his Calvin Kleins. 'I'm truly, truly sorry. I really didn't think she would pull anything like that. You've got to believe me!'

I sat up as he slumped on the bed. I wanted my orgasm back. The guns, the warnings, the whole doubt wagon charged into my head like the riot police.

'It was her – Mitzy, the woman who's suing me,' he explained.

It hit me then just how little I knew about this man. This bloke who had taken me to heaven with his tongue, this man who preferred his women unplucked, his coffee black and his orgasms sunny-side up. He was a stranger to me really – one up from a one night stand but, anyway I chose to construe it, I had just heard him admit that he was using me for sex.

I thought about Rory's warnings, and of the gun in my bag, as I watched him pull out a cigarette and light it. Cupped in his hand the flame illuminated his face – lined with a lifetime of street-cred cool and *savoir-faire*. I was drugged with a need to trust him. So what if he was using me for sex. Use away. I was hardly fucking him for his shorthand after all. Judge not, lest ye be judged and all that.

'Mitzy was here? But how did she know where you were?' I asked, not entirely sure I wanted to hear the answer. First rule in cross-examining witnesses – don't ask questions if you don't already know the answer.

'That's the thing – I really don't know. I think she's obsessed.

She's completely off the planet, she's got to be. I mean why else would she pull a stunt like this?'

'I'm calling the police,' I told him, groping for the mobile. 'I mean she was way out of line. How dare she come here! If she thinks I'm going to take this lying down she's wrong. I'm your counsel and this is harassment.' I reached over the bed and into my bag.

'No, don't. Please! Forget it. She's gone now. She won't come back.' He had grabbed my arm with the speed of a gambler grabbing chips at the same time as I had inadvertently pulled out the gun, mistaking it for the phone. I closed my eyes like children do when they hide from grown-ups. My colon was prolapsing in fear. As I shoved the gun back in the bag, I was silently chanting, 'Please don't let him have seen it. Please don't let him have seen it.' The whole time he was looking into my eyes, registering nothing but desire.

'Let's just forget it,' he pleaded. 'Besides I don't want the police turning up in the middle of what I have planned for you.'

'Oh?' I whimpered, as he slid under the covers and started snuffling around my erotic zone. I tried to get my anatomy to do what it should when a madly attractive man starts kissing my nipples, but I felt like I'd been handed a Rubik cube with missing pieces. 'Ah? I, er, saw the Mitchie Wanhato show last week,' I blurted. 'Talk about jolt. Tell you what, my focus was knocked to smithereens.'

CHAPTER TWENTY-SIX

i'm no sharon stone – nor was I meant to be!

While Matt went forth to discover my *kundilini* under the duvet, I began to face the full enormity of my dilemma. And it was extremely enormous. Middle-class girls from suburbs of privilege in Sydney, with a first from Oxford, do not belong in situations like this.

Let's get this much clear, I am a passive, not an active seeker of action and thrills. I am one of those unashamedly boring people who watch TV if I want drama – I don't *do* it. I'm no Sharon Stone – nor was I meant to be. A bit-part actor that's me. If I feel in the mood for stalkers, private eyes, coded messages and guns, I get myself to a Tarantino film.

Give me hyperreality above reality any day. Puh-lease, I'm not even equipped for the strain that accompanies mundane action. I lose it if I break a nail. I bitch to my therapist if I can't get the latest Gucci belt in time for a party. I'm not even embarrassed about it. Put it this way I don't watch the news and burn with jealousy when I see people kidnapped or murdered.

So who did I have to turn to? Charles and Sam – well that was another can of worms. I should call Charles, she was always a stalwart in times of trouble, but I didn't know what to say if she really *was* having an affair. Surely it wasn't true – not good old Roedean, hockey-playing Charles, not good old no-nonsense, give it here and I'll iron it, Charles?

I was facing limited options in a scare scenario. In fairy-tale speak – the wolf was at my door and there wasn't even a twig bivouac, let alone a brick condo for miles. Where was I meant to run? To Rory? I think NOT. Gran always said never trust a man who says 'trust me'.

That left Giles, my ex in the insteps. Give me a break, that man was as ready for a gun and a stalker as the Virgin Mary was for Brad and his two-foot penis. Face it, I was alone in all this.

'I get the feeling your heart isn't in this,' Matt said, coming up between my legs for air.

I was about to say, 'Oh sorry, I forgot you were there,' but knowing how thin-skinned blokes are about stuff like that since we got equal pay, I thought I should save his feelings. I mean, I didn't want him regressing into the foetal position of perceived impotence and demanding I mother him at this stage of the proceedings.

'I'm sorry, I'm just thinking about Mitzy. I can't help it, I just don't understand how she knew where I lived?'

'Shh,' he said, putting a finger to my lips. 'It's me who should be sorry, scaring you like that, but I promise, I honestly didn't think she'd do anything as half-witted as that. I bet she saw us at Harvey Nichols and followed us back. I'm as pissed off as you, believe me,' he said, sitting up beside me. 'I told you I had a bit of a thing with her. It's the old "God hath no fury like a woman scorned" scenario. I'm serious,' he said when I looked at him like he needed a double dose of HRT. 'I wouldn't be surprised if this whole suit she's throwing at me isn't just an excuse to get back at me for not sleeping with her anymore.' There was a long pause while we both sized up the situation. 'Look, how about I try the coffee again?' he suggested eventually.

There were a lot of submissions I could have made, disputations I could have put forward in mitigation, but looking back I don't think I was looking for answers as much as hope. I snuggled back down under the sheet and tried again to tell myself it was OK. Poor Matt was just being persecuted – stop! It was a messy business dating clients, perhaps I had been a bit unwise.

And then the facts crystallised – God, if Candida found out about the goings-on today my life wouldn't be worth living. At the very least I would be taken off the case. Everyone would hear about it. My reputation would be vomit. The writing was on the wall for Matt and me.

This possibility sent me into a tail-spin of decline. I started weighing up whether my life was worth living without my new-found sexual despot and lightly toyed with the idea that maybe the time had come to get stuck into the temazepam and sleep my way out of it. Suicide and I had been circling one another for as long as I could remember. Call me mad, but death and immortal life have always struck me as a whole lot more fulfilling when measured against a life cycle of menstruation and menopause and HRT. My therapist is always nagging me about my pretensions to suicide. 'Who do you want to punish with your death, Evelyn?'

She was always asking moronic questions like that. If I called her and told her about all *this* stuff that'd been going on, she'd probably say I was delusional, a compulsive manic depressive, a paranoid schizophrenic with a persecution complex – and charge me ninety quid. As if that would put me off orchestrating my own death? Hello?

Not for the first time I wondered why I hadn't become a psychologist instead of a barrister – or even an astrologer? That's where the money was – and the power for that matter. No one sent analysts or astrologers notes about covering up their cleavage. I had hardly got into my full paranoid stride on all this when I heard more raised voices in the kitchen. Mitzy must have returned.

The shouting voices were even louder this time and accompanied by banging and crashing and finally smashing. Now yelling was one thing but knocking about my Conran paraphernalia was the proverbial last straw. Even Miss I-Hate-Confrontation Hornton drew the line there. If drama was going to seek me out and start smashing up my kitchen – such as it was – I was bloody well going to face it head on. I didn't go to kick-boxing classes in Bethnal Green for nothing!

Pulling on a Nicole Farhi top and Gucci drainpipes, I was hyperventilating like a berserk Sufi, psyching myself up for battle. If there had been any hallucinogenic mushrooms handy I would have scoffed them down and daubed my body in mud. Storming out to confront my intruder, I was hit with more than I had bargained on though.

The sight before me wasn't remotely close to the one I had mentally prepared myself for earlier; i.e. a refined woman with a deficit of a few million quid in her account. There was a woman, yes – an Irish-sounding woman. A plumpish middle-aged woman in an outfit I think you call a muu-muu – a swathe of fabric in bold colourful patterns. She was struggling with Matt who was still naked – over Brad (also naked).

She had Brad in a headlock while Matt was pulling on his lower torso. She was screaming, 'Rape! Rape! Rape!' Which was a bit rich I thought. I mean, I know Matt's a master of sexual tyranny and all, but I got the feeling earlier that his erection was feeling a bit tired and emotional. In fact I wouldn't have been at all surprised if he'd faked his last two orgasms. I doubt he was ready for a go at madam in a muu-muu here anyway. Brad wasn't looking too keen on the ménage either.

But whatever was going on, one thing was clear – my initial bold plan to hurl a few well-deserved home truths at Mitzy's ego seemed inadequate now. I mean, get real, this woman was not built to have *anything* hurled at her. She was a hurler rather than a hurlee so I huddled by the toilet cubicle, thinking that Matt's taste in women wasn't particularly great before I realised how un-PC I was being.

Their tug of war was all over in seconds. Matt seemed to be winning, right up to the point when Mitzy grabbed Brad's member giving her a clear advantage. The feminist in me was half in a mood to cheer, but her dominant position was not to last – because, as Matt made a lunge to regain the vital organ, Brad burst.

'Yer filthy fuckin' villain,' Mitzy swore in a thick Irish brogue. 'Now look what yer've done!' She shoved Matt's naked body into the makeshift sink Paddy had installed and for a minute I thought he'd been impaled on the hot tap, but it was just one of his internal organs being displaced.

There is very little dignity in being a naked forty-something bloke with long hair and a withered penis being shoved by a flame-haired Irish woman in a muu-muu.

'*I've* done?' retorted Matt incredulous. He was holding the remains of Brad to his groin like a fig leaf but Mitzy had already run off. He looked like a pathetic caveman who'd just been blamed for putting out the fire.

'What the fuck was that?' I asked him, coming out of my hiding spot. 'I really am calling the police this time. Mitzy has gone too far.' I was livid. 'Those blow-up men don't grow on trees you know – they can be bloody expensive.'

'Mitzy? That wasn't Mitzy!'

'Well who the hell was it then?' I asked.

'I don't know, I've never seen her before in my life,' he screamed. He was verging on hysteria and small pockets of spittle had gathered at the corners of his mouth. I knew I was probably being really shallow, after all the poor bloke had had a nasty shock, but I couldn't help dwelling on how quickly men lose their cool under pressure. He should try a stalker for size.

I gathered myself together feeling suddenly superior. 'Well, I can assure you, I've never seen her before. She's probably one of those people that do head counts for the council or something. You must have done something to upset her. What if she's my new neighbour?'

He was taking on a deathly pallor and as I watched him,

naked and luminous in the fluorescent light of the doorway, I thought he looked rather less like a sexual tyrant and more like a dilapidated and lost old man. He was still clutching what was left of 'my very own Negro lover' to his groin and his Australian twang was thickening. He was one of those blokes who get mucusy under stress. 'She knocked on the door,' he explained. 'I thought it must be Mitzy again but it was her. She said, "Can I have a word with Miss Hornton," and then saw the rubber doll and went ape!'

The black rubber rag that had once been Brad snivelled about his groin. Looking at him I felt a distinct cooling of my loins – although that could have just been my spermicidal gel running. I was still standing there trying to take it all in when Rory walked through the open door.

CHAPTER TWENTY-SEVEN

even my libido was beginning to question my motives now.

'Yer kidding ain't ya?' Rory asked, leaning in the doorway, chewing gum, his tobacco pouch sticking between his jeans and washboard belly. OK, so I've heard of designer shab but this was pushing the point a bit far – besides who had designed his shab anyway? Certainly not Paul Smith.

'This isn't, like, for real is it?' he asked.

I presumed he was being rhetorical and ignored him. 'The Neanderthal is back,' I muttered. 'You don't get it do you? When I said I never want to see you again I was as serious as Emily Davison when she said she wanted the vote and was prepared to die to get it.'

'Doll, you are one kooky lady, you know that.'

What a contrast he made beside Matt – only not specifically at this minute because Matt was still naked – holding the tattered remnants of Brad to his groin. Pathetically inadequate, it looked more obscence than full-on nudity, mainly because Brad's willy was the only recognisable part of his anatomy now. A sort of shrivelled pizzle and testicles with realistic hair. Basically I couldn't help thinking that Matt wasn't putting his best foot forward just at the minute.

'Playtime at the porn farm is it?' Rory enquired, raising one eyebrow like Simon Templar. He was leaning against the wall, propping himself up with one leg – not that I could actually remember ever having seen this man upright without a supporting wall.

'Ah well, you see, you've caught us at a bad moment,' Matt explained, spreading Brad's hideously smiling face around his loins. Then he turned to me and gave me a knowing smile which I returned with a brave one. The truth was though my libido was already beginning to question my actions of the last two hours. He just didn't look like the same man that I had taken to heaven with my lips only an hour ago. In fact at that minute the only place I felt disposed to take him was to the door.

'Is that what it is?' Rory asked sarcastically. He looked vaguely threatening, if you discounted the cherub tattoo partially visible through his unbuttoned shirt. That was another thing, why couldn't this bloke do up a button every now and then – was he dyslexic or something?

'What category of bad moment would you classify this as, Matt?' he asked. I looked from one to the other riveted by the tension.

But Matt just muttered something about needing to put some clothes on and scuttled off. Which was a bad move – huge as it happened because, as Rory and I watched him disappear down the expanse of my loft, the little flesh there was on his hairy buttocks jiggled. At that moment his credibility as an attractive man with fuckable prospects was lower than any man I have ever gone to bed with.

'Unless I'm mistaken that bloke's got cellulite,' Rory laughed as soon as Matt was out of earshot.

'Can it, Rory.'

'I'm not canning anything until you tell me what the fuck you are doing?'

'What the hell has it got to do with you?' I hissed.

'Didn't I warn you?' he hissed back. 'Even you can't be as stupid as you're pretending to be.'

'Have you thought about a vasectomy recently, Rory?' I riposted.

He grabbed my shoulders and shook me, which is like the most annoying thing you can do to an ovulating woman. 'What do I have to do to get through to you?' he asked. I grimaced and rolled my eyes back in a look of sheer boredom. 'I mean it, Evvy. This bloke is a heavy character! You could be in real danger!'

'Would you mind letting go of my shoulders? What do I have to say to get through that thick head of yours? My name is Evelyn. E-V-E-L-Y-N as in Waugh!'

This was all getting too complicated and I wanted out. I was going to seek a new minimal lifestyle – free of blow-up dolls, stalkers and private eyes. A simple pared-down existence where form followed function. 'I mean it, Rory, I don't want to know. I've had enough. Enough of you, enough of enough.'

'Enough of enough?'

'Piss off! Is that simple enough for you?'

He grinned superciliously. 'It's not even as if you're getting paid for this you know,' I told him as I heard the shower start up in the background. Why was it that every bloke that made his way into my flat felt free to take a shower and move in? Did I have a B&B sign on the door or something?

Rory laughed – not his usual warm Guinness laugh. This was more like your cold arsenic laugh. A new tack. 'You got a penchant for arseholes or what? This guy's done time you know and it wasn't for nick'n fuckin' cars. He's got a gun – well you've got it now but there is no saying he hasn't got a whole arsenal hidden somewhere. And you're here with him, romping around like Bambi and Dumbo with a blow-up man.'

'It's not my blow-up man!'

'Nothing would surprise me with you,' he smiled. 'You are one kooky doll, you know that?'

'So you said. Would you mind dropping this *doll* business? I am not a toy that you can just play around with!'

'Sure, doll, but don't you just love it when I wind you up?'

Ah yes, wind me up. Rory had the ability to wind me up

like no other man before. He managed to get under my skin, up my nose and every other place I didn't want him. This bloke was as invasive as a virus.

We didn't say much else before Matt returned fully clothed, we just sort of circled one another and bared our teeth.

'Well, darling, I think I'd better get going,' Matt said sweetly. His wet hair was tied back which made him look slightly *Reservoir Dogs*ish.

'Good shower, man?' Rory enquired.

'Very good,'

'Doll here's got brilliant nozzle power hasn't she?'

Matt ignored him – in fact he ignored us both.

'You don't have to go,' I told him, looking accusingly at Rory.

'It's OK,' he said, studiously avoiding eye contact, like our spaniel used to do when it had nicked a chicken bone from the bin. 'I've got an appointment anyway.'

When he had gone, Rory punched the air and I decided it was time to knock a few home truths into this blockhead's brain. 'Look, Rory, I don't know where or why you got the impression I was in need of your assistance but I'd like to make it clear that you are no longer required. My stalker has vanished and so, you see, any spurious justification you may have had for hanging around is no longer an issue. I don't think putting it gently is going to cut the grass with a bloke like you, so watch my lips and I'll spell it out. Piss off, Rory. I don't want to see you again.'

He grinned and chewed his gum loudly.

'Are you completely insane?' I asked him.

He winked at me. 'You're great, doll. I can't believe it, I never loved a woman in anger so much. Tell you what, why don't you nip over there and put them sandals on for me again?'

'That's it, I'm calling the police,' I screamed.

Still his belligerent form leaned against my door. 'You do that, Miss Evelyn, and while you're at it show them these.'

And that was when he gave me the clippings – which to say the least were to put a sinister emphasis on the events of the last few hours.

CHAPTER TWENTY-EIGHT

you can tell a lot about a woman from her footwear.

After Rory left, I lay twisted, cocoon-like, in my duvet staring at the clippings he had handed me. The man in the photograph from the 1984 Sydney *Morning Herald* was undeniably Matt Barton, despite the fact that the caption read 'Daniel Morry wanted for questioning for the embezzlement of two million dollars from J.D. Steer and Co'.

The other clipping wasn't dignified with a photograph. It merely stated that a Kenneth Brown had been sentenced to two years for the manslaughter of a co-worker after a struggle with a handgun. There was no evidence to link Matt to this clipping but it was there – in my hand stapled to a clipping that connected him to a very serious charge. It was a case of guilt by staple.

On top of this I had the incriminating evidence of one handgun licensed or unlicensed to persons unknown which Rory had supposedly found in Matt's glove compartment. If I was to believe Rory – and despite myself I was starting to – I was right to be seriously scared. I had just had sex with an embezzling murderer while his gun lay concealed in my PP bag at the foot of the bed.

I had never regretted an orgasm so much. Face it, girl, I told myself, you are heading towards the fate of those women you read about in tabloid papers and say 'poor, stupid, sad, bitch'. Women who took a wrong turn down the cul-de-sac of ruin, who end up either dead or snapped by photographers going into court, looking bleary-eyed and bloated.

Your nieces and nephews will ask your sister, 'Whatever happened to Aunt Evelyn?' And they'll be told to say Hail Mary's for you. I ruminated on all this while consuming vast quantities of Belgian chocolates and crying. When I looked at my face in the mirror it was bleary-eyed and bloated. I sobbed some more.

What I needed was company, someone to say 'don't worry it's probably just a bad patch'. I even half regretted not asking Rory to stay the night. No! I told myself – you still have your pride. Well more or less. Anyway it was during this bleak moment of lonely desolation that someone knocked on the door.

A cold trickle of chocolate ran down my chin as my intuition warned me that this was probably not the tooth fairy. Even though I have the intuition of a lemming, I knew that whoever it was out there, I didn't want to see them. I crept over in stockinged feet to the door and lay down to see if I could tell who it was by the shoes. You can tell a lot about a person by their footwear.

'Who is it?' I asked, pressing my face to the floor and peeking through the crack. But all I could see was fluff and shadow.

A muffled woman's voice replied, 'It's me, remember, I rang you up this morning. You know – the flowers?'

Oh my God! It was the sock voice without the sock – she who wanted to make amends. She who more than likely wanted to do me great harm!

'I've got a gun,' I warned her in my deepest most threatening voice.

'Oh dear,' she said. 'Don't do anything rash.'

'Rash? Hello? Get a grip, woman, I just said I've got a gun, all right? A veiled threat to do something rash if ever there was one. And I mean it! Just leave or, or, or I'll blow you away.'

There was a silence which my paranoia took full advantage of, plunging me into a feverish state of terror. Oh shit, what kind of career move was this – blowing people away – just as I was starting to have a bit of a success at the Bar? Then I started evaluating the circumstances of her visit more carefully and panicked because it was just as likely that she'd come armed herself?

After all, this was London – hailed as the hippest city in the world. And you don't get those sorts of accolades on the quality of chop houses and bagel bars alone. When people talk 'hip' at the end of the millennium they usually imbue the word with the promise of edgy danger. OK so the shopping's pretty good on Bond Street and our bands are topping the Pops but the fact is a city doesn't get noticed internationally unless you've had a few drive-by killings and an arms shipment or two gone missing from your ports. Admittedly there was a time when I would never have pegged London as a gun-toting city but then again in those days Londoners still called cappuccino fluffy coffees and policemen 'bobbies'.

'I mean it,' she insisted. 'We have unfinished business. There are things we need to sort out. Like I said, I intend to make amends. You've got to let me in! I'm not going away until I've said my piece.'

Shit, was this broad on a twelve-step programme from hell or what? Or maybe when she talked 'amends' she meant it as a threat, maybe her idea of amends was my idea of GBH.

'What do you want with me?' I asked her. 'I haven't done anything wrong. I haven't got a clue who you are but this really isn't a good time. I've got a lot of other shit on basically. Heavy shit.'

'I've had enough trouble over you too,' she said more quietly. 'I just want an end to it so I can get on with my life, just let me in.'

She had to be joking. She had about as much chance of getting in here as Salman Rushdie had of having a relaxing holiday in Iran. 'Put it in writing.' I suggested, my legal training coming back to me.

There was a dissatisfied grunt on the other side which made me very nervous. Shit, I didn't want to rub her up the wrong way. This was a woman who thought nothing of stuffing socks in her own mouth, so heavens knows what she was prepared to stick in mine. Best to keep things friendly I decided, deeply regretting the gun threat earlier.

'Or, um, you could make an appointment with my clerk,' I offered. 'Not that I don't want to invite you in, but you really wouldn't want to come into this mess. Hell no. To tell you the truth this flat is swarming with builders at the moment. Yes that's it, big, strong, muscular, tattooed men who aren't used to, er, women's company. They're nice enough in their way but I couldn't account for their actions. They tend to get a bit hyper with more than one woman around.' What the fuck was I talking about? 'Just thinking of you, more or less,' I assured her.

She laughed, a sharp, bitter laugh that chilled me to the core. I was still on my hands and knees on the floor trying to get a glimpse of her shoes – as I said you can tell a lot about a woman from her footwear and hers was revelatory, terrifyingly so. Any chance that we might have anything to chat about disappeared as I made out, not a pair of Blahniks or Choos, or Guccis, or Westwoods – but gentlemen's felt slippers. This was ominous stuff. Felt slippers, while fine for flapping down hospital wards on Zimmer frames, are not the sort of footwear you wear when you want to impress.

'What builder?' she asked nastily.

She'd thrown me. 'Huh?'

'What fucking builders are you talking about?'

'Oh the usual, they never come in ones do they, not builders? Always a team. A veritable horde of beefy, heavy-drinking, tattooed men, all muscles and smells.' I pounded my feet on the floor making what I hoped were the sounds of a team of large, tattooed men on the verge of a riot. 'In fact it's so dusty in here with all the work they're doing.' I gave a little dry cough. 'Not a situation in which I can receive company. Even if you were the Queen I'd turn you away. Even Hugh Grant. So as I said, give my clerk a ring – he'll be only too happy to make an appointment for you to see me in chambers. You have the number.'

Things went quiet as she seemed to consider this. At first I thought she might even have gone, her pause was so long – positively Harold Pinterish in fact. 'What are they doing here at this time of night?' she said eventually.

'What?'

'The builders. Why are they still in there?'

What was this woman on about, was she a labour relations officer or something? Come to think of it I hadn't paid Paddy for so long, it wasn't inconceivable that he might have reported me to some sort of tribunal.

'Oh it's quite all right,' I reassured her. 'They're all on time and a half, er, double even. It was their choice to come in at night.'

She responded with another one of those bitter laughs.

'In fact they earn far more than me – I'm just on legal aid most of the time. I mean a fraud hardly pays my dry cleaning bill let alone my shoe habit,' I prattled nervously, as I continued to grapple with her footwear. They were the sort of worn out tartan slippers I'd seen on a Channel Four documentary about asylums.

This was either a case of grunge taking itself too seriously or she was a really twisted psychopath escaped from a mental home. In fact, I remembered in a horrid cold attack of fear that this building used to be a mental asylum until thirty years ago. She was probably once an inmate, a loony homing pigeon returning to the scene of the countless atrocities that had scarred her life. And now she was outside my flat very probably with homicidal intent. Out for revenge. That's why she'd flipped when she heard I was overworking my builders

– locking them up in this den of erstwhile torture. Oh my God, this was serious. Who did I dial?

'I'll be back,' she snarled. 'You can tell him, I'll be back. I'm not to be cast aside. I was prepared to admit it was my fault. Well, you can tell him from me . . . Oh forget it.'

'Consider it forgotten,' I barked. 'My mind's a veritable sieve. I'd forget my head if it wasn't screwed on, I employ a man specially to ring me up on my VAT deadline to remind me to pay . . .' But her slippers were already scuffling down the stairs.

I disintegrated into a jellied heap of designer wretchedness and sobbed. This was what alcoholics refer to as a 'rock bottom' and I had landed with a thud. At this point an alcoholic would get himself to an AA meeting and set out on the path to sobriety – the refuge of teetotaldom. Unfortunately there are no self-help groups for people on hit lists. People with bounties on their heads are fairly much left to their own devices. The only thing that was going to help me now was a Kalashnikov.

That was why I decided to sleep with the gun in my hand. Well, not my hand exactly – then any delusional old attacker could grapple it off me and use it against me. Face it, even a hundred-year-old woman crippled with arthritic joints could disable me if I was tangled up in my duvet badly enough. Nonetheless I was of a mind to sleep with the gun nearby, under my pillow or something.

The problem was, when I sprung open the clasp of my bag, it became apparent that bad had morphed into hideous. Someone had stolen my handgun.

CHAPTER TWENTY-NINE

that was all I needed – a couple of blokes in tourniquets wielding gold cards.

The nuns back at the convent probably never imagined that little Evelyn Hornton would be so upset to discover herself gunless. I mean I was the girl who headed all those disarmament demos on the hockey field at the Loreto College for Gentlewomen in 1987 when we should have been playing St Gertrude's in a to-the-death tournament.

I was the one who did three weeks' detention for putting up the WHY OWN A GUN IF YOU DON'T PLAN TO KILL? posters all over school.

Oh callow youth, I sobbed into my pillow. Now here I was in London, threatening to blow mad old women away and cavorting with convicted manslaughterers. 'Forgive me, Lord,' I told my maker, 'but even you have to face it – this is not the time to face life unarmed.'

I was now at the hitherto unprecedented point of wanting to contact Rory, only I didn't have a clue where to find him. He was typical of his sex in that respect – never there when you need them. It was ten thirty at night – too late to ring Paddy and I wasn't going to ring Giles and have him roaming around in his insteps.

What I needed was serious backup and support. In short I needed a woman. I dialled the girls and they weren't in. That left me Orlando – in the hat that can hold a drink? Or the Notting Hill junkies I used to live with? Now I was really scraping the barrel – I could just see them turning up in their designer tourniquets wielding gold cards and trying to buy heroin. I must have been dangerously desperate even thinking about them. I had to contact someone – but not the police. Not yet.

After a long process of elimination and trying and retrying the girls and gorging my mouth with some grade-B chocolates I'd discovered in my knicker basket, I did something that contravened all sanity regulations and dialled Candida. It was an incredible, daring act that I should have taken class-A drugs before attempting – but for those of you who haven't got the point yet, I was living dangerously.

She answered the phone in a sleepy, soft voice almost devoid of the asperity I was counting on. I was lulled. 'Hi, Candida – just me,' I breezed.

Her voice came down the phone and throttled me. 'If this is one of your drugged ideas of a joke, Evelyn, might I suggest you look for a new career?'

'Candida, we have a problem,' I told her firmly.

She didn't respond so I ploughed on, not really knowing where I should begin and how this would end. But I decided to start with the stalker and why I'd hired the private eye and how he'd found the gun and how now he'd given me the newspaper clippings. Then I went on to detail the disappearance of the gun and the woman in bed-slippers turning up at my door and threatening amends. I erred on the side of safety and left the shopping and sex with Matt out.

Candida had maintained her silence throughout and I had a feeling she was probably taking notes. I could just see it in print in *Counsel Magazine*. She would make sure that I ended up like one of those barrister wraiths you see skulking about the Inns of Court. Men and women who made an inappropriate remark about a particular judge's fitness to sit on the bench, or an ill-advised comment about the equal opportunity pendulum having swung too far the other way, now doomed to hear their names whispered about the Temple as if they were a sanitary item. Pathetic creatures no one really knows but everyone knows of. I would end up pursuing hopeless cases against newspapers and eating my lunch on the kitchen-staff table in the Inner Temple.

At the end of my rant she exhaled loudly and all at once I realised how my recital made the comings and goings of my existence sound *preposterous*.

I had heard Candida damn people with that word before. In chambers' meetings when Warren put forward his brave plan for the clerks to call the barristers by their first names. 'Preposterous!' she had cried. And Warren had bowed his head, no doubt praying that the silence surrounding this expostulation would swallow him up. And now, as I waited for the word to make its way down the phone line, I bowed my head and cogitated on my doom.

Instead she spoke to me in a purr. 'Darling, would you give me ten minutes? You've rather caught us at it, my dear. The Duke was kindly about to present me with his orgasm when you rang and I really shouldn't leave him dangling like this, darling.'

'No,' I agreed. 'Absolutely. Crucial that you, um, that you, well, see to him. Well what I mean is, I'll wait for you call.'

Putting the phone down I was feeling unjustifiably optimistic, probably struck with joy by the cosy intimacy of her revelation. I mean this woman didn't even discuss what perfume she wore – although it was unmistakable. She never even told us where she spent her holidays or where she grew up and now she was revealing the ins and outs of her sex life to me. What a compliment.

I lay on my futon comatose with excitement . . . for about two hours. And then the inevitable doubts set in as I sat staring at the phone in my lap like it was a lamp and I was waiting for the genie to pop out. God this guy was a marathon orgasmer.

Three hours later I began to know how the Persians felt at Marathon that day. I changed the battery in case that was the problem, then I dialled directory inquiries to make sure my phone company hadn't been liquidated in a takeover bid and then I panicked – thinking that she might have called while I was checking the line. Despair moved in like a leaking gas main to encompass me.

CHAPTER THIRTY

here I was being flanked by every misogynist's worst nightmare.

By eight o'clock the next morning, I was in chambers asleep on my desk. I had drifted off into a dream of terror, betrayal and homicides – where people in slippers were out to get me. It was so vivid it was like watching a film – *Revenge of the Slipper People*. Only the lead victim was me.

Candida charged in shortly after eight o'clock. I looked at her feet, half expecting to see them wrapped in tartan Hush Puppies but her patent Walter Steigers shone more or less innocuously. After her no-call last night I had basically convinced myself that she was part of the plot to destroy me. Well, actually, I had always thought that – only now I was certain I had the circumstantial evidence. How Rory or Matt or the slipper woman linked up to Candida, I couldn't be sure but as far as I was concerned she was in the frame as a suspect.

'Here you are, darling, where have you been? I've been trying to reach you all night! I rang your number and there was no answer and then when I did get an answer it was that Charlotte woman who said you'd moved.'

'I moved months ago – I did tell you. My number's on the chambers list.'

'Did you, darling? Well I expect you may have mentioned it in one of your mousy little commentaries, but well, frankly, I have such a lot on my mind. Not like you young things – all fluff and flounce, bubbles and bounce. Enough of that though – are you still alive?'

'Still here,' I said somewhat pointlessly, standing up and throwing my arms out in a sort of Dada-like gesture that didn't quite come off, given how low I was feeling.

She stepped back and looked at me like I'd just sicked on myself. 'Well, there we are then. So my sleepless night and my concern for your welfare were wasted. I suppose you knew what a high state of panic you put me in when you rang. I've been beside myself, darling. And the Duke has been beside himself too.'

I stood there looking at her like a fish on cocaine and tried to tell myself I was dreaming. I mean this was Candida, aka The Bitch, That Cow and The Virus – the all-time anti-girlfriend, the bitch in heels who planned my downfall like insurance agents plan endowment policies.

'I even had the Duke out looking for you on the streets of Soho!'

Well this was more like it – a geographical reference to my morals. I suppose it wouldn't have occurred for her to look for me in Hampstead or Putney or St John's Wood. But come to think about it she did look kind of worn out and old, not the usual immaculately turned-out, starched from head to foot in Poison, Lucrezia Borgia I knew and feared. Even her hair looked, well, fluffy.

But did I trust the fluffier version any more than I trusted the starched one? Obviously I didn't. Resoundingly and emphatically no, no, no. I was more than ever on my guard.

'The Duke has contacted people who can help with these things. He has been fantastic, darling. Simply superb. Make no mistake I suspected that Barton from the start. That solicitor and her biscuit bingeing will get short shrift from me in the future. Now, the first thing is to show me these clippings you spoke of. If you are in danger we must go to the police more or less straight away – of course.'

'Of course,' I said, with a firmness I didn't feel. The Bar has an innate distrust of the police. Verbals and forensic tampering, that was how I felt about police. But I was treading water in this new role Candida had cast me in – victim of her concern.

She looked at me warily as if I might make a sudden move again. 'Well yes, plenty of time for the police later though. First thing is to get the clippings.'

'They're in my flat,' I said.

'Right, well as the man appears to be armed I've taken the precaution of hiring a few bodyguards to keep a close eye on the two of us until we get this whole mess sorted out. Of course, you should have told me about this private eye fellow's findings sooner rather than later, my dear. I will need to speak to him as well but in the meantime we must be prepared. These Antipodean gangsters can get quite ruthless when you rub them up the wrong way.

'Antipodean gangsters?'

'It doesn't do to be naive, Evelyn. Not at your age. I'm not going to harangue you about your involvement with this Barton man, although heavens knows it makes me shiver. Nonetheless, the die has been cast and now we must do what we can to mop up the mess.'

I swallowed. 'Mop up the mess?'

'Now you must take six bodyguards for yourself and I'll keep the other nine here, for heaven knows what tortures he has planned for me as your leader. They are the best in the business, darling. Ex-army women who'll know what to do to a creature like Barton. As the Duke says, one can't be too safe – only too sorry.' Then she gave one of those chilling antifreeze sighs of hers and opened the door.

'Come in then, don't loiter,' she called out. 'We don't have all day – quick march and all that!'

I watched, amazed as my small room filled up with half a dozen beefy broads in leathers.

'This is Kim, Dingo, Bill, Stevie, Lazza and Anne. Girls,

meet Miss Hornton. They've been instructed to flank you as
long as I deem necessary, darling. My treat – apart from dietary
requirements. You'll be responsible for feeding them, obviously.
They won't sleep as they'll change shifts every eight hours, but
all that will be seen to without you needing to notice. Just give
them plenty to eat, darling. What I mean is don't go to any
trouble. Good plain food is all they require. Isn't it, girls?' she
asked loudly and clapped her hands as though she was Brown
Owl speaking to a deaf brownie pack.

They nodded robotically. They were a healthy-looking
bunch, all big teeth and massive limbs coated in leather.
They wore feminine shiny bobs that belied the carnivorous
looks on their faces. They were bloody intimidating basically
– they reminded me of the Israeli women soldiers with their
Uzis on buses in Tel Aviv. No idle observer could mistake their
shared penchant for casual violence.

They gathered around me with arms folded and I couldn't
help feeling that they were waiting for Candida to give the word
so they could kick my skinny butt.

'As I say, Evelyn, if you're popping into Mezzo or the
Oxo Tower, the girls will join you, darling. Nothing special
for them.'

I nodded dutifully. Candida seemed to have gained some
of her old style back now as she fluffed up her bouffant and
pulled a Chanel compact from her bag. 'Run along then, I'll
wait here in case Barton phones you. First sign of him, and Kim
has been instructed to call the police. Any other developments
will be reported to me first. Is that clear?'

'Crystal-ish,' I said.

'Run along then, darling, chop chop.'

I shuffled hesitantly to the door, flanked by my trained
killers. I didn't want to be alone with them basically. 'I'll see
you when I get back then, shall I?'

But she didn't reply, she was already sitting at my desk
logging onto my e-mail, so I jostled my way through to the

front of my bodyguards and took off down the corridor. I had
expected them to follow at a respectful pace but they had a
separate agenda in which my self-esteem didn't feature. Kim
and Lazza strode on either side of me, squeezing me against
the book-lined walls so that my assertive pace was reduced to
a waddle.

I was beginning to see the hitherto unsuspected pitfalls of
Candida's concern. Is this how it was for the Duke? Did she
authorise and monitor his strokes in bed, I wondered, trying not
to giggle. Not competently enough to get a marriage proposal
out of him, I consoled myself.

Orlando appeared at the top of the passage in one of his rare
pinstriped guises. The girls, no doubt keen to impress me, went
into automatic defence mode. Bill charged out in front and did a
few things with her hands that looked like warning karate poses
but which Orlando interpreted as groovy dance moves.

He fell to his knees and emulated them himself.

'Inexorably superb, Evelyn!' he cried out. 'This is brilliant!
Phenomenal, how I worship you!' But before the words were
out of his mouth, Bill had him spread-eagled against the wall.

Squeezing past I heared his giggles while she frisked
him with her baton. 'Seriously cool, seriously cool,' he was
murmuring. I kept my head down and acted like ministers
do when they've been caught with a rent boy in Shepherd's
Market. This was a red letter 'no comment' day for me.

At reception I saw the wisdom in ducking below the window
to avoid being seen by the clerks' room. A girl has her image to
keep up and mine certainly didn't need half a dozen leather-clad
women on either side of it. But as I stooped, I felt Ann and
Lazza's arms holding me upright so that my legs began to
paddle in mid-air, presenting me to my amazed clerks as one
of those girls in an Ecstasy coma being thrown out by nightclub
bouncers.

Warren dropped his head and looked meaningfully at his
screen-save. Brilliant, I mean what if I was being led off to a

death camp? I was paying this bloke to be my virtual guardian yet here I was being woman-handled by every misogynist's nightmare. Right! Next chambers meeting I was going to be lending my weight to Vinny's arguments to end Warren's ten per cent!

Owing to acute embarrassment, I jogged down Clerkenwell Road, trying to get the whole ordeal over with as quickly as possible. I would get the clippings, take them back to Candida and politely decline her bodyguards for the future. Kim et al jogged along beside me, talking on those phones you see security guards in banks with – reporting passing trees and incredulous pedestrians to one another.

A tourist group on a tour of Legal London got very excited and started taking photos. People laughed and nudged one another – so much for British reserve. Thank God I was wearing my beige Armani – at least I was exonerated on the sartorial front. What on earth had possessed Candida to hire six of them? As far as we knew Matt was a one-man operation and not a very muscular one at that. OK so he had a handgun but six ex-army tank girls seemed a bit OTT. I suppose I should have been impressed, or grateful even, but the thought of feeding them even 'good plain food', on my woeful finances, petrified me. My last remaining credit card had been cut in half and Warren hadn't looked too keen to give me any cheques last time I saw him.

In a nutshell I was now living in fear of the words, 'we are feeling peckish'.

CHAPTER THIRTY-ONE

despite his speech impediment he did seem to be an in charge sort of bloke.

We retrieved the clippings without incident and ran them back to chambers – the girls' steel-capped boots echoing on the cobbles like a snare-drum roll. Every member of the judiciary going about the Temple that morning stood aside and watched our running procession – only no one was applauding, they were more likely passing silent sentence.

I wanted to stop and explain, to reason, to excuse myself to my judicial friends or even to blame Candida, but what could I say? The reality was they'd be dining out on this story for months.

I left Kim et al on the leather chesterfields in reception while I took the clippings in to Candida. I discovered her sitting on the Duke's knee in my room. I'd never met him before, up until now he had been no more than a name on the card attached to a baby-seal-skin coat or a Lacroix jacket or a room full of orchids. Although he had been courting Candida for years, no one had ever sighted him. In the darker moments of my feelings for Candida – and there had been some pretty black spots – I had hinted bitchily that the mad, mad extravagant duke was a myth.

Looking at him now as he stood to greet me with a formal little bow, I saw a grey diminutive man – shorter than Candida

– shorter than most people basically, with thinning grey hair, a deep tan and a propensity for talking with his mouth half closed. He looked like he'd just had all his teeth taken out.

'Ah, Evelyn, at last. Allow me to introduce his Grace, the Duke of Billingsgate.'

'How do you do, your, um, Holiness,' I stuttered, uncertain how to greet a 'Grace'.

'Mmm mm m mm mear,' he mumbled.

'Just call him Duke,' Candida interpreted for me. 'The Duke doesn't stand on ceremony.'

He didn't stand on a dais either I noticed. Basically he stood at about five foot in shiny black Church's. He was one seriously weird little guy and not at all the sort of bloke you could imagine sending off Lacroix jackets and exotic blooms to a woman like Candida who was known to eat cab drivers for breakfast. This was the mad, mad extravagant duke in person. The perpetual suitor. Still waters run deep, I guess.

Candida seemed bowled over with pride, linking her arm in his and interpreting for him as he explained how he was having some of the chaps at The Yard dig up the dirt on Matt. I presumed he meant Scotland Yard and not the funky gay bar in Soho the girls like to descend on for Sunday brunch.

Despite his speech impediment he did seem to be an in charge sort of bloke, I decided as he presented his procedural plan, point by point. Although he was completely unintelligible, I couldn't help but be awed. He sounded like Sam buying options with a mouth full of marbles. And I could see in a bizarre kind of way how Candida might fall for a short man like the Duke who needed someone else to speak for him. He had a title.

But he represented so much more than that to me, for he was Candida's Achilles heel – the weak link in her reputation as a woman who always gets what she wants. Because she wanted this bloke to propose to her more than Moses wanted a plague of frogs visited on the Egyptians. And he was obdurate.

I guess this Duke bloke had his own mind and that was no mean feat where Candida was concerned. No one who came into contact with this woman was their own person. She could suck out free will and self-esteem with a look, not even Supreme Court judges were safe. Certainly I was her creature. No, this Duke bloke had hidden depths as far as I was concerned. I looked up to him – metaphorically, obviously.

'So, Evelyn, I have managed to knock off a few of your advices while I was waiting. I'm going to be tied up entertaining his Grace the rest of the day. We'll call you if we uncover anything. You really should spend more time on your advices you know, solicitors appreciate a thorough treatment. I was just saying to Carol at Clifford Chance how shabby you young female lawyers are these days. All things considered you may as well take the afternoon off and do some more shopping.' She sighed as if that was what I spent my time doing – instead of advices. Needless to say I hadn't had the guts to tell her where to stick her bodyguards.

I did as I was told and went off to collect the girls from reception where there was a bit of a fracas going on. Vinny, our chambers bore, had descended on my girls in my absence and attempted to engage them in a little light tedium and, like others before him, he had found more than he bargained for.

By the time I walked in, Lazza and Dingo had him in a neck-lock while Warren and Lee were observing the sideshow through the window of the clerks' room with a mixture of fascination and amusement. Vinny's tongue was spilling from his mouth and his glasses were hanging lopsidedly off his face. Apparently they'd been holding him there for the duration of my absence and, what's more, none of the other members of chambers walking through had suggested intervening. When I ordered his release he scuttled away like an embarrassed witness who's been caught lying and Warren and Lee came out to congratulate the girls.

It was while under the influence of acute embarrassment

that I decided to take them to lunch at the Japanese Tuckshop on St John Street. I know we are talking major brain bypass here but I was weak with humiliation. I couldn't have my clerks get any more ammunition on me. But why did I opt for sushi? It was a question that was going to keep me awake for weeks, I just knew it.

I mean sushi's the sort of food you eat as an art form – an expensive foray in cuisine minimalism. It didn't take a sociologist to see that these were the sort of sheilas who could suck up the sashimi and sake like sumo wrestlers. The little bloke cutting up the stuff couldn't work fast enough.

All dreams of not having my loft repossessed this month were history by the time the girls ordered their third lot of sake. I picked disconsolately at a piece of seaweed and berated myself for being stupid enough to ring Candida in my hour of need. But it was too late to turn back now, she had taken on my case with the enthusiasm of a missionary and it was on a runaway course. I was starting to reminisce on the good old days when all I had to worry about was my stalker turning me into a hotpot

By the time the girls had licked the last bit of nigiri maki off their plates and slurped the last drop of sake from the jugs, I was starting to wonder if I'd ever shop again. That was also the moment when Sam walked in with Rory.

This was a weird turn-up from a lot of angles. One, because Sam loathes Japanese and secondly what the fuck was she doing with Rory? Thirdly, they didn't look in the least bit surprised to see me. Not that either of them acknowledged me.

Rory leaned on the door and looked on indifferently as if we were greyhounds in a race he hadn't bothered to bet on, while Sam marched straight up to Kim and confronted her with a shove.

Kim rose to the challenge and managed to make the art of swallowing a lump of sashimi look as terrifying as a vampire's fangs, while her comrades gathered around doing their various martial art practice moves like some sort of aggro Tai Chi class.

Dingo stuck her baton in her teeth and started growling.

'Bloody hell!' I cried.

'You've been messing around with my girlfriend,' Sam yelled.

Two mid-forties women in goat's wool home-spun cardigans, who'd been happy enough to show off their liberal N1 politics by smiling at us over their udon noodles earlier, dived under their table. The little bloke who had been serving us, ducked under the counter. I decided to err on the side of caution and join him – which was a bit mad basically because it exposed my lack of allegiance to the girls. All six of them.

I looked over at Rory who had started rolling a cigarette with one hand.

'I suppose you're the sort of bitch who thinks possession is nine tenths of the law do you?' Kim sneered, puffing out her chest. She was definitely on for a fight and Sam looked lamentably inadequate as her wrestling partner. She might talk and walk like a Panzer division on the move but she was only five foot tall with no martial arts training whatsoever. Basically she was used to talking and buying her way out of trouble.

'I think you should stay out of my relationship,' she warned, edging in closer and giving Kim another shove. This was getting nasty – not that it was nice before but the girls were starting to look frighteningly sick of shadow-boxing. I had that feeling I usually get just before I throw up.

'I'm not interested in your cloying relationships, shorty!' Kim jeered, hands on hips. Dingo started to circle Sam.

Rory lit up.

'We've got a kid!' Sam reasoned – maybe even she had started to size up her disadvantage and thought that talk of innocent children might pacify them.

'I don't care if you've got a fucking orphanage, you sad old leso. I don't like being told what to do.'

By this stage I was feeling guilty about hiding behind the counter with Ramos (he'd introduced himself during the orphanage dig). I mean it wasn't very loyal of me. Maybe I should remind the girls just who it was they should be minding. So I stood up and approached Kim. Lazza and Anne moved aside to let me pass. 'Look can we discuss this later, I—'

'Fuck off, straight girl!' Kim spat with a venom that sent me scurrying back to the counter.

'Nice try, kid,' Ramos said kindly. My intestines felt like they were being squeezed through a udon-making machine.

'Right, that's fucking it! I've had enough!' Sam screamed.

Phew, thank God it was over. She'd had enough and was going to leave. I said a silent prayer of thanks.

'No one fucking speaks to my friend like that,' she added as she punched Kim hard in the eye with a right cross.

So that was what she meant by 'that' being 'it' I moaned. 'It' was when I saw my best friend pummelled to death by a bunch of leather lesbians. My responsibility was clear – this was where my legs were needed. Thai kick-boxing in a Japanese restaurant? Culturally warped but, who knows, it might take off I mused as I checked my heels. Only as it happened I never got the chance.

Before I had stood up, Rory had Kim and Dingo in a headlock and by rights Lazza, Anne, Bill and Steve should have been onto him like Aussie Rules footballers in a scrum, only that was when my stomach decided to give up the fight.

I threw up on the lot of them.

'Nice one!' cheered Ramos.

CHAPTER THIRTY-TWO

the art of staying cool when the adrenaline radiator has just burst.

Rory seized the opportunity to get Sam clear of danger. That left me significantly alone with my bodyguards, who were none too pleased with me. I guess dealing with projectile vomit attacks wasn't in their job description.

The women in cardigans had snuck out during the disturbance without paying their bill, so I more or less had to do the right thing by Ramos and foot the damage. My bodyguards went to the loo to wash off the noodles, leaving Kim and Lazza with me, muttering darkly about 'straights'.

Ramos gave me a pat on the back when we said goodbye while simultaneously admitting that it might be best if I found somewhere else to eat my sushi in the future. Face it, you're going to be starved out of this town, girl, I told myself as my self-image reached its lowest nadir since Paddy had walked in on me in the loo.

As I was being chaperoned back to my flat, I felt like a prisoner not a mindee and I was nothing if not a little nauseous still. I just wanted a long bath, a couple of Enos and an overdose of Secanol but when we actually got inside I was compelled to lower my dreamscape yet again. By then I would have been happy with a safety latch.

My door had been jemmied open and lying outstretched on the floor was Matt, with the woman who wanted to make amends standing over him. (I recognised the slippers). To hell with that, I recognised the muu-muu.

My bodyguardesses went into action like the trained professionals that they clearly were. Within moments, the unconscious Matt was cuffed and the muu-muu was spread-eagled against the wall like a billowing yacht sail. She couldn't have been more than forty – and while she'd looked a trifle cross when we'd arrived, the outfit was kind of at odds with the archetypal demeanour of the gangland moll. Basically this outfit was at odds – period! The muu-muu is one of those designer grudges that some bloke put together to further his cause to make women look as stupid as he was.

She started to whimper. Lazza took a swatch of her grey-flecked hair and pulled on it brutally. 'Cough up then! Go on cough up!' she yelled, like my doctor does when he wants a phlegm swab.

But Muu-muu didn't look like she had anything to cough up. She was making the sounds of one truly bereft of phlegm. Something in my forgiving Catholic nature went out to her. 'For the love of God have mercy,' she was sobbing.

'We'd better call the police,' I said, taking out my mobile.

Kim, the guard possessed of both brain and body, grabbed the phone. 'I don't think we'll bother the pigs just yet. Let's face it, the police can be a bit limited in their powers to get answers. We can take care of this.'

By this time, Dingo had managed to jam the door closed and, as she leant against it and folded her arms, I got the shivery frightened feeling that I normally only get when megalomaniacs start singing, 'I Did It My Way'.

Were these steroid monsters supposed to be making me feel safe? Forget it. I was right not to buy Candida's concern shit. I was in trouble and the only person I trusted in this country anymore was a woman sweating so profusely she was going to win the Miami Wet muu-muu competition.

I was so scared I was calm. If the last four years at the Bar had taught me one thing, apart from refusing any food that comes with yellow sauce, it was the art of sounding cool when my adrenaline radiator has just burst. Barristers get pretty adroit at that, especially down in the cells at the Bailey where I spent most of my pupillage. 'I'll just check this guy for ID,' I announced.

The girls looked impressed at my girl guide spirit and were probably relieved that I was prepared to deal with 'the bloke'. I could tell they were the sort of bullies who preferred their victims to be in a condition to kick back.

'Right, luv,' Kim agreed. 'You check the arsehole on the floor and we'll check the back of this place. Are there any hear exits?'

'No,' I admitted.

'OK Bill, Lazza, you watch the caftan.'

As I eased my hand under Matt's unconscious torso he let out a grunt – much the same sort of grunt he had made when he orgasmed on top of me yesterday. The sounds of sex lose their quality of amour in the cold light of antipathy, I thought as I found the first passport.

Bill and Lazza went back to bullying the poor trembling Irish woman. She might have intimidated me with her slippers but at least she hadn't clocked up a two hundred and fifty pound food bill at the Japanese Tuckshop!

'I'm sorry about this, Miss Evelyn. It was Rory who give me the key . . .' she sobbed.

My spine slumped. Rory? Was he advising half the female population of London or what? I found another passport.

'I only came to get what was mine. He had no right to give it away.'

'What did you say?' I asked. 'Who had no right to give what away?'

'Come on, cough it up,' Lazza urged although I could tell she was basically losing interest. She was sitting on one of the velvet vulvas now with Bill. Muu-muu, like the good victim she was, kept her place against the wall.

'My gear. The things I bought with my money. They were mine, not his to give away,' she said.

'What are you talking about?' I repeated, as I went to work on Matt's next pocket. Lazza came over to check out what I was doing. I had so far unearthed three passports, all of them from countries the French don't like giving visas to. Australian – in the name of Michael Finn. Botswana – Chuck Brewster and a South African – Dylan Thomas.

'I'd better give this shit to Kim,' she said as I passed her the ID.

'He gave them to you didn't he?' Muu-muu asked.

'Who?'

'Paddy, my husband. That was why I was following you all that time. I thought the two of you were on together because of the way he kept giving you all my stuff. Only when Rory came back he set me right. He said Paddy was like a father figure to yer. That was why I sent you them flowers as a way of . . .'

'*You* were following me?' I asked, as I discovered a bunch of credit cards and a gram or so of white powder. A booty which paled into insignificance as it dawned on me that I had lain awake at night in terror because I was being stalked by a woman in tartan slippers and a muu-muu! I had been stalked by Paddy's wayward wife – Rosy? It was mortifying. And at that point I hadn't even stopped to consider the implications that Brad must have once been '*her* very own Negro lover'!

'In the trench coat and sunglasses? It was you?'

'Do you know 'er then?' Bill asked.

'Well, er, yes, that is to say sort of.'

'Well keep your eye on 'er then, I'll go and tell Kim.'

'So you were the one stalking me all that time?' I whispered.

'That's right. I was fuming, specially when he gave you the baby feeding warmer. We couldn't have kids you see and then when he started giving you all my stuff, the stuff I bought with my money from the teaching job, it broke my heart it did. I thought he didn't want me. I only left him to show him. To show him how he needed me.'

'But you broke his heart,' I told her as I tried Matt's trouser pockets.

'I didn't mean no harm or anything. When Rory told me what was what, I chucked it in. He give me the keys see to get the stuff. It's my stuff, all of it. He had no right t' give it away. And then while I was gathering it all, yer man here broke down the door and I had to hit him with the sandal.'

So Rory had known all along that my stalker was no more than a sad woman in a muu-muu who was jealous because her red-haired husband was showering me with her blow-up dolls and lawn sandals! This was the sort of news that took a while to sink in. But as my hand wrapped around the familiar cold metal of the gun, I found I had other things on my mind.

CHAPTER THIRTY-THREE

guinness, cigarettes and gum.

On Candida's instruction we removed Matt's handcuffs and left him groaning on the floor to slowly regain consciousness. Without calling the police we were really in no position to hold him; basically Matt was now in a position to lay criminal charges against me should he care to.

I would have liked to have been a fly on the wall when he came round to find himself stripped of everything that makes life in the free world liveable – i.e. passports, credit cards, cocaine and gun. All it took was one body search to turn him into a nobody. If only I could wreak such conclusive revenge on every man who crossed me.

Rosy was permitted to scuffle off in her slippers – profusely apologising and promising never to darken my doorstep again. I hadn't told anyone about the gun and had no intention of doing so – it was getting so that I didn't know who to trust anymore. Looking back I can't blame myself – forget chaos theories, my life was a *mandelbrot*.

We returned to chambers for further instructions from Candida – 'base' as the girls called her. She was closeted with the Duke and didn't want to be disturbed. Poking her head around her door, I got the impression she wasn't wearing her Yves Saint Laurent blouse any more.

For want of a better place to leave them, I took the girls with me back to my room where Rory was waiting on my swivel chair

– he was shirtless too. He also had his cowboy-booted feet on my briefs. I asked the girls to leave us alone which they agreed to pretty readily. I figure they knew when they met their match, especially Dingo who still had welts around her neck from her struggle with him at the restaurant.

Rory didn't get up, or take his feet off the table, or put down the brief he was reading. Gentlemanly flourishes were superfluous to a man who still hadn't advanced beyond the *Homo habillas* where women were concerned. I reminded myself that this was the bloke who thought the suffragettes were a female soul group from the sixties. But then I noticed that he had undone a pink ribbon from around a brief and my anger bubbled up inside me like a pot of rancid stew.

'You've got a nerve!' I said as I shut the door. I didn't want Vinny interrupting my ABH.

He swung his legs off my desk and came over, pinioning me to the wall with his smooth brown arms – was he waiting for a calendar to discover him or something?

'So what do you have to say for yourself? Hey?' I demanded, slightly unnerved by the proximity of his bare flesh. 'You knew who my stalker was all along didn't you? It may interest you to know I just found your sister ransacking my flat.'

I could hear my voice climbing the decibels range. When that happened I always hit shrill high notes. 'Just mouth the words, Hornton,' Sister Carmel used to say in choir practice. Well I wasn't going to mouth these words – I wanted answers and I wanted them now. By catching me unawares and refusing to call me doll he had dislodged me from the driving seat. Just the same I was in no state to be having this conversation and we both knew it. I was like a drunk driver demanding her right to drive.

'What is it with your family? All I wanted was a bit of plumbing and carpentry,' I told him. 'Nothing fancy! And what do I get instead? A stalker, a private eye and a guy in a red moustache who wants to relocate his wife's possessions to my flat? What is it with you? Are you trying to carve out new territory in the latest accessory field? Hey? Hey?'

He folded his arms and leaned against my desk. We were only inches away from one another. I could smell his breath – Guinness, roll-up cigarettes and gum. He still hadn't said a word but I detected a trace of mockery in his dark brown eyes with their flecks of green, which only made me wilder.

'And what was all that business with Sam? I suppose you know you've broken up the most decent couple in London! What do you think you're playing at? Hey? Well?'

I could hear the second hand making its rotations around the clock in Judge Hawkesbury's kitchen above. These ceilings were paper thin. Rory didn't answer. I thought about all the time I'd ever spent with this man and how I had never been certain of my footing with him. He had always seemed irritatingly sure of his.

There was a stray lock of hair that was hanging over one of his eyes, making him look so adolescent and sweet and, without stopping to think, I reached out to push it away and that was when he gathered me in his arms and snogged me.

I grabbed him by his hair the way Lazza had done to Rosy and tried to dislodge him but his face had a grip on my larynx that a leech would admire. He had me wrapped in his big brown chesterfield arms and, besides, despite myself it was bloody nice. Unexpected. Outrageously presumptuous, but definitely nice.

He kissed me like I figure angels kiss, with an assurance that was so gentle my throat just said 'what the heck' and gave up its secrets. Even though I planned to slug him as hard as I could once it was over, I couldn't help but enjoy it for the time being. It was like I was being kissed all over – his whole mouth seemed about to swallow me up. My legs went weak like those astronaut people that have been in orbit for years. And then he lifted me up as if I was no heavier than the black Gucci frock I'd changed into at the flat (beige doesn't really suit me) and put me on the desk.

I couldn't tell where his lips ended and his hands began as they roamed my body – this was masculinity with the gloves off. I had never felt so utterly helpless with a man before, stripped of power and ego and the nagging self-conscious feminism that underwrote everything I did and thought.

It wasn't that I was thinking about domestic drudgery or how long before this bloke made me barefoot and pregnant, it was just that I didn't give a shit about the balance of power any more. All I cared about was where his hand was going to caress next. I was giving myself up to unrepentant, mindless pleasure for the first time in my life – well the first time that day anyway.

When it did finally stop we just looked into one another's eyes, sizing up one another's thoughts like combatants in a war game. Then I slapped him as hard as I could across the face and he walked out.

CHAPTER THIRTY-FOUR

to be cool in london is to look and live like a junky without actually taking heroin.

As a precaution, Candida packed me off to Notting Hill for the night to stay with the girls, while the bodyguards were sent to stand vigil at my flat to keep an eye on whatever Matt was after. I guess it was taking a while to sink in that my loft was currently surrounded by tank girls because all I could think of was how my hand still stung from the slap I'd delivered to Rory. All the way along the traffic pile-up on the Westway I wondered where he was, what he was thinking and why I had allowed him to kiss me.

Charles was home alone with Johnny, bopping away to dance music in a pair of pale blue Chanel hot pants and a matching bikini top – nail varnish coordinated. She greeted me with a cuddle and a martini, forcing me to review my grave fears for her relationship with Sam.

'Darling, how marvellous to have you back, it'll be just like old times. Bruce is off for the night so it will just be us three.' Bruce was the Norland Nanny. Her name was Penny Bruce really and she wasn't a bit gay but she called herself Bruce because it sounded cooler.

'That's great,' I agreed. 'Just like old times.'

She crinkled her nose. 'Except you'll have to sleep on the couch because Bruce is in your room now. But I'll do a Marks

& Spencer's Italian and we'll drink ourselves rotten, paint our
nails and gossip our way into the morning on the balcony.'

I told her my door was being rehung and she didn't ask for
any further explanation – I don't think I could have given her
one even if she had. My day had been disturbing enough without
reliving it. Besides I didn't know what emphasis to place on the
Rory incident.

I was just glad to see that she was her usual self, not in
the least bit withdrawn or devious looking. This, I told myself,
was definitely not the behaviour of a girlfriend cheating on her
lover. Maybe what happened this afternoon with Sam was just
the result of a bad period cramp or something. These girls went
together like Chanel's Rouge Noir and nails, like Philip Treacy
hats and Ascot, like gin and vermouth. Their relationship was
impregnable, unassailable. Bloody rock solid basically.

I relaxed into the Mae West lips sofa with my martini and
made some raspberry noises for Johnny while Charles clattered
about in the kitchen. His infectious chortling was a huge boost to
my ego, proving I still had the power to impress – even without
an uncut credit card to my name. I kicked off my shoes and
gripped the familiar domesticity of the flat we'd all shared for
two years like a life raft.

All that changed when Sam got in.

Did I say life raft? Did I say rock solid? Try quicksand. The
way she looked at Charles was so acid it burned the make-up
off her face. Suspicion cut through the atmosphere like a razor
blade through a line of coke as Sam slammed her briefcase
down and thrust a bottle of something bubbly into Charles'
hand. Cyanide possibly? Then she strode wordlessly over to
the stereo and turned it off. 'I didn't expect to see you here,'
she groaned.

'I've had a break-in at my flat so I'm having the door fixed,'
I explained.

'Oh, darling, you didn't tell me you'd had a break-in –
anything stolen?'

'Er, no, nothing stolen, just kids probably.' It was a lie which spoke volumes about how uncomfortable I felt at that minute. When you can't even tell your lesbian girlfriends that a bloke you trusted turned out to be a gun-toting bastard with a criminal record, you know you're alone.

'Well of course you're always welcome here,' Sam replied sarcastically before striding off to the shower.

After that I stuck to the corner of the room with Johnny like an au pair without a work permit. Even changing nappies was a fragrant joy compared to the stench of bad vibes emanating from the girls.

As we sat down to pasta, one part of me wanted to pull them into my ample bosom and tell them how much I loved them and knock their heads together and make them see what a great couple they were. Tell them how I was sure that with a bit of honesty and respect for one another's feelings we could work this out – LA group-therapy style. But I figured I had more chance of getting Rafsanjani to admit that Salman was his brother, so I stuck to blowing raspberry noises for Johnny.

From then on things went from miserable to intolerable. Somehow I got embroiled in one of those, 'Could you ask her if she'd pass the salt please, Evelyn?' things. I mean the stuff was right by my hand so I just passed it over myself, but just the same Charles countered by saying, 'If she finds it empty you can tell her it's because *she* never fills it.'

This must have been how nuclear warheads felt in the cold war. If this was what keeping the peace felt like, maybe disaster was better. Either I was going to lose it and kill them both or they were going to forget I was there and kill each other. Either way Johnny was going to be exposed to homicide at a very young age.

Johnny was the only thing that made me keep my cool and stopped me saying anything. The food coagulated in my throat and after my third glass of wine I left the table and went back to making rude noises for him in his bouncy until he showed signs of becoming sleepy. That was when I began to wonder what would happen when he went to bed? Would détente end?

I offered to bath him, change him and read him his story. He fell asleep halfway through Little Red Riding Hood but I read on into the Ugly Duckling just to keep out of the living room where the silence was deafening.

'I thought I might go and visit Nick and Ben,' I told them when I walked out to find them sitting at opposite ends of the balcony. The night sky was splashed with stars and a full moon as silver as a zinc-topped bar in a Conran restaurant and I thought about Rory and wondered if he'd seen it and if he'd thought of me.

'The junkies? Whatever for?' Charles asked, amazed that I couldn't find perfect peace there on the balcony while they played a vicious game of Cain and Abel.

How about because you two are enough to drive anyone into the arms of a strong narcotic? I should have said. But by the way Sam didn't even turn around to look at me I guessed that they knew.

'So, er, don't wait up,' I said. 'I've still got my key.'

Neither of them replied. Had I unwittingly joined this war or something? If so whose side was I on? I looked from one hardened face to the other. It didn't look like there were going to be too many toenails painted on this balcony tonight.

It has been said that London is a city of over twelve million people all trying to live the life of a junky without ever having taken heroin. But they don't know the half of it. It's not all falling asleep over mugs of coffee with lit cigarettes in your hand. I should know, I made a study of it when I lived with Nick and Ben for six months before I bought my loft in Clerkenwell.

They were successful bond traders for two city banks and, having seen their lifestyle first hand, I can assure you that this junky lark is more boring than art. Even William Burroughs would have headed for the nearest NA meeting if he'd met this particular couple of smack-heads.

By the basis of any social quiz test you care to name, I was
heading for the party black spot of London that night.

CHAPTER THIRTY-FIVE

the notting hill junky, i.e. armani underwear, pink's shirts and burberry tourniquets.

Nick and Ben were in exactly the same state that they were when I had left them six months ago. Like dissipated opium addicts of the 1990s sitting in their cold steel Alessi kitchen in Armani underwear, Thomas Pink's shirts unbuttoned and their silk ties around their arms as tourniquets.

They were having their after-dinner heroin hit.

I knocked and when no one came I used my key. They looked about as thrilled to see me as a milkman is to see a bottle of milk. Emotions don't run very deep in a junky's veins – which is their great strength I guess. So I sat at the table and pretended that what they were doing was no different from drinking beer. There was no point trying to distract them or entertain them and, unlike more social drugs such as alcohol or cocaine, there was no offer to join them. Heroin is as far from the proverbial good-time drug as you can get.

I had watched them going through this vein-chasing, bloody ritual for all the months that I had lived here, until shock was replaced by indifference, and finally boredom. Despite this there was something clinically gripping about the ritual. I mean, I bet these blokes could have had a thousand gun-raiding bastards in their flat and they would have reacted with complete contempt.

That was how they survived the bond market – by rising above it on a narcotic high.

Eventually the blood surged into Ben's syringe, alerting him that the vein had been successfully excavated and he sighed in relief. What I would have done for a sigh like that, I realised. I hadn't exhaled for like hours! Days even! Weeks!

'So, Evelyn, how goes it?' he asked, pulling off his Burberry tourniquet while Nick wound up his own injection.

'Sure, OK, if you don't count blokes with guns breaking into my apartment,' I replied matter-of-factly. 'I'm staying with Sam and Charles while my bodyguards clean up the mess basically.'

'Yeah?' said Ben rubbing his face to keep his eyeballs from rolling out. 'How are the girls?'

'That's why I'm here, they're arguing. Mega disputations going on down on Ladbroke Square. I can't believe it really, Sam thinks Charles is having an affair, can you believe it? She even hit one of my bodyguards.'

'I loved the effect they did to their walls,' he replied. Nick seemed to have passed out with his tie still around his arm. 'Yeah, (nod, nod) really added value to the place.'

'Their wall treatment?' Hello?

'Best move they ever made buying that place. That square has quadrupled in price in the last few years.'

'I see.' This was not the dialogue I was looking for as a follow-up to my pretty startling explanation for being there. I mean I had practically defied them to balk with that last reference to bodyguards. Basically I had imagined that even two smack-heads like Nick and Ben would be able to grasp the crucial alarm element here.

Had Notting Hill had a complete life bypass or what? Was W11 fortified against reality by its bastion of wine bars, restaurants and designer smugness? Had real-life danger been superseded by interior decorating and property prices?

'Yeah (nod, nod) emulsion with an oil base wasn't it?

I saw Sam then ... (nod, nod) ... other day (nod, nod) and she ...'

I waited patiently for him to finish his sentence – like a word junky waiting for the next fix but it didn't come. His hand was all over his face now, pulling on it like it was a rubber one he was trying to take off.

'Yeah (nod, nod) excellent,' Ben exclaimed, coming to like a wind-up toy.

'Yeah, excellent,' I agreed, but I don't think they really noticed the sarcasm.

'How are you anyway?' Ben asked, suddenly waking refreshed from his nap.

'What, apart from armed attackers and a flat full of lesbian bodyguards? Completely fine. Never been better. Hardly a care in the world. Now that I know who my stalker is and where the gun is, my anxiety levels are down by, hell, about ten per cent on last week,' I breezed.

But Ben's chin was running down his neck like ice cream. I watched them for another half-hour as they nodded into their designer stupors, then I checked their vital signs and took myself into the spare room where I curled up in my old bed and waited for the night to pass. I didn't even try and kid myself that the girls would have waited up for me.

I opted not to stay for breakfast though. Watching Nick and Ben in the mornings was like watching feeding time at a transport cafe. Fried eggs, bacon and sausages whizzed up in a pound of extra virgin olive oil and served with a loaf of organic bread. Forced down every morning precisely at six with a gallon of Darjeeling tea before they went to the gym and pumped up their veins for a new day.

Charles and Sam on the other hand usually had a more civilised meal of coffee and more coffee. I staggered in around eight, desperate to be part of the ritual. Bruce was running around the room giving Johnny a helicopter ride in a scene of domestic felicity but I didn't get a chance to take it in for long or to get a coffee because as I arrived Sam was on her way out. There was another tube strike today and if I wanted to get to work at all – now was my big chance.

CHAPTER THIRTY-SIX

my profligate saviour.

As we drove down Bayswater Road, I offered Sam some girlfriend nurturing. I told her that if she needed anything – anything at all – even LA group therapy, I would be there for her. I even offered to share my Prozac script. She was as tight-lipped as the sphinx though and snapped at me to shut up before she ran up the arse of the Volvo in front.

These tube strikes were striking at the heart of London's commuter rage and I was part of a growing group of dissenters, plotting train driver lynching that summer. Like the rest of my generation I didn't care about the welfare of the worker, I just wanted one of those life styles that people in Calvin Klein advertisements have. As long as I could avoid knifings as much as possible, and not live in a borough that wanted half my yearly income and never took away my garbage, I was happy. Sometimes I get the feeling that London is the focus for some lunatic dictator with a cruel but effective plan to make life despicable.

I outlined this theory to Sam who drove like she lived – on the edge, along the pedestrian sidewalks basically – mowing down anyone or anything in her path. We terrified more horses that morning than a pack of loony hunt sabs. I mean, seriously, this was not a journey to be taken without a high coffee intake.

The very idea of talking to her about her relationship was laughable – proving how out of whack LA-style therapy was in

London. Prozac couldn't even skim the surface of this summer of tube-strike stress. We were heading for disaster as surely as Sam was heading for that horse, I realised as I staged my mutiny – grabbing the wheel and steering us into a gaggle of cyclists.

'It's OK, I'll walk from here,' I told her as she took hold of my neck and started shaking it. We were at Marble Arch and even the cyclists I'd mown down felt compelled to remonstrate with her. I suppose a cycle courier knows better than anyone how a murder on Marble Arch can hold up the traffic all day. They probably saw my salvation as a career move.

I was only two miles from chambers now but I was in such an acute state of terror I forgot my bag with my mobile and just about everything else that makes this city remotely liveable. All I had left was the gun stuck in the enormous pockets of my Ozbek pantaloons. These trousers had seemed just the thing last night when I found them like forgotten treasure in one of the cupboards in Sam and Charles' flat. Now they made me look and feel like a frazzled traveller back from her gap year in India.

Bombay and Calcutta at least had their transport systems happening. There was anarchy on the streets of London. As I shoved my way through the crowds I tried to cheer myself with thoughts of the summer term ending. Today was the last day of Trinity so a *laissez-faire* dress code would prevail at 17 Pump Court, which was a relief because there was no way I felt safe to go back to my flat to change. Not until I was certain that nothing more than a stark minimal space lay in wait for me.

It was around eight thirty in the morning but the crowds were from another time frame – around middayish. Frightened Japanese and American tourists were already clustered nervously in shop doorways, seeking safety from the bus queues that snaked dangerously down Oxford Street. When people start sticking to the pavement in London the crime rate soars. This is what declarations of 'coolest city in the world' can do to a place. Even the *Big Issue* sellers knew better than to come in to work today.

I arrived in chambers a little after nine. 'Miss Hornton, nice little capitalist/builder dispute for you. You're the capitalist,' Warren smiled as he handed me my brief.

'Thanks, Warren – you know how I love to play the bastard.'

'Now, now, Miss Hornton, a pink ribbon's a pink ribbon. Don't go getting sniffy about your briefs now, I've had enough of that down the years from Miss Raphael.'

The word 'sniffy' held particular connotations for me at that moment. I hadn't showered for twenty-four hours and, after my grapples with bodyguards and unconscious villains, I needed soap and water like a claustrophobic needs space. Chambers had installed a shower in the kitchen at Warren's insistence and I headed for it posthaste.

As the power shower surged down my back and the soap suds gathered at my feet, I tried to get my seemingly insurmountable problems into perspective – talking myself up and telling myself my adrenaline could probably do with the exercise. I am, at the end of the day, of a positive disposition. A fighter, not a thrower in of towels.

Speaking of which, I noticed there was a distinct lack of flannel about the place as I turned off the taps and peered out of the steamed-up glass. There was a damp pencilled sign on the shower door. TOWELS CAN BE OBTAINED FROM THE CLERKS' ROOM. The closest approximation of a towel I could see was a wet tea towel and a roll of paper towels with about two sheets left on it.

So it was that, with each ineffectual dab with the paper towel, my blood pressure rose and my positive affirmations dissipated like the steam on the glass. By the time I pulled on my pantaloons and felt the heavy bulge of the gun along my leg, I was in the mood to use it. I toyed with the idea of marching out to the clerks' room and shooting up my briefs.

The look on Warren's face would be worth it. He'd be born again all over again. Then maybe I'd go into the conference room and shoot up the chair where Matt had sat – and the Fortnum and Mason biscuit tin. The only thing stopping me was that I had no bullets.

I made myself an espresso thick with sugar and some toast in the Dialite toaster that Warren had harangued chambers to buy. That day I saw the great wisdom in all Warren's spending drives. How had I ever thought to object to this profligate saviour? From now on I resolved to encourage him to spend my colleagues' and my money to his heart's content. This toast was worth the one hundred and sixty pounds the toaster had cost – worth more because it cheered me up.

I was just putting in a last slice by the time Vinny discovered me and began to ply me with boring determination about the petty cash figures. Trust him to be in early on the last day of the summer term.

'Vinny, I really don't have time for this, I'm sorry. I have an important case on.'

'Well, Evelyn,' he warned. 'It is precisely because members of chambers put their heads in the sand that the clerks' room is able to get away with such flagrant spending. I mean that toaster for instance – one hundred and sixty pounds.' He pointed to it with thin-lipped satisfaction as my toast burned.

'He told us it would never do that,' he smirked.

I wondered what would happen if I pulled the gun on Vinny now and demanded that he hit the floor. Or better still if I held it to his temple and told him that if he ever bored me with his small talk again, I would blow his brains out. This tableau gave me a sudden surge of *joie de vivre*. Basically this gun thingamee was doing more for my confidence every minute.

'Do what?' I asked as I took out the offending toast and applied liberal strokes of butter and marmalade. 'I set it to burn,' I lied. 'I think this toaster is one of the greatest advances seventeen Pump Court has made this century. Anyway, Vinny, I honestly have to run.'

'Yes, I noticed there was a fellow in your room earlier when I came in.'

I shoved the toast into my mouth and dashed off in excitement. Rory had returned to finish what we started, I thought, tossing up whether to hit him again or not.

But through the open crack in my door I spotted not Rory but Matt sitting in my room, his shoulders slightly rounded as he stared out onto the square. My clitoris kicked my conscience in the shins. How had I ever been aroused by this effigy of man's inhumanity? He reminded me of those Mexican dolls they suspend for children to viciously stab until sweets pour out of the impaled insides. Rory had been right all along, the man was a creep.

CHAPTER THIRTY-SEVEN

what he needed was a metaphorical bobbit job.

Now that I actually had one of these Smith & Wesson's pressed into someone's head, it was dawning on me that empowerment was a whole lot easier to come by than any of the feminist dialectics that I had read suggested. Mrs Bobbit must have known this feeling. The possibility to cause a man some serious physical harm, exponentially changed my perspective on a lot of things. Basically I was now wondering how I'd ever got by without one.

Watching Matt perspiring like a pot of boiling kidney beans, I felt as powerful as one of those TV bitches who's got a hold of some bloke's balls with her teeth. I was flying! This was better than cocaine, better than sex, better than Prozac even – although I suspect just as addictive. I had wasted my life in the pursuit of a career, love and the best heels in town, when it seems I could have done more for my self-esteem with a .38 calibre handgun.

'You know, Matt, it's a funny thing,' I drawled. (Guns kind of make you drawl.) I just felt *really* relaxed. Like I was about to snuggle down to a good old chinwag with my analyst at ninety quid an hour. Come to think of it, who needs analysts when you've got a gun in some bloke's ear?

On the other hand, Matt didn't look relaxed. He was shaking so much he'd have lacerated himself if he was shaving. Which was very satisfying from my perspective. He was looking distinctly low on his 'suave' reserves. Face it, he was about to shit himself. Can I say here that, satisfying or not, this was a little less than I expected from a Darlo Bar regular.

Men are a constant letdown are they not?

I pushed the gun deeper into his ear canal, hoping this would lubricate his power of speech a little. I felt totally safe about this because for one the gun wasn't loaded and even if it was I was doubtful of my own ability to fire it, given my innate reluctance to ruin my manicure.

In the silence upstairs we could hear the quotidian sounds of Judge Hawkesbury plugging in his kettle, talking to his dog and shuffling tea bags. Judge Hawkesbury is one of those judges that hates crime and it made me feel guilty knowing he'd probably take a very grim view of what was going on below him. He still thought that 17 Pump Court had a reputation to uphold – he was none too keen on the empowerment of women idea either, I dare say.

Matt looked up to the ceiling. I could see what he was thinking – that if he yelled loudly enough, help would come. So I laid this hope to rest by explaining that in the eighties Judge Hawkesbury had made a name for himself by giving a whole bunch of IRA bombers hefty prison sentences. Since then he has survived several near misses with car bombs which have left him deaf.

I completed Matt's disappointment briefing by reminding him that the clerks were on the other side of the building and as it was the last day of term it was pretty unlikely that anyone besides Vinny would come in. They would all be in court or enjoying a sleep in. 'No, Matt,' I told him, 'you have me all to yourself.'

'What do you want, Evelyn? Can't you put that fucking thing away? I don't know what your problem is – really,' he told me in a sort of huff that suggested he was no longer about to shit himself.

'Matt, Matt, Matt. See the thing is when I woke up this

morning,' I explained, 'I just wasn't in the mood for this *shite*.'

'What have I ever done to you, Evelyn? I thought we had a good thing together. What's going on?'

Had I really once thought this bloke was suave? I pushed the gun deeper down his ear, basically it was in as far as it was going to go, but I was unnerved now, starting to lose the insouciant high this weapon had evoked earlier when Matt had looked so vulnerable. A little bit of terror on his part was all I was hoping for which seemed a fair exchange after all the aggravation I'd gone through.

He looked me in the eye. 'I'm sorry, Evelyn, you don't know how sorry I am.' He didn't look too sorry especially when he gave me a patronising smile and told me that I was being 'plain silly'.

'Silly? People holding a gun to your head don't like being called silly, Matt. You don't walk into a gun shop and say "give me a gun that will make me look *silly*, please". Guns are more or less seen as a silliness-prevention accessory. God, didn't they teach you anything in the Darlo Bar?'

'I promise you, Evelyn, it's not how it looks. I wish you'd just give me a chance.'

He was back in the hot seat now so I pressed home my advantage. 'Well, you see, that's another thing, Matt. I'm not handing out a lot of chances these days. You could say you used up more than your fair share of chances long ago. Like before you broke into my flat, like long before you involved me in a shonky fraud suit. How about you stop asking for hand-outs, Matt, and start giving a little because, as of this moment, you are no longer one of life's receivers. Start being a giver, Matt.'

I could see he was impressed. 'Evvy, please.' (He was pleading now; that was good.) 'Doesn't what we had together mean anything to you? Look, put the gun away. I'll drop over to your place later with a nice bottle of claret and we'll talk this over.'

I think the word he was looking for to describe his condition was sad. I told him so. 'You're sad, Matt. If you're trying to con me into letting you off with anything less than a hole in your head, you're going to have to mitigate your balls off. When you refer to what we "had together" I presume you mean the sex. Even you, in your supreme male arrogance, can't think that sex, however good, can get you out of this shit?'

He smiled at me to hint that he did. Now isn't that men all over?

'You've got to admit it was pretty good,' he said.

Oh this was rich. This was so rich it was making my stomach turn. It was bad enough that I'd sucked this sleazy bloke's dick in a moment of what I could only describe as libido-induced insanity. Now he wanted me to have a full reason bypass. Like a lot of blokes I had met down in the cells of the Bailey, Matt was long overdue for a metaphorical Bobbit job. 'You left the seat up, Matt.'

'What?'

'The toilet seat! You left it up. Very disappointing.'

'What are you on about?'

'No, like a lot of your gender you were a big disappointment,' I sighed, readjusting my legs. 'The cunnilingus was effective I grant you, and such enthusiasm is to be admired in a man your age. But overall your performance lacked finesse. Women of my generation expect more you see, Matt, your post-coital behaviour in particular was a big turn-off.'

'My what? What are you on?'

'On? What am I on? Not enough frankly. But let me give you a sketch of my lasting memories of you, shall I? You left your pubic hairs all over the bed, a used condom on the floor. You used my shower without asking, you wet my towel and you left the bloody loo seat up. So basically any residual afterglow I may have felt after our orgasm exchange was all used up by the time I cleaned the bed, slipped on your condom and broke my nail using my tweezers to flip down the loo seat.'

'Tweezers? Oh, give me a break. You're mad.'

'Hello?'

'Screwed. Lost it. All men leave the seat up. Just deal with it. You're neurotic, lady. Seriously neurotic, you know that?'

'Whose got the gun, shit-face?' I asked him.

'Oh come on, Evvy, you're not serious? Is that what all this is about, a fucking bog seat?'

'Neurotic or not, I've got a gun pointed in the general direction of your brain, so I'd take it as read that I want to be treated like an extremely sane woman. Don't push me any further and force me to redress the repressed anger of millions of women through the ages that have put down the seat without a murmur.'

He laughed, he sneered. 'Get a grip,' he told me.

I really didn't like this man and I wanted to make it clear that he was not in a position for sneering so I tried to cock the trigger. I wanted to make a clicking sound that would suggest he was seconds away from having his brains blown out. I had seen this ruse used to great effect to scare the pants off people in movies, but despite my best efforts the gun was silent.

'Drop the attitude or I'll waste you,' I told him. 'Just tell me who you are and what you were doing to Mitzy – and to me.' Did I sound like a cool gangster or what?

'I told you, Mitzy lost her money on the markets.' His slow, even, irritated tone made me furious. It was official now, I was starting to lose my edge. Maybe he had remembered the gun's lack of bullets after all.

I became more determined than ever to make the gun make a clicking noise like it was ready for action. I wanted him to be scared, sorry and, well, shitting himself basically. Where was the fun in pressing a gun to someone's brain if they continued to speak to you like you were on tranquillisers? I pulled the pistol nose out of his ear and shook it.

Matt spun around as if to grab it but I shoved it up his nose.

'What the fuck are you doing?' he asked, now looking and sounding more agreeably nervous.

Fact is, I didn't have a clue what I was doing. I know less about guns than I know about the mating habits of snails and, let's face it, threatening people wasn't really part of my psychological make-up either. I could see now that I would have done better not to cover my eyes during the tense bits of *Pulp Fiction*. 'I was trying to make the gun ready to fire,' I told him truthfully.

'Oh fuck, Evelyn,' he whimpered in an altogether more promising tone. Just to be on the safe side I tried once more to make the gun make a noise. If I could keep him nervous, I stood half a chance at getting the truth.

The resounding explosion took my eardrums out and blew the painting Mark Sidcup's wife had lent me to smithereens. Thankfully the force of the shot had also made my aim swerve and Matt was still there unharmed. Stunned, blinking, but alive. Judge Hawkesbury's dog was barking madly upstairs.

'What the fuck was that you stupid bitch? You could have killed me!'

I shoved the gun barrel back into his temple before either of us had time to reassess the situation properly. 'Just shut the fuck up, will you! I'm the one with the loaded gun, so I get to say who gets called stupid, right? Christ, Matt, what did they teach you on the streets of Darlinghurst that a girl from the North Shore has to spell this shit out for you?'

My adrenaline was turbo-charging through me now. I mean it's not every day that a girl gets to intimidate a bloke who leaves the loo seat up like this. I owed it to every woman that has ever played the victim to make this moment count. Anyway, that was when Vinny turned up.

I heard the door handle turn behind me and then I heard Vinny.

'Oh good, there you are. I thought I heard a noise in here. I've got some figures which might interest you, proving once and for all that Warren has been fiddling chambers' petty cash. I knew there was something shifty going on with those chocolate . . .' He broke off as he grasped the situation – if not fully, at least sufficiently to alarm him.

I aimed the gun at him and ordered him to shut up and sit down.

Vinny shut up and sat down. I gave Matt a look as if to say – that's the sort of rapid response I want from you, dickhead.

'I'm going to say this once, Vinny,' I told him in a voice he had never heard me use before. 'I have my period. So do as I say and you won't get hurt. Matt here has something important to tell me, so you just sit there quietly with your audit sheets and let him speak without interruption.'

Matt swallowed hard, so I kept the pressure up by grinding the pistol nose into his temple. I was staying clear of his cranial orifices as a safety precaution, in fact I didn't even have my hand on the trigger, but he couldn't see that. He was shaking again. Very satisfying. Vinny nodded his eagerness to listen.

'OK, maybe I did do some creative accounting with Mitzy's money, but hey it happens.' He smiled and shrugged his shoulders, as if Vinny was a man of the world who could understand. Boy had he misjudged his man there. I mean Vinny was in a tizz over misappropriation of chambers' coffee money, which he believed had been used to buy chocolate creams. Vinny was psychopathically tight-fisted, not the man to understand multi-million-pound frauds that's for sure.

'OK, so I was wrong, but I wasn't the only one.'

'Get on with it,' I told him.

'Things started to go wrong when Mitzy got involved. For a man, business is business but women always let their emotions get in the way, know what I mean?'

'Save us the new-lad semantics, Matt,' I warned him.

'I'm sorry, but that's how it was with her. She wanted to make her husband suffer – he'd been cheating on her, see? You can ask your friend the private eye, he got the goods on him in the first place. But Mitzy's not the sort to let a bloke off with anything as easy as a divorce. She wasn't going to be happy with anything but ruin. I should know, eh?'

The mention of Rory made several of my mental pathways gurgle to a halt. I shook my head as if I could jiggle my thinking back into place. Rory was involved? 'So why was she suing you?' I heard myself ask.

'She checked out of America with his fortune – I helped her lay her hands on, how shall I say, a little more than just his personal wealth. Amazing what you can do with a password and a pension fund.' He was looking at Vinny as he justified himself. 'Look, it wasn't my idea, I was helping a damsel in distress to seek her revenge. I would have thought a feminist like you would have applauded.'

'Save it, Matt,' I ordered. I was thinking about Rory and damsels in distress and wondering how he was linked. I was afraid that maybe no one was innocent in this whole débâcle – not even me.

'Anyway, it all went wrong when she discovered I was seeing someone else. Let's just say I like to till love's field. I did my bit on the understanding that all she got out of it was two million and revenge. The rest was meant to be mine. I invested the money and lost it, actually it does happen, that part is all true and the money wasn't strictly speaking hers.'

Vinny rose to leave. 'There we are then. All cleared up. I'd best get this circular around to the other members of chambers—'

I waved the gun at him menacingly. 'Sit!'

He sat down.

'What about the manslaughter charge?'

'The what?'

'I saw the clippings. You absconded over an embezzling charge in Sydney under one name and killed your wife under another name and did time in jail.'

'My, you have been busy.'

'I'll tell you when you can be sarcastic.'

'I've never had a wife, dead or alive. Seriously. I thought you were joking.' He looked really rattled now. He looked at Vinny for support but Vinny was examining his figures with rapt interest. 'Look, I swear. I might have been a bit dodgy on the financial front and I did get away with a fair bit in Sydney. But I've never been stupid enough to tie the knot, let alone kill someone. I promise you, I've never had a wife. I'm a swindler not a killer. Give me some credit,' he said.

Vinny raised his eyebrows and held up his papers. 'I really should be getting these figures circulated,' he warned me. I had to give it to the man. He had a certain fatuous style about him – impervious to excitement even when it came at him with a loaded gun.

'OK, Mr Squeaky Clean, how about the gun? I got this out of your pocket yesterday when you broke into my flat. Or hang on, maybe you just came round to put the seat down. Is that it?'

'I found the gun in your bag. It made me nervous, I mean what's my brief want with a loaded gun? And what with that shady private eye you've got hanging around I didn't feel safe. Put yourself in my position for a minute,' he smiled reasonably. 'Look, Evelyn, OK I'll admit I've been a bit dodgy but you're kind of involved yourself now if you know what I mean? Have you thought of that? You can't keep me here all day, and I don't think you want the police involved do you? So why don't we just forget this ever happened? You keep the gun and we'll talk later on when you don't have your period, OK?'

'I'd better just run along now . . .' Vinny stood to leave.

I was ruined. My one moment in life to play the person in control and I'd blown it. Even with a gun, I was disempowered. 'Fuck off, both of you,' I snapped. It was time to call in the cavalry, well Candida to be precise. With or without a gun, at least she would be able to hold her own.

CHAPTER THIRTY-EIGHT

every second of silence took a metaphorical inch off his dick.

Candida walked in about ten seconds later with the Duke, by which time I had RSI from holding the gun to Matt's head. Keeping up the intimidation didn't look this tough in *Pulp Fiction* that's for sure. I was surprised to find that I had never been so glad to see her inimitable brand of cold judicial charm and Knightsbridge finesse.

It didn't take her long to take stock of the situation.

'Evelyn, put that wretched weapon away,' she ordered. 'You look so common wielding that pistol. Put it back in your purse. You're not in the East End now and I don't think the Duke appreciates that sort of behaviour, do you, Duke?'

The Duke smiled and made one of his closed-lip, muffled noises. I had an urge to wedge an iced-lolly stick in his mouth and prise it open. This bloke made Prince Charles look like the big-mouthed frog.

'Vincent! I hold you responsible for this,' she informed him.

'Sorry, Candida, I was, er, just coming in to show Evelyn my figures. It may interest you to know that Warren has been buying biscuits with the coffee funds. The petty cash accounts he's been keeping are riddled with discrepancies.'

She turned on him like a snake uncoiling. 'And it may interest you to know, Vincent, that I am a Queen's Counsel not an accounts clerk. And you my learned friend are supposed to be a barrister. We are both above figures unless they hold a direct bearing on a case.'

Vinny looked appropriately stunned and scuttled out.

Then she turned on Matt. She didn't say anything at first, just sort of sized him up like he was a pile of garbage the council hadn't taken away. Matt went bright red. I was pretty sure that his focus was getting a good jolt now.

This was a woman who was in total control – and I mean T-O-T-A-L. If she had said clean my shoes with your tongue, he would have been on to the task like a shot. But instead she said nothing and each second of silence took a metaphorical inch off his dick. My admiration for this woman was skyrocketing.

Finally she sat down on my side of my desk and leaned across, exposing a long expanse of Wolford stocking as she shuffled through my drawer for a nail file. Then, without facing us, she began to file her nails. It made a sound like a hairpin being pulled across a blackboard.

It was only after all her talons were sharpened she met Matt's eyes. 'Tell me, Mr Barton, do you think it should require a gun to make you explain what is, after all, information incumbent on you to hand over to your legal counsel? Mmm?'

Matt's face lit up. I could see he thought he was home and hosed as he unslumped his shoulders and met her gaze with that look of brazen cheek I had once found such a turn-on. 'Nail on the head, Miss Raphael, I'm with you all the way on that. It's all been a misunderstanding. As I was telling Evelyn here, everything I told you was the truth.'

She smiled kindly and curled her lips into a girlish pout that even I, at twenty-seven, felt too old to carry off. 'Well not quite *everything*, Mr Barton. Mmmmm?' I couldn't believe it – was she nuts? Had the woman overdone it on the atomiser this morning or something? The man was a gun-wielding bastard. How could she flirt with the enemy?

'Come now, Mr Barton, *everything*? Surely that is a vast, vast realm.' She waved her hands around in the air – the nail file glinted as it caught the light. 'Why, *everything* includes all the little things you took such care to conceal. *Everything* includes all the naughty little omissions mentioned in the reports I have here from Interpol,' she purred, patting her pilot case.

Matt looked like a junky who can't find a vein.

'Um, I don't know what you're talking about.'

Candida touched his chin with the file and smiled. 'Oh I think you do, John Henry. Or should I say Nelson Frederick or even Dylan Thomas? Your schizophrenic lifestyle has caught up with you, Matt, or rather a few disgruntled husbands have. I also believe there is an extradition order for your arrest both in Australia and the States. Oh and another little thing we chanced upon was two million pounds hidden in Evelyn's account.'

'What?' I screamed. I mean all the other stuff – fine. I was prepared to take that on the chin. I had just slept with a no good, embezzling, murdering scumbag. It was a groin kick to the old dignity sure, but I was made of stern stuff. An ancestry that traced its lineage back to the Tyburn Martyrs, that's me. The scars would heal – my heart felt like a bladder now but it would recover. But to hide millions in my account, thereby implicating me in his crime and possibly jeopardising my career, that was unforgivable.

'Sorry about that, Evelyn,' he whimpered, turning to me like a dog that has been kicked and beaten and is desirous of a pat. 'I just thought you wouldn't mind me cheering up your account a bit. Hell, I thought you'd be grateful. I really did enjoy sex with you, Evelyn – that's the truth.'

If Candida was appalled she didn't show it. I just sat there and did what, in theory at least, should be impossible without gills.

'I'm glad you brought up the truth, Matt,' Candida continued. 'It seems to have been something you have a remarkably creative flair with, but you must take more care when using the word truth to a barrister. We are nothing if not pedants,' she told him, putting the file back in the drawer.

That was when Matt made his lunge for the door – shoving Candida roughly out of the way like he was off to the Harrods' sales. The Duke politely stepped aside allowing him a free passage into the thickly set chests of Lazza and Bill. It was not a good morning for Matt.

'Excuse me, ladies. Er, Miss Hornton, are you in there?' Warren called out from the back of the crowd.

'Through here, Warren,' Candida replied, as if welcoming a guest to her cocktail party. 'Ladies, step aside for Warren.' The girls were already doing what they did best, holding Matt spread-eagled against the wall while they frisked him.

Warren walked through showing no interest whatsoever in the sideshow. 'Sorry to disturb you, Miss Hornton, Miss Raphael, Duke (he bowed his head) but I've just had Judge Hawkesbury on the phone. Seems he had a bullet go through his floor. Shattered his light fitting. Apparently there are sparks shooting out all over the place. I don't mind saying he's livid, Miss. Got Special Branch up there with him and now the place is being overrun. Claims the bullet came from your room. I've tried reasoning with him. "What would Miss Hornton want with harbouring IRA terrorists in her room?" I asked him. But he's in a right state so I thought I'd better warn you. No doubt Special Branch will want a word. He's pretty incensed, I don't mind saying. Called me a blighter and he's never done that before – always very polite is Judge Hawkesbury.'

CHAPTER THIRTY-NINE

a girl without a credit card is a girl without power.

What happened? I asked God. One minute fire, brimstone and lesbian bodyguards were raining down on me like disco biscuits and the next minute fate had transported me to this chauffeur-driven Roller. After the police had taken Matt away and taken our statements, Candida had insisted I accompany the Duke and her on a shopping expedition.

Not that I was moaning – I couldn't stop myself from bouncing up and down on the big soft back seat, basically.

Candida looked on aghast. 'Are you all right, Evelyn?' she enquired after I'd practically sent myself shooting through the roof. I could see she was regretting her moment of largess as I blinked at her as if she was a hallucination. How many Prozac had I taken this morning anyway?

'Me? Never been better. Just, um, checking the, ah, spring of the upholstery – in case I'm ever in the market type thing.'

The Duke smiled at me benevolently before staring back into Candida's eyes. Talk about love struck, this bloke was a dribbling mess. So why hadn't he popped the question?

'Well steady up, Evelyn, I don't want you making the driver nervous. It's his first day.'

'Oh sorry.'

'He's Armenian,' she mouthed silently. As if the double handicap of newness and Armenian-ness were too much to take on top of bouncing passengers. What did she think he'd

do, swerve into an oncoming lorry – or drive off into the East
End? Just the same, I kept myself firmly seated and tried to
act like chauffeur-driven Rollers happened to me every day.

As we floated along in this tasteful, civilised way, I gave a bit
more thought to all the problems of the last few weeks and how
a good deal of them had vanished with no real harm coming to
me. In fact I was back where I started with an unpaid builder's
bill, an outstanding mortgage and a lot of cut-up credit cards.
And no Rory.

Candida interrupted my reverie. 'Let's do Bond Street,
Evelyn? The Duke said he'd love to do Chanel and Cartier.
Then he'll take us to the Ivy for lunch,' she trilled, like the best
girlfriend she'd never been.

'How kind he is,' I replied, even though I hadn't heard the
Duke mumble a word.

I couldn't remember Candida and me ever going shopping
together. Shopping is the holy bonding preserve of girlfriends
and Candida had never been that. She'd taken me to get my
hair cut once – something I'd lived to regret for about the six
weeks it took to grow out. Still, I didn't think she could do
much harm to me on Bond Street. In fact no one could do
much harm to me on Bond Street today. I didn't have a credit
card on me – not even a cut-up one and, as any post-feminist
shopper will tell you, a girl without a credit card is a girl
disempowered.

Actually I didn't even have a lipstick compact on me and I
was still wearing those ridiculous pantaloons which had looked
like a great idea when I bought them and swished around W11
and the Portobello Road record shops the first few times, but
tucked up in a Rolls-Royce with an impeccably dressed duke
and a woman who looked like an ad for the Lanesborough, I
felt like an ethnic, gap-year reject.

'First thing to do is to buy you something to wear,' said
Candida as if reading my mind. 'The Duke told me he wants
to make a gesture.'

I looked at the diminutive little man, waiting expectantly, but not so much as a nervous tic escaped him.

'After all you have endured quite a lot and the Duke admires pluck, don't you, Duke?' She nudged him in the side so that he emitted a small muffled yelp like a stuffed toy that had been sat upon.

'Tell him he really mustn't,' I said, feeling another bounce coming on.

The Duke took his hand out from his breast and patted my knee. Was that it I wondered, was that the gesture? I patted his knee back and smiled subserviently, the way I imagined dukes expect bouncing barristers should.

I was finding all this a bit embarrassing basically. Growing up in Sydney didn't really equip me for dealing with royalty. Shit, I panicked, maybe I shouldn't have touched him? But I looked over at Candida and she was smiling kindly on me.

'So good to see you two getting along,' she cooed. I looked around for a hidden camera or something. The Duke and she were both grinning violently, like I was some sort of orphan Annie they were bestowing their benevolence on. Well sure, basically I was.

We pulled up outside Chanel and, as the chauffeur came round to let us loose on civilised shopping London, the little guard at the store entrance bustled by the door polishing up his handles. The Duke got out first allowing Candida and me to trip over one another in an undignified rush to be the second one out. Candida naturally won the battle and glided over me to the Duke's side and whispered something. I saw she was holding a sort of car blanket thing in her arms. As I climbed out she held it against me.

'The Duke didn't want you to feel out of place, my dear,' she explained, as she attached the said blanket to me with a safety pin like it was a makeshift straitjacket or something.

'You mean like being the only one floating into Chanel wearing a car rug, type out of place?' I asked.

'Well you can hardly float in wearing those pantaloons like an extra from *Ali Baba and the Forty Thieves* can you, darling? At least in this you look like you've been involved in an accident.'

'They were Ozbek's,' I explained, feeling slightly guilty about referring to the designer's creation in the past tense.

'I don't care if they were worn by Tutankhamen for his funeral. I didn't want to have to spell it out, darling. I tried to spare your feelings, but if you insist on brutality you will get it from me from now on.'

I could tell I was trying her patience by the rising tone in her voice and I really didn't want to do that. She'd turned up trumps in getting the armed embezzler bastard off my back and I wanted to repay her in some small way so I simpered, 'Sorry, Candida, I was being silly.'

The Duke patted my arm.

'Never mind. I expect the strain of the last few days has chafed your sensitivity,' she said firmly, buffing her hair in the full-length mirror.

'Does madom require any assistance?' a French matron in a prim little dark Chanel suit enquired.

Candida turned around and appraised her. 'Madam does not require your assistance as much as you are required to give it, my good woman,' she told the assistant frostily. Mitchie Wanhato had obviously never encountered Candida on the spend. Otherwise he might have entitled his opus – 'Shop Assistant Beware'.

'What are you, a sixteen?' she asked so loudly that everyone in the shop turned to see what sort of kooky fatso thought she could find something to fit her in Chanel.

'Please, madom,' the matron whispered fanatically. 'Six-teen is not a Chanel size.' Basically she was terrified that word would get out that Chanel did off the peg for the obese.

'I'm a tall ten,' I offered, hoping to ease the tension. 'Well sometimes even an eight when I haven't been near a Belgian chocolate for a few weeks. That's a six in America actually.'

'There you are then. A ten! Run along now, that's the sort of thing we're after. I haven't got all day!' Candida snapped her fingers and clapped her hands.

The Duke seated himself comfortably and smiled the smile of a man resigned. I was really starting to care a great deal about this duke bloke. It was slowly dawning on me that he was really quite a good hat.

CHAPTER FORTY

somewhere between cartier and chanel, I had become a yoked woman – a tiller of fields, a loadbearer.

The Duke's gesture ended up costing me as much as a long case in the Court of Appeal. He had bought me a powder-blue Chanel suit and, let me make it very clear, it was not the sort of suit I was ever likely to wear again. I was in the invidious position of not being able to turn it down but knowing there was no way I was ever going to pay him back unless I agreed to work for a Russian brothel in Soho.

The assistant handed me the Ozbek trousers in a Chanel bag.

'Just throw them out, I won't be requiring them again,' I told her grandly.

She wrinkled her nose as if I had made a bad smell. 'Madom had best take care of the matter herself,' she responded, as if we were talking about contaminated waste someone could get fined over.

It was agreed that the next stop should be Cartier.

'Should we walk?' Candida enquired – wrinkling her nose and shaking her head.

The Duke smiled vacantly up the street.

'No, you're so right as always, my dear,' she agreed, stroking his cheek. 'Too much sudden exercise for a young woman like, Evelyn.' Then she sighed heavily as if she was at a charity dinner discussing whether or not to send Rolex watches to Ethiopia.

She turned to me and repeated the theory. 'The duke is worried that you aren't fit enough for a walk up Bond Street. Your generation has never pushed itself as hard as ours.'

Hello! We was talking about a stroll up the street, not the London to Monaco Grand Prix here. I turned to the Duke for support but he was staring poignantly ahead in the direction of the lounging sculpture of Winston Churchill – not emitting so much as a mumble. I mean, I had to make a stand on this one. A stand for my generation's ability to make it up Bond Street on foot.

'I love exercise,' I assured them both as the pleasantly bustling shoppers streamed past us – smart-suited men and well-heeled women whose commitment to the latest accessory glazed over their eyes like a bad case of malaria.

Candida rolled her eyes at the Duke who concurred with one of his stuffed toy grunts. 'Come along, Evelyn, don't take it personally. The Duke and I were speaking generationally.'

A lot of conversations seemed to be taking this tack, wherein my generation and age would be attacked by the Duke – via Candida – as being too feeble or too scatterbrained to cope with minor challenges the older shopper can take in his or her stride.

It was easiest to agree.

So we took the Rolls-Royce and on the way I agreed with Candida (or was it the Duke) that life simply couldn't go on if she didn't immediately purchase a diamond Baignoire watch.

Not wishing to be too profoundly pedantic or anything, I felt it wasn't really my place to remind her that even a QC in a reasonably lucrative chambers does not bring in the kind of throwaway money required to buy this particular watch with diamond encrusted face.

Cut me some flack on this one – as yet I hadn't seen the

Baignoire expedition for the ruse it was. Baignoire turned out
to be the code name for another far wilier plan she had hidden
up her Yves Saint Laurent sleeve. I worked that out as soon as
she got inside Cartier. Instead of making for the watches, she
tripped through a muscular crowd of Arab women cloaked in
swathes of black fabric who were all bent over another cabinet,
chattering excitedly. At first glance I thought they were nuns
discovering a new holy relic.

What could it be, I mused as I cut my way through – a phial
of Christ's blood? A strand of thread from the Virgin Mary's
garment? Mohammed's sandal? I dived in to see. Elbowing my
way through to the epicentre, I found a cluster of hard-faced
Italian women whose bright eyes were glinting as sadistically
as gold credit cards.

Candida was already at the front when I broke through –
practically prostrate, virtually weeping as her finger pointed
and her lips quivered at the exotic arrangement of engagement rings.

'Oh aren't they adorable?' she gooed to the store at large. A
score of eagerly nodding, commission-reliant assistants agreed
that they were just the thing to put a smile on the face of the
most hardened human.

Basically the deal was this. This perpetual courtship lark
of the duke's was getting a bit bloody perpetual for its own
good. Lacroix jackets and seal-skin coats are all right as an
interim measure, but this wooing business had been going on
for years.

At late forty-something, Candida wanted five-carat commitment, not a wardrobe stuffed full with gifts from a mad, mad
extravagant duke. She wanted her title and she wanted it now.
Her subtle hints had obviously got her nowhere so she must
have decided it was time to hammer out a deal using more
obvious manoeuvres.

I could tell though from the look of acute agitation on the
duke's face that he would rather urinate on himself then and

there in preference to noticing those rings. He was looking longingly at the door with the most feeling I'd ever seen him express. His mouth was practically moving for Christ's sake. For the first time in our long acquaintance I actually felt sorry for Candida who, mesmerised by a particularly big sapphire ring, hadn't seen the duke's wince. She repeated her question.

That was when I knew I had to do something. The Italian women were egging her on, nodding excitedly and gasping, virtually manhandling her to make a purchase. The Arab women were focusing too, making frenzied guttural sounds at the back of their throats. It was like being in a crowded room waiting for a woman to give birth. Basically everyone was revving up for a sale, not least of all the shop assistants who were fingering the credit slips by the tills.

Get real! I wanted to yell out to them – I mean had these people had a sight bypass? It didn't take twenty-twenty vision to see that this duke bloke would prefer a bad case of piles to a case full of engagement rings at that moment.

There was no getting away from it. It was my duty as a fellow woman to shield Candida from what I knew would be an embarrassment no amount of diamond Baignoire watches could cure. It was a dirty thankless task but it was the sort of favour every woman owes her sisters – saving them from humiliation in the marketplace.

'Oh my God! Is that the time? Oh my God! Duke you have to help me,' I pleaded at the top of my voice, throwing myself on my knees and giving him my best Orphan Annie beseech. 'I simply must get back to my builders!'

Candida turned round to see the Duke's jubilant smile as he instructed the guard to open the door. The whole store fell to a hush. I knew it could be years before she would appreciate the charitable significance of my little selfless act but just the same I wasn't prepared for the look she bestowed on me as the other shoppers turned their back on her.

Her gaze burned through my Chanel makeover like battery acid.

Three washed-out-looking Hare Krishnas tinkled past the car as we pulled out and I had an urge to jump out and join them. But I wasn't stupid, where Candida was concerned, I could run but I couldn't hide. I was locked into her fate now. My friendship with the all-time anti-girlfriend had just bitten the dust and there would be no salvation until I got her married off.

My mind harked back to textbook pictures from geography class at school depicting African agriculture. Black and white snaps of Brahman cattle humping these big wooden structures on their backs so that they could pull carts and till the fields. That was me now, I was a yoked woman. Some time between entering Chanel and leaving Cartier I had managed to become a load-puller, a field-tiller, a proverbial W1 Brahman cow. The burden for Candida's marriage was on my back and it felt heavy.

I looked at the Duke with new eyes as he gave me a weak but grateful smile – one yoked Brahman to another sort of look. Don't relax yet, I wanted to tell him. It's not over till the fat cow sings.

CHAPTER FORTY-ONE

she made youth sound like a nasty case of impetigo.

The Volvo was gone. Clamps, tickets and Resident Committee complaints, gone. Suddenly that car seemed like a metaphor for Rory. Rejected, scorned but now desperately wanted and loved.

'Well, Evelyn, there you are back among your builders,' Candida remarked snidely. I felt like a tadpole that was being released back into the native habitat of its swamp after a brief spell in the clear waters of the glass jar. This was the first thing she'd said since I'd dragged her away from Cartier and yet my cheeks burned as much as if she'd been striking them with cruel jibes all the way home.

Truth was, getting the Duke away before he revealed his engagement ring antipathy, was the first favour I'd ever done my long-standing anti-girlfriend. Let's face it, rescuing Candida's dignity had never been a priority with me before. Don't take it personally, I wanted to tell her – it was a gender thing. Sometimes even we anti-girlfriends have to put our own sex first.

'The Volvo's gone,' I remarked.

'The what?' she snarled.

'Oh nothing, I just had a Volvo here.'

'Well, hardly something you want to make known, my dear. But I suppose you're young,' she conceded, managing once again to make youth sound like a dose of impetigo. Nasty but probably curable with strong antibiotics.

The Duke accompanied me to the door of the building while Candida waited, sulking in the air-conditioned opulence of the Rolls.

'I must thank you for your company,' he said. Not that it was coherent to the untrained ear or anything. But I got the gist.

'Well yes, sure, your, er, Duke, I mean, Duke. Good to meet you. Take care of Candida. You know something, she's not as tough as she looks – I mean seems. Not that she looks tough in the Hells Angel sense or anything. Hell no, she's as far from looking like an HA as a duchess.'

He laughed and kissed me a few times on both cheeks. For some reason I felt choked up to be suddenly saying goodbye. It was like a chapter of my life was over – the luxury chapter – a short but brief interlude. Now it was back to life in a loft shell.

I tried to tell myself that I wasn't the sort for Rolls-Royces and accounts at Cartier, but that theory washed as much as telling myself I was glad to see the back of Rory. My sense of loss was further knocked into perspective by the scene I found in the lobby of my building. *My Beautiful Laundrette* had mobilised. Bundles of stuff wrapped up in sheets chocked the stairs – like a Sudanese family on the run.

Clambering over the swathed bundles, I realised that this was not what Karl Lagerfeld wanted for this neat little powder-blue number. He had probably envisioned sweet little tea parties and lunches with the girls at Daphnes as he oversaw the stitching of the Chanel label and finally waved the garment on its way. I also wondered at the familiar smell of the stuff. Gaultier perfume? 'Sam?' I called out taking the stairs two at a time.

'Finally. Where have you been?' she yelled from the landing upstairs.

'What are you doing here?' I asked as she handed me Johnny.

'Go to your godmother, fatso,' she told him.

'What's going on?' I repeated through clenched teeth the Duke would have been impressed by. A voice inside me said, Run! Run back as fast as you can – maybe the Rolls hasn't left yet. But I had Johnny now and he wasn't of a weight that could be hastily moved.

'The nanny will be here soon, she's getting supplies. What do you do for supermarkets around here?'

'What's going on?' I pleaded yet again, thinking that maybe if I chanted it enough the whole hideousness would disappear – or at least I'd fall into a hypnotic trance.

'I've walked out,' she said.

'Oh, Sam!' I sat on the cold dusty cement stairs beside her in my new Chanel suit and put my arm around her. I'm nothing if not a brilliant girlfriend. 'Sam, what is going on with you two?'

'I told you, she's got someone else. That bitch you were with at the Japanese place.'

'Kim the sumo? Nah not Kim, she's not, well, she's not her type.'

Sam laughed. 'Is she anyone's? The whole lot of them seemed pretty sexless to me.'

I gave her a squeeze while Johnny walloped me in the eye with a fist the size of Frank Bruno's. 'Ow. Shit, Sam, what are you feeding this kid on? Mega Mass?'

'Tit milk, but that's all going to stop as of today. He's draining the life out of me. Seriously, I'm worried he's going to start picking up cars and eating krypton.'

I took advantage then of our bonding and decided to go for broke. 'I'm sure Charles loves you too much to risk your relationship with an affair.'

Her body slumped into my shoulder. 'What the hell is happening, Evvy?' she said, bursting into tears.

I pulled her to me in one of those sticky cuddles this suit wasn't designed for. She let out a big sob followed by a worryingly moist snort into my powder-blue bosom. Johnny took a handful of my hair and yanked it.

This girlfriend shit can be heavy going. I bet blokes never put one another's Gieves and Hawkes or Armanis through this sort of rough treatment. Sam started really blubbering and Johnny got one of his man-sized fists around my ear and twisted.

'Sam, darling it's OK. There, there,' I offered gently as I frisked my pockets for Prozac. I mean this was my girlfriend of the razor sharp wit, with the Panzer-division logic and the barbed tongue. This was my friend who could kick a bloke in the balls when he wasn't even in the same city! Skinheads with pit bulls crossed the road when they saw my girlfriend coming.

When I went to see a therapist to deal with the emotional fallout from my break-up with Giles, Sam had said, 'What's emotional fallout then?' And when I'd tried to explain she'd said, 'Bloody hell, I'm glad we couldn't afford that shite in Hackney – sounds like a right fucking load of ovaries.'

Before I'd moved in with Sam and Charles I'd never met anyone like Sam before. Basically I related to Charles, we were on the same dose of logic. Sam was just a woman who came with the Charles package in the beginning, but now I realised I loved her as fiercely as others feared her and I honestly would have done anything I could for her. I just would have liked to come out the other side with ears.

So I took her inside and made tea. We lugged in her bundles and stuck Johnny in his mechanical jerking swing. 'Have you spoken to Charles about all this?' I asked tentatively after I'd changed back into my pantaloons. Face it, a kid like Johnny can decimate those powder-blue tea-dance suits in an afternoon.

'Of course I have,' she snapped.

'Well what does she say? Does she admit to having an affair?'

'No.'

I walked over and hugged her. 'Well maybe she isn't? Gees, Sam, you're always so bull at a gate.'

'Have you spoken to her?' She spun around as if stung.
'No.'

'Good. I mean, I don't want you doing one of those "you're both my friends" numbers. I can't handle that shit. You're going to have to choose, Evv.'

'What, so I have to choose between my two best friends?' I asked, terrified at what I was about to hear.

'Yeah, like the women with the baby in the Bible you told me about. The ones who the King told to hack the kid in half.'

'But I love Charles.'

'I love her too, but if you try to please us both you'll be hacking the kid in half.'

I looked over at Johnny, alarmed.

'Not Johnny, you cretin. I was speaking metathingamee.'

'Metaphorically? That's not like you. You've never used metaphors before.' That's when I knew we were really in trouble. First tears and now metaphors.

She gave me a brave tear-stained smile. 'Yeah so, I've never been a single mother before. I've got to live on my wits now. You got any music?'

'Yeah over there,' I said pointing to the stereo. That was one battle I had won at least – I got my stereo back. Sam put on some Elastica and started to dance with Johnny. I looked about my loft space and sighed. I'd had such optimistic hopes for it when I moved in – a minimalist Mecca – that was the look I had dreamed of when I'd bought this place. White walls, ethereal open space and polished wooden floors.

Looking about the floor I had gouged up with the lawn sandals and the walls my builders hadn't got round to painting yet, I realised what madness my dreams had been. My lifestyle was too complicated for minimalism. Flooded with Sam's possessions, some humped together in sheets, some strewn out like slashed haggis, my 'space' had more in common with a Bedouin camp than Mies Van der Rohe. Maybe I'd had bad Feng Shui advice or something.

My reverie was broken by a knock on the door, and the fantasy that it was Rory gripped me like a vice. Maybe he'd just taken the Volvo for a drive and now he was back? My imagination took off, my expectations soared. What would I say to him? What would he say to me? I wouldn't give in too easily. No, I'd start with being super cool and sophisticated.

He'd no doubt call me doll and pull me to him. His smile would be hard to resist but I'd retain a little frostiness to start with. But then his strong arms would hold me tightly against his warm brown chest. I shivered with anticipation. He'd probably say something teasing until eventually my *froideur* would thaw.

OK, so the truth was I was going to throw myself into his arms sobbing joyfully about how glad I was to see him and plead forgiveness for slugging him. I flung open the door. But it was Bruce the nanny.

CHAPTER FORTY-TWO

i kept yelling, 'give him your tits! give him your tits!' like some psychotic porn film director.

The next few days were trying. It was a long weekend and the four of us cohabited with a fair amount of stress and a maximum of fatigue. For a start we were all broke. Although some were broker than others. Sam was broke in the, "owning your own three bedroom garden flat in Notting Hill, a Ferrari, annuity plans in every drawer, a couple of hundred thousand in the bank and rich horizons ahead" sense. OK, so she'd left all her cards in Notting Hill.

Bruce was broke because Sam hadn't paid her and I was just plain broke – as in no money, in danger of having my place repossessed and very little work in the foreseeable future apart from a landlord and tenant dispute in which I was acting for the bastard landlord.

We wouldn't have survived without Bruce. She was brilliant. Sam's bundles of stuff made us feel like the place was closing in on us and, what with the rain which started the day she arrived, it was like London had declared a siege. Basically neither Sam nor I were survivalists. Left to our own devices we would have subsisted on baked beans and chocolate and generally bickered over whose turn it was to change the nappy.

As it was, Bruce ran around after us like a human dynamo, giving Johnny helicopter rides by the hour and making delicious meals out of these bags of sticky vegan stuff I'd bought at a health food shop when I first moved in. Way back when I had vowed to turn over a new dietary leaf.

No one rang, no one called – not even Paddy. I tried not to get uptight about it but, on the third day, the keys I'd given him arrived in the mail with a note, "Here, keys." I gave way to feelings of desertion. There was still no word from Rory. I didn't really feel it was something I could discuss with Sam so I brooded away quietly to myself white trying to talk myself out of the madness of being attracted to a private eye who thought the emancipation of women was something to do with 'that time of the month'.

Eventually Sam started to go stir crazy. She spent her time on the phone to Charles, hurling abuse and refusing to listen. I was more and more convinced that this was just a quarrel that had blown out of control but I didn't dare suggest that to Sam. I mean here was a woman used to having her ego massaged by making millions an hour for her bank and now her life revolved around changing CDs, speculating on the colour of her next vegan meal and doing relief helicopter shuttles for a ten-stone child.

The worst bit was that on top of everything else she had decided to wean Johnny. Everyone's nerves were on edge. I found the nights the worst – when he would scream blue murder and no amount of swing jerking or helicopter rides would shut him up. I admired Bruce who agreed to deal with him so that Sam wouldn't be tempted to give way and offer her breasts.

If I'm honest I was less supportive than I might have been. When things got really bad at around four a.m. I'd start screaming out, 'Give him your tits! Give him your tits! For Christ's sake give him your bloody nipples!' like some psychotic porn film director. Now I could see what you were getting when you paid for a Norland Nanny. Because shaved head, pierced nose, dungarees, bare feet and all, Bruce was a Norland Nanny through and through. She stuck it out without a complaint.

Out of admiration, I stayed up with her for some of the night and volunteered the odd helicopter ride. It was during one of these manic sessions at four in the morning that someone knocked at the door for the first time since we'd started our siege. Bruce, Johnny and I jumped out of our skins when the rapping started. In fact, Johnny sucked in so much air his crying stopped altogether for what seemed like the first time in days.

'Who can that be?' Bruce enquired in her perfectly clipped St Paul's vowels.

'Who are you?' I demanded, hoping against hope that it wasn't Rory – not now that I was back in the Ozbek pantaloons. Back in? Bugger that, I had put them on on day one and I hadn't taken them off. Worse than that, I wasn't wearing lipstick, eyeliner or even a bra for that matter.

But it didn't sound like Rory who called out. 'Smmme!'

'Who?'

'Smee!'

'Do you know anyone called Smee?' asked Bruce, holding the still-stupefied Johnny on her head.

'Smee who?' I persisted, but there was no response.

'What should I do?'

'Let them in I guess. Maybe they're good with kids?'

Just then Johnny got his mind around the job at hand again and started yelling his head off – screaming like we were walloping him against a wall or something. Panicked about being dobbed in to the Child Protection League, I opened the door.

Orlando fell in with a thud.

It was very odd indeed. It wasn't that he was clutching half a dozen bottles of Veuve Clicquot – two of them empty – that shocked the hell out of me, or even that he had seen fit to enter my flat unconscious at four in the morning. Both these things were perfectly in keeping with the Orlando I knew and loved.

The flaw in this scenario was what he was wearing. I

thought I'd seen it all – the rubber outfits with nipple clips, the Gaultier micro-kilts, the Vivienne Westwood platform slippers, the bondage trousers and the hat with a drink stand on top. But this outfit topped the billing in shock value. A pair of sand-coloured trousers, a maroon Ralph Lauren shirt and a navy blue blazer and dock-siders.

He started to get up.

I introduced them. 'Bruce the nanny, meet Orlando the barrister.'

They shook hands. 'Outrageous name,' he said, still sitting on the floor looking up.

'Thanks, it's not my real name though,' she shouted over the top of Johnny's bawling in her ear.

'Wow! How cool!' he drooled as he got up. 'What's up with the kid?'

'He's not allowed to drink breast milk any more,' I explained over the top of the cacophony.

'Brilliant! How outrageous!' Then turning to Bruce he said, 'Don't the most bizarre things happen around this place?'

Bruce nodded her agreement, a little too eagerly for my taste.

'Like, have you seen the sandals?' he asked, mindlessly passing me the empty bottles. 'Here, I bought you this.'

'Gee thanks.'

'Sorry, I meant these ones here,' he explained, passing over the full ones. 'I got thirsty waiting for you to answer the door. I thought you must be having a party.'

'You drank two bottles of champagne on your own? How long were you out there?'

'What?'

'It's four o'clock in the morning, Orlando, we were just trying to get Johnny to settle.'

'Sure. But look, what I have to say won't take long. Do you think we could talk alone somewhere?'

CHAPTER FORTY-THREE

the post-feminist/new-lad romance – to snog or to slug?

I led Orlando to the shower cubicle which was still the nearest thing I had to privacy. Standing there, crowded awkwardly in the white-tiled compartment, I was wondering impatiently where all this was leading – I mean was he going to offer me more drugs? I'd more or less decided to accept them if he did but as it was he started snogging me senseless.

'What the hell was that for?' I screamed when I got a chance to breathe. I was tossing up whether his actions warranted a full-on kick to the groin or just a slap across the face.

'Can't you see, I'm madly, inexorably, passionately, irrevocably in love with you, Evelyn?' he asked, his eyes bulging from their sockets like two pregnant fish about to give birth. Then he did it again. Snogged me.

I opted for the knee-in-the-balls option. Wham!

Most guys sort of collapse and make soundless expressions of agony or groan pathetically when you whack them in the sperm bank. Not Orlando.

'You are so excellent! So unpredictable. So perfectly outrageous,' he moaned in a painfully joyous voice. Then he crumpled into a writhing heap and nursed his manhood. 'You're one terrific woman. God, I'd love to drop acid with you,' he gasped.

Now here was a true individual, I mused – not many men would applaud a woman who kicked them in the testicles. Maybe I should consider his proposal more carefully – like not!

'You sure you're not on acid now?' I checked.

He looked at me, wounded. 'Don't tell me you don't know of the feelings I've harboured for you since the first time I came to chambers? Look, Evelyn,' he said, becoming more animated, 'I'm more serious than I have ever been. I'll fly to Australia and ask your father.'

'Ask him what?'

'For your hand.' He stood up to give me the full force of his argument, using gestures and facial expressions that I had to admit were pretty convincing. I'd never seen him perform in court but I was prepared to concede that Mossad had chosen the best man for the job.

The points he put forward for our perfect union were unorthodox but solid. 'I know you're a gentile and a pork eater, but I love you. I want you to marry me! Or at least to sleep with me on an exclusive basis for a long time. I'll even refuse birth control if that's what your faith demands of me.' Then he threw himself at the plughole like he'd lost a contact lens and started kissing my feet, slobbering between my toes like a pig hunting for truffles.

I mean what was I to do? I was an amateur at this sort of thing. Marriage proposals didn't exactly fly at me like kangaroos at bull bars. I felt embarrassed. I mean marriage? OK, so I've read the newspapers, I knew the term – SINBAD (Single-Income-No-Boyfriend-And-Desperate). But this was taking the solution a bit far. Orlando was still licking my toes – a happening that as a post-feminist empowered woman, I should be revelling in, but realistically speaking it was pretty unpleasant.

I observed that the hair on his crown was thinning and a more sympathetic mood overwhelmed me. After all he was only twenty-four and it seemed pretty damn lamentable that even the young were ageing so fast these days, and then I remembered the confusion I had made over Orlando's feelings for me such a short time ago.

'Orlando what's got into you? I'm way to old for you,

remember? You told me that yourself when I thought you were offering to sleep with me.'

He looked up at me like a berated child. 'I was just embarrassed that you'd outed me. I didn't have the courage then. I was terrified of rejection. I had to be sure my feelings were reciprocated you see.'

'Seriously?'

He grabbed my knees. 'Oh, Evelyn, you have made me the happiest man alive. Your acceptance means more to me than my Barmitzvah.'

Right ho, I thought. And then – shit! I obviously hadn't handled this as well as I could have. How was I going to break a rejection to him now I had been compared to a Barmitzvah? I was toying with the idea of another kick to the groin when Bruce yelled out that there was someone at the door. What was that saying – opportunity only knocks once?

Looking back I can see how insane I was to throw my arms around Charles like that – I guess I wasn't thinking too clearly. I just cuddled her like the saviour she was without giving a moment's thought to my previous promises to Sam to avoid her on threat of Johnny being torn in half. The worst part of it was that Sam had woken up somewhere along the line and staggered out to witness my *faux pas*.

When I turned around, she was bearing down on me like Boadicea ramming a Roman chariot. Thankfully Johnny distracted Sam from her hostile intents by hooking on to her neck as she passed him. With a lightening fast manoeuvre, he had connected to her tit.

After that my flat became a Tower of Babel as everyone spoke over the top of everyone else and Elastica added a bass drone to the lot of us.

'You traitor! How could you?' Sam yelled, Johnny suctioned to her breast like a prosthetic limb.

'Oh shit! I'm so sorry,' Bruce cried, trying to pull Johnny off.

Sam: 'How could you let him get on my tit like that, you stupid Norland bitch?'

Charles: 'Don't talk to our nanny like that!'

Sam: 'What the hell do you want at this time of the night anyway, bitch?'

And so on and so forth – absolute chaos. 'I have an announcement to make!' Orlando shouted above the din, clapping his hands together and looking at me proudly like I'd just given birth.

'Evelyn, we need to talk,' Sam told me in a warning voice.

'Oh no! I think he's done a shit,' Bruce moaned, as sure enough a brown squidge appeared around the leg of Johnny's nappy.

And then on top of everything my mobile rang which shut everyone up while they all searched for their respective phones.

CHAPTER FORTY-FOUR

i've got you under my skin – or is it just my eczema again?

'Hiya, doll?' he said, as all the drama going on around me became irrelevant.

'Shut up!' I told everyone.

'What?'

'Not you, Rory. I've got a lot of people here.'

'Party huh? Well listen, doll, I hope I'm not interrupting? It's still early here in NYNY. I was just wondering how you were hanging?' he asked.

My throat was paralysed with joy. 'Fine,' I managed to croak.

'Great. Listen, I saw they got Matt. I'm sorry I didn't get a chance to say goodbye before I left. Thought I'd call and check how you're doing, I don't want you thinking I abandoned you or nothing. I was there watching your chambers when the police led him away. Looking out for you, doll.'

'Oh,' I said.

'Saw you drive off in a Rolls. And I figured, hey, you'd be too upwardly mobile to fit a down and outer like me in your schedule.'

There was silence as a verbal coma took hold of me. A thousand things I should have said got stuck halfway up my oesophagus. There was a neon sign flashing on and off in my

head like a migraine, saying 'TELL HIM YOU LOVE HIM!
TELL HIM YOU LOVE HIM!' But I didn't.

'Are you still there, doll?'

'Yeah.'

'Hey, you're not still pissed with me about that kiss are you?
I know I was way out of line.'

I think I managed to get out a 'no'. Now was the time to
dive in and admit that my libido was his, but I was in a mess.
I mean it was still sinking in how far away he was and how I'd
never see him again. One part of my psyche was telling me to
slip into one of those five-year comas I'd read about.

'Say, did Paddy move that car like I told him?'

'What?' I asked, dragging the word out like a reluctant
witness. 'Oh yeah, sure.'

'I told him you weren't too keen on it,' he laughed. 'I guess
I kind of wound you up a bit over that bomb, didn't I? But
when Rosy asked me to come back because Paddy was having
an affair and then when I spoke to Paddy and he asked me if
I'd do a favour for a friend – you got to see it from my point
of view. I mean Rosy thought you were after her man. Can
you believe it? He should be so lucky. Anyway I should've
told you the whole story but I let my feelings kinda get in
the way. When I saw you were hot for that creep, I just
slipped a disc.' He dropped his voice. 'You got under my
skin, doll.'

There was another silence. I wanted to dive in and swim
across the Atlantic and kiss him stupid, but I remained mute.

'Listen there are a lot of things I should have explained,' he
went on.

'Like what?' I asked expectantly, thinking he was going to
tell how he loved me and was going to fly back on the next
plane if I said the word.

'I mean about Barton and stuff.'

'Matt?'

'Look, I should've told you what you were dealing with.

That guy's been screwing people for a long time but, hey, that clipping was a dud.'

'What clipping?'

'About the guy that killed his wife. He's one of those guys with an ego so big he thinks he can cream a few mill from his investors and no one will notice. But he's never killed anyone. I just threw that in to scare you.'

The five-year coma seemed more seductive by the minute. This bloke I was starting to think I might want to reproduce my chromosomal structure with had actively set out to deceive me. 'The gun went off. I could have shot myself! Or killed someone.'

'Na, doll, it wasn't loaded. Ya think I'd give you a loaded gun without telling you? I swear it wasn't loaded. You gotta know that.'

I did know. I knew so much now that I started having one of those reclaimed memory shock thingamees – the realisation that Matt, a man I had desired and lusted after and eventually taken to my bed, had put the bullets in that gun. He had broken into my flat for some target practice and if not for the fast actions of a woman in a mum-muu, he might have succeeded.

'Doll?'

'Uha?'

'You OK?'

'Uha.'

'I've got you under my skin.'

He was making me feel like I was a case of eczema. If I was under his skin, what was he doing a Concorde flight away? But still I didn't say anything that might give him a clue as to how I felt. Charles, Sam, Johnny, Orlando and Bruce were looking at me like I was a stuffed exhibit in a museum that was showing signs of life.

And I mean this was probably the most exciting transatlantic phone call I'd ever had on this phone. Face it, this was the sort of thing I was hoping for when I agreed to buy the damn thing.

Gorgeous blokes calling from Manhattan. It sounded great on paper. So why couldn't I enunciate any of this elation?

'Well, I guess I'd better sign off then,' he said after the silence became too uncomfortable to bear. 'I guess you're still kind of pissed with me about that kiss?'

I could have said a lot of things then, even something really basic like 'no' would have sufficed.

'Did you get the keys I sent?'

They were from him? 'Here, keys.' That was all a man who had me under his skin had to say? It was time to ask them to get the drip on stand-by. This coma was definitely digging in.

'So promise me you'll take it easy, doll?'

I promised. It wasn't until I put down the aerial and shut the mouthpiece that I began to see what a mess this coma thing had got me into. Like why didn't I ask for his number? Why didn't I tell him I missed him? Why didn't I ask anything? Because I was a pork-eating, low-life skin affliction who didn't know what she wanted. Who always chose Mr Wrongs and didn't know a good thing when she fell for it.

I was in love, for Christ's sake.

Yeah but I was in love with a man who called me doll. Shit, what would Germaine say? All her hard work, all that campaigning and bra burning. Women had starved themselves to death and run out in front of horses so that I could say no, so that I could have a choice, so that I could escape from men like Rory.

He was a post-sexist who had given me a gun I had almost shot Judge Hawkesbury with. He had lied to me. Face it, Evelyn, he's worse than a sensitive-new-age-bastard. He's a new lad. And there was something else I was going to have to face – he was back in the States and I was never going to see him again.

Orlando came over and put his arms around me. Taking in the still-silent crowd he announced, 'Friends, strangers and breast feeders – I have an announcement to make.'

The hopeful faces of my friends opened in amazement. 'You are looking at an engaged couple.' Then, in case there was any confusion, he pointed to himself and then to me.

'Oh fuck!' I said and burst into tears.

CHAPTER FORTY-FIVE

alcohol may not be an answer to life's problems but it's a bloody good retort.

There was a stunned silence, a few muttered congratulations and then Sam gave Johnny back to Bruce and took me to the far end of the loft. Charles followed. I threw myself on my futon and sobbed while they stroked my back and said soothing things like, 'Evvy, there, there, what's the matter? You can tell us.'

Embalmed in the comfort of the closest thing I had to family in London, I let everything out – spiced with a fair degree of self-pity and shame. I told them about Matt and the gun and his ultimate capture and how I had fallen in love with a no good, egotistical Irishman, and how I didn't care that he was the sort of bloke I signed petitions to get castrated.

'So how did he get rid of the stalker?'

'She was Paddy's sister.'

'She was involved too! He got his sister to stalk you?'

'No, that was something else, just a coincidence I guess. She thought I was after Paddy.'

'Paddy?'

'My builder.'

'You were after Paddy, Evelyn? Oh my God, we never knew,' Charles cried out as if I told her my preference for sex ran into the realm of the bestial.

'And now you're engaged to Orlando!' Sam reminded us.

'My God, you're like a bitch on heat!' Charles proclaimed.

A bitch on heat? Hello! Excuse me, but these girls were straying off the girlfriend nurturing path – like in mega-leagues. I pulled out the last few dusty chocolates from under the bed. I mean for a moment there, I thought I was really on to something – uniting my girlfriends in my misery. But a dog on heat went beyond my Florence Nightingale remit. 'I love Rory!' I wailed.

'She loves Rory?' Charles mouthed to Sam. 'There, there,' she soothed. 'Tell us all about it.'

Sam grabbed my hand. 'But don't you see that's great? He loves you too, Evv, he loves you too!'

Charles and I both looked at her in total bewilderment.

'He told me about the whole thing, about Matt and the gun and how he was really worried you were involved with this creep.'

I had to wedge myself up on my pillows to deal with this one. I mean, I wasn't used to being reliant on Sam telling me which bloke fancied me. Then I remembered the Japanese Tuckshop. 'Is that what he told you on the way to the restaurant to beat up my bodyguard?' I enquired with a certain acerbity to my tone.

'What's all this?' Charles asked, rightfully confused.

Sam looked embarrassed. She spoke quietly into her hands. 'Look, it wasn't like that. I saw you with Kim. I had Rory track her down.'

'What?'

'Don't look so innocent, you were having an affair. Don't you see, I had to confront her.'

'An affair?' Charles repeated like she'd never heard the term before.

'Well, I saw the two of you holding hands at Café Bohème! What was I meant to think?'

Charles looked incensed. Barristers are good at the incensed look – it comes in really handy when you make an objection knowing you haven't got a leg to stand on. A look of hurt outrage can be enough to throw the judge. 'You mean you saw me in Soho with Kim a few weeks back?'

'Holding hands!'

'She's a friend of my old girlfriend, you fool. You remember Jane – you met her at a party once.'

'The drunk solicitor with red hair you lived with for two weeks about ten years ago?'

'Yeah, well she's got AIDS. I was just comforting her girlfriend. If you'd trusted me, if you'd asked me, I would have told you. Is this what all this is about then, your moods, your disappearance? You thought I was having an affair?'

Sam grovelled about Charles' legs like a spaniel that's just done a whoopsy. The focus was shifting from me faster than the duvet does at night when you bring home a new man. I decided it was time to give it a bit of a tug and recap on my misery.

'Now I'll probably never see him again,' I bleated.

They both looked at me briefly. Charles patted my knee. But the focus was beyond my control. I swallowed the last linty Belgian choc as they turned their attention back to each other.

'How could you think I'd be so low as to cheat on you with her?' Charles said vehemently.

'You told me you'd confronted Charles about the affair,' I reminded Sam, resigned now to being a bit-part actor in their drama.

But they ignored me completely. I had to face it – there wasn't even a walk-on role for me in this tragedy. I toyed with the idea of leaving them to sort it out but I didn't want to face Orlando again, so I fluffed up my pillows and arranged my magazines. Then I stuck my head under the bed to check for any last chocolates I might have missed earlier.

'Why should everyone else know apart from me?'

Were we doing Shakespeare here or what? I looked to check she didn't have her hand on her brow – these criminal barristers got away with the cheapest emotive ploys. I blame it on the jury system.

After a particularly dramatic pause, during which I found that lost choc I was searching for, Sam had thrown herself into Charles' arms and was sobbing. 'Oh forgive me. I'm so sorry. That was why I bought the stupid car. Can you ever forgive me?'

I got the impression that Charles was going to forgive her – I also got the impression that it was time for me to leave. After six lint-covered chocolates and a marriage proposal, I didn't have the space on my mental disk drive required to comprehend why someone buys a Ferrari because they're ashamed?

At a time like this Gran would have said, 'Alcohol is not an answer to life's problems but it's a bloody good retort.'

So I wandered out to join Orlando, Bruce and Johnny to get absolutely blotto.

An hour later we were all singing Auld Lang Syne, watching Bruce do these amazing stunts she'd learnt at Glastonbury. There was this thing where she balanced an empty bottle on her nose while juggling another three above her head.

Orlando kept trying to grope me so I had taken over the helicopter rides for Johnny. I was going to have to face our engagement sooner or later but I'd decided it might as well be after I'd lost consciousness. Charles and Sam held hands and looked into one another's eyes during the chorus which we all forgot and improvised in our own different ways.

Orlando did this really neat warbly baritone and Charles improvised the deep bits by trying to sound like Dame Nellie Melba.

We thought we sounded really cool and kept singing it over and over, trying to get the whole thing to sound professional. There was vague talk about finding a name for our group and getting an agent to find us gigs. That's the sort of self-delusion you're paying for when you buy vintage champagne. Eventually we collapsed into fits of laughter and Orlando came over and put his arms around me.

Oh this was a dreadful mess.

CHAPTER FORTY-SIX

the glastonbury
knowledge.

We were watching dawn break over London. St Paul's was lit up like a great fiery ball in an orange smog that romanticised the morning way out of proportion. For the first time in ages I remembered why I bought this place. My Feng Shui might be stuffed and Mies van de Rohe might be ashamed of me but the view was to die for. I was living slap bang in the centre of the funkiest city in the world and everyone around me was gooing and gaaing.

Bruce was up on Orlando's shoulders doing high kicks. Johnny had crashed out about an hour before, so all our giggling and singing was being done in whispers. We'd all changed into our underwear somewhere around four in the morning because our cavorting was making us hot. We were taking turns at teaching one another a dance. In between a rumba and a limbo, I got the opportunity to corner Charles on Sam. 'So is it all OK between you two now?'

'She just assumed, Evv, that's what hurt. There's no trust in our relationship. Did you know all about this?'

'Well, er . . .' I admitted.

'Oh this is great. So basically not even my friends trust me any more. Why didn't you tell me about this?'

'Well I suppose . . .' I suggested lamely.

'Yeah sure. We've been together seven years, you know, we've got a kid together and yet I feel no closer to her than a stranger.'

'But you love her,' I reminded her.

'Yeah, that's the fucking fly in the ointment isn't it? I love her.'

It was a pretty simple thing to say. In fact I think she'd said it before but as she walked away to join the group it struck me across the face as surely as someone slapping a hysterical woman. I was in love with Rory. He was the fly in my ointment.

He needed a wardrobe consultant, a hair cut and a copy of *The Female Eunuch*, but I loved him. It had been so obvious to hate a man like Rory – a man with no grasp on the concept of women as his equal – that I had. And now he was gone, instructing my builder to remove old Volvos and sending keys in the mail.

I wanted my Volvo back and I wanted those arms around me, those great big pecs with their smooth brown skin. Instead I was engaged to a man who could usually be found gravitationally challenged by bondage trousers and platform slippers.

I was leaning against the door wrapped in pensive thoughts such as these – watching my friends gyrating in their underwear. That was why I was the only one who heard the quiet tapping around seven. This time I didn't even bother trying to fool myself into believing it was Rory.

The Duke looked very sheepish when I opened the door. 'Please accept my apologies for calling at such an early hour, Miss Hornton, but I couldn't stay away.'

I blinked at him as if he might just be a mirage of an exceedingly short grey man in a Prince of Wales check suit. I grabbed his arm and checked his Rolex. Yes, it was seven a.m. and I had a duke at my door. Oh brill, don't tell me I had another unwelcome suitor? 'Come on in, Duke. Welcome to my Lonely Hearts Drop-in Centre. I hope you're a vegan.'

'A what?'

'A lover of nut-meat cutlets – it's what we subsist on.'

'Oh? What a lively young woman,' he commented to change the subject as Bruce went pirouetting off into the distance.

I was only able to interpret his muffled communications as long as I didn't watch his mouth. It was the spooky stillness of his lips that really put me off. Now that my vision was slightly crossed from my all-night champagne binge, I was finding it a lot easier.

'That's Bruce. She learnt it all at Glastonbury last year.'

'Oh really?' he asked in a tone of marked indifference. 'I would never have guessed.'

'So, Duke, can I offer you Champagne of the Season dregs?'

'Charming offer, my dear, but I don't think I will. I was rather hoping we could go somewhere private, don't you know. I had something of a rather delicate nature I was hoping to put to you.'

I eyed up the shower cubicle that the gang were running around – like a Calvin Klein commercial – using it as a sort of maypole for their futurist fertility dance. Deciding that my shower couldn't take more than one proposal a morning, I shrugged my shoulders and told him that private was doubtful.

'I know a delightful little breakfast spot not too far from here,' he offered and I agreed. Breakfast seemed like a remarkably attractive idea – mopping up the champagne with a bit of greasy egg was just what I needed.

'Now I can see what Candida sees in you, Duke, my man.'

I didn't want to interrupt the others so I decided to just sneak out. It wasn't till I reached the Roller and saw the expression on the chauffeur's face that I realised I was still in my underwear.

CHAPTER FORTY-SEVEN

i regretted not coming armed with a straitjacket.

Gorgeous waiters wafted around with platters of kedgeree and crumpets. On one side of me a man in full morning suit was spreading a thin veneer of marmalade on a piece of toast. The soft soothing strains of Liszt massaged away the headache that had been threatening to strike on the way there in the car. Here I was breakfasting at Claridge's with a duke, wearing the Azzedine Alaia I always knew would come in handy. I felt like Holly in *Breakfast at Tiffany's* – only something told me this scenario wasn't going to end up as a film. Unless we were talking cutting-room floor.

To start the ball rolling towards disaster, the Duke was so agitated he'd dropped half his kipper down his front. At first I tried not to notice but as he grabbed at the greasy red mass, it spread and it spread. Eventually I felt the onus was on me to comment – to say something reassuring like, 'Don't you just hate it when kippers do that?'

'Never mind – perhaps the waiter can provide you with something?' I soothed.

'Can't you see this is all Candida's doing?' he cried out petulantly at the top of his voice. For a moment you could have knocked me for six – I mean this was the first time I'd seen his mouth fully opened. Not only that but it was full of kipper.

A woman in her eighties at the table adjacent to ours in a

bright floral dress and large Jackie O sunnies, looked disgusted by my duke's manners. The bloke in the morning suit munched his toast obliviously. I don't suppose he'd come here for the sideshow.

I hid behind a piece of toast, gathering my thoughts, waiting for the kipper, the woman and the impeccably hovering waiter to go away. But the Duke kept insisting, 'It's her, it's her, it's all her doing!' His voice was getting louder and louder.

I mean, I had been waiting for this bloke to open his mouth since I first met him – but now I was prepared to offer him every cut-up credit card in my bag to shut it.

The woman in the glasses said, 'Well!' in a seriously pissed-off Victorian tone of voice.

I patted the Duke and hushed him. I mean give me a break, the first time a duke takes me to Claridge's and he goes and opens his mouth and distresses people.

'She's doing this to me!' he repeated. Clearly the guy was upset. I mean who wouldn't be? Half a kipper down the front in a room full of well-oiled money isn't easy to take on the chin. But let's get real – even hating the woman as I did – Candida was in the clear of any breach of duty on this one.

'Well sure, granted her influence is pretty far-reaching but seriously, Duke, you can't blame *this* on her,' I suggested gently.

'No you're right. Of course you're right,' he lamented, grasping my hands. 'From the mouths of babes.'

'I thought you loved her.'

'Love?'

'Well I just thought . . .'

'I worship her,' he cried, trembling through every microfibre of his little grey body. 'I worship her!' Gee these aristos don't do anything by halves.

'That's what I meant!' I told him.

'But where does it get me? Where? Where?' he wailed

'She thinks the world of you, Duke,' I encouraged him,

wondering how he'd take it if I put my hand over his mouth and gagged him. The woman in the Jackie O sunnies was apoplectic with rage.

'I am just her p****!'

'Her what?' I asked. His mouth had sort of seized again.

'Her plaything!' he repeated through tightly clenched teeth.

The woman in the bright dress *tut-tutted*. 'Well, hardly plaything, your Dukeness. I mean Candida takes life pretty seriously in my opinion.'

'Oh, but you're young,' he moaned, summoning a huddle of well-wishing waiters. 'What does youth know?' Seriously, these youth jibes were getting to me.

'Look, your Dukeness, can I be frank here?'

'Frank?'

'Open. Free and easy,' I explained. I mean what did he think I was offering at seven in the morning – a role-playing session? I'll be Frank you be Ginger? Puh-lease!

'Be my guest,' he said patronisingly.

'Well, maybe I'm wrong but basically I get the feeling Candida is getting a bit anxious about this perpetual courtship deal you've been offering.'

'She's commented on this to *you*?'

'Well indirectly yeah,' I admitted. He grasped my hands in his and took them to his lips and kissed them, leaving a bit of kipper on my knuckle.

'Miss Hornton, you have made me so very happy. Can't you see,' he expatiated, waving his arms expansively. 'If I could be sure that my proposal would be met with acceptance, I would be on one knee tomorrow, today even. It has been the risk of rejection that has kept me so tight-lipped. A rejection from a woman such as Candida would be more than my heart could bear.' He looked me in the eye. 'In short it would destroy me!'

'Well hesitate no longer, your Dukeness. Take the er, um, oestrogen by the horns, old boy. Basically I'm no expert, but judging by the way Candida was eyeing up those engagement rings at Cartier, I think you can be as confident as the next man that she will say yes.'

That was the moment at which he grabbed the woman in the bright frock by the upper arm. I can see in hindsight it was just an action brought on by the excitement of the moment but at the time I regretted not having brought the straitjacket and a mouth vice.

'Sorry about this. I'm so sorry!' I told her, jumping over the table and grabbing the Duke's hand. I shook it roughly, like you do with kids who put their hands in lion's cages. But it was too late. The woman let out a blood-curdling scream, summoning every man, woman and cloakroom attendant Claridge's had hired in the last fifty years.

'Toodle-pip,' I reassured them as they descended on our table – on foot, diving from great heights and waddling over on Zimmer frames.

'Nothing to worry about.'

But the bitch in the bright dress bellowed, 'This man t-t-t-ouched me!'

'This man happens to be a duke!' I told her and when she rejected that as an excuse, I made some unfavourable references to bargepoles.

'He manhandled me! Look at the mark he left.'

Sure enough there was a grease ring on her blouse. 'Here let me dust that off,' I urged, going at the mark with my napkin – bits of kipper flying all over the place. Shit this stuff was like splinters of the cross – it was everywhere.

'He meant no harm, he was practising his proposal!' I explained to the staff.

'He t-t-t-touched me!'

'He's going to propose,' I announced to the restaurant at large. 'A terrific QC leading me in a case at the moment in the Royal Courts of Justice. What a girl – if you ever find yourselves in a tricky litigation, call her. Damn it call me!' I

opened up my bag and started dishing out the cards. Well, in
for a penny in for a pound.

But my oppressor was having none of this. 'He grabbed at
my person,' she entreated but the day was won as everyone
started shaking the Duke's hand and offering their congratulations.

CHAPTER FORTY-EIGHT

the unsophisticated london weather had no respect for azzedine alaia.

I must have fallen asleep on the way home. Even with the accessories of the rich and successful, this city takes it out of a girl. The chauffeur woke me with a cruel shove when we got to my building. The first thing that struck me was the pouring rain. The second thing was that the Duke was gone. Then I remembered that Rory was gone and last – but most poignantly painful – I remembered that Orlando hadn't.

'He said he was going to make a marriage proposal like. Said to tell you the car's yours till tomorrow,' the chauffeur explained. 'And I come with the car. S'pose you think it's your lucky day? A girl like you – never thought you'd be so lucky, did you?' He turned around, rolled his eyes and grinned at me apishly.

'Lucky? Me? I don't think so,' I replied haughtily, as if Rolls-Royces were something I just took in my stride. I was also weighing up the advantages of having a Roller with the disadvantages of having this creep at my disposal. He was only about twenty-five years old so I decided to be generous – maybe he would grow out of it, I told myself. Basically, I'm ashamed to say it – call me a shallow materialist – but there was a lot I was prepared to put up with for the sake of a Roller.

'Only as you're not a duke I don't need to wear my hat,' he went on. 'I checked that with base like, so don't go getting haughty or anything 'cause this boy knows your station and it's not warranting a hat. Take it or leave it.'

'Pity the attitude doesn't go with the hat,' I muttered, as I got the sleep out of my eyes and my feet back in my shoes and tackled the realisation that I was going to have to go out into the rain. 'You haven't got a brolly have you?' I asked.

''Fraid not. The Duke took it with him.' He turned to me and gave me the eye-rolling ape look again – this time with his tongue sticking out the side of his mouth. 'And anyway brollies are extra.'

It was a lashing ferocious summer storm with all the elemental extras – hail, thunder lightning and wind. The sort of turbulent weather environmentalists warned us about decades ago. London's weather had never had the *savoir-faire* to appreciate Azzedine Alaia. Within a split second of walking into it, this little frock wasn't just clinging to me, it was being absorbed into my skin.

I might as well have been naked.

Taking a look back at the chauffeur, I could see he thought so too. His eyes were swinging from his sockets like pendulous breasts. If I'd thought to call up *Penthouse* I could have made some seriously crucial money out of this gig.

Bruce met me at the door, babbling incoherently about how the girls had made up and gone home. She had the furtive air of an Olympic sportsman on steroids being asked for a urine sample. I mean if I didn't know she wasn't a Catholic I might have thought she was guilty or something.

Not only did she not register that I was wet but she wasn't seeming to grasp the concept that I wanted to get something to dry myself off with. Even though I said the word 'towel' repeatedly – and with some energy.

She reminded me of witnesses who claim they didn't know that when they signed the statement they were admitting responsibility. Obstructive I call them. And that was Bruce that morning, bloody, irritatingly obstructive. What's more she was doing her best to block my passage to the other side of the loft where I had a decent chance of finding a towel.

'So what are you still doing here?' I asked as I tried to get around her.

'I just had a few things to, er, clean up,' she muttered as she bobbed from side to side, blocking my path.

'Oh right. Well feel free to leave now. I'll handle it all. You just get back to the girls before they start bickering about who's going to change the next nappy,' I urged her. 'I'm going to hit the sack – I'm all ovaried out.'

Despite her best efforts I had managed to traverse half the loft when she scuttled under my feet and I fell flat on my face.

I struggled up without her assistance. Something was going on here but I wasn't sure I wanted to get to the bottom of it. I asked her to move aside so I could get a towel. That was when she began to physically shove me.

'Excuse me?' I said, on the verge of losing my sense of *noblesse oblige* that prohibits hosts slugging guests. 'Could you let me pass? I need to get to my futon.'

'You don't want to do that,' she said.

'Hello – are you insane?' I asked her as I peeled off the dress and passed it to her. 'I've just installed a paddling pool all over the floor of my flat. I need to dry off. And then I intend to go to bed. Now move aside before I bludgeon you to death.'

She took hold of the wet pulp that had once meant more to me than my mortgage. But she didn't budge. 'You can't go through there. Um, well, we had quite a lot to drink . . . we didn't know when you'd be back . . . Orlando . . . well that is to say. I . . . oh God, how do I say this?'

But she didn't have to say any more. Orlando said it all. I had pushed my way through her barricade and discovered him – naked, stretched out, asleep and snoring. There was a used condom by the bed.

'Oh indignity of indignities!' I cried out in grand amateur dramatics style. 'My fiancé has been screwing around.'

Bruce burst into tears and flung herself into my cold, wet, naked body.

'Shhhh. Now don't cry. I was being facetious. It's OK. I really don't mind.'

'I'm so sorry,' she sobbed. 'It just happened. I'll probably lose my job. You'll tell the girls. I don't blame you for wanting to flush my career down the toilet.'

I muttered a few reassuring things as I scanned my gear scattered all over the floor, searching for a towel. Bruce blubbered away into my Alaia, oblivious to all my protestations.

'Heck, calm down. So you screwed my fiancé – hardly a hanging offence. I promise I won't even tell the girls.'

'Don't you understand? We betrayed you!' she cried, flinging my Alaia on the floor as if willing me to do a jealous-lover routine.

'Don't worry about it. I don't mind really. Um, if I could just get something to dry myself on?'

She looked at me dumfounded. 'You don't?'

'No. It was just a spur of the moment decision to get married. We really weren't suited,' I explained. 'Now if you could just see your way clear to giving me a towel?'

'You mean that?'

'Sure. Look, why don't I go out and make myself scarce while you two get your things together? Just give me the towel, that's all I require.'

'You're being very good about this.'

'Not at all. Like I said, we weren't really suited. It was madness from the start – his cabalistic relatives and the Pope would never have allowed it,' I assured her trying to dampen her doubts. 'Not that he isn't a catch and a half of course. Towel?'

'You don't think he's a bit straight? Only he's pretty conservative compared to the guys I usually date,' she said, chewing on a strand of her hair.

I began to panic that my lack of fury had cooled her interest – basically I was falling into a P.J-Wodehouse plot better suited to a Bertie Wooster.

'I mean, I've never been with anyone as straight as a barrister before,' she added.

'Straight? Orlando?' Hello, are we talking about the same creature here?'

'Well he's so, so, so . . . Aquascutum isn't he?'

I saw then what was happening. This girl in her blissful ignorance had no previous experience of Orlando's usual guises – his nipple clips, bondage trousers and platform slippers. She'd only met him last night in his dock-siders and sand-coloured chinos. 'Believe me, Bruce, looks can be deceiving,' I promised her. 'Orlando's much more than he seems. I mean, ask him to show you his bondage trouser collection for instance. Girl guide's honour – Orlando is a dark horse, wild, outrageous, phenomenally so. In fact that's why it would never have worked between us – I'm too straight for him. He probably thought he could change me – lure me up the great heights of his platform slippers type thing but at the end of the day I'm just a boring barrister.' I finally got my hands around a towel. It was wet.

'Sorry about that, it's wet,' she explained noticing my chargin. 'We kind of had a shower together. To cool off, you know?'

Sure, I thought. Why not? Practically compulsory in this place. Orlando let out a loud burp and turned in his sleep.

'He is kinda cute, isn't he?' she sighed and I nodded furiously, realising what a lucky break I'd just had.

CHAPTER FORTY-NINE

trust us, all this indignity and humiliation – it's for your own good!

That was how I got to be sitting with the chauffeur from hell outside my loft at nine o'clock in the morning, waiting for my ex-fiancé and his bit on the side to leave. I had done the decent thing and presented them with the cocaine I'd found in Matt's pocket just to show there were no hard feelings. I think that was what finally convinced them that they were doing the right thing.

I was using the time to take stock of my life. I mean look at me – a Rolls-Royce at my disposal and what did I do? I watched my flat like a stalker. Basically so much had happened in the last fortnight and yet so little had changed. I was going round in circles.

The misery of my predicament must have led me to talk to myself for I had accidentally spoken out loud. 'I should have listened to Rory from the beginning. Oh why did I allow my stupid pride to get in the way? It was just that he caught me off guard in those bloody lawn sandals and after that I more or less held it against him. Now, I'll never see him again.'

'Well you know what they say – tis better to have loved and lost than never to have whats'it before,' my chauffeur said, shaking me to full awareness and humiliation.

'What? Er, did you say something?' I was trying to pretend this wasn't happening.

He turned around and winked. 'I was just sayin, luv, it is better to have loved and lost etc, etc. Gees I thought a bird like you woulda heard that before.'

'Great, so now I've got a philosopher for a chauffeur.'

'Well! Sorry for breathing, ma'am!'

'Oh forget it, I was just thinking out loud.' A bit later I had the misfortune to say, 'la-de-da'.

My chauffer was on to me like a scud missile. 'Lally what?'

'Nothing all right, I was just musing.'

'You know something? You're A-musing!'

'Hello?' I said, offering him the chance to shut up. 'How about a bit of respect here? I'm sure the Duke wouldn't want you speaking to me like that.'

'Oh la-de-da,' he sang, looking at me in the rear-view mirror. 'She wants respect now does she? Well respect is extra.'

'Where'd the Duke find you, the circus?' I asked him in my most cutting, sarcastic tone.

'You're a funny bird.'

'The attitude is free right? Just my luck!' I folded my arms and made a glaring face in his mirror.

'It's OK, doll, keep your panties on. I was just havin' a bit of a laugh. A lad needs something to keep his pecker up in this job.'

I felt the colour drain from my face. Doll? Did he just say doll? I felt like I'd been punched in the heart. But I didn't get a chance to check the placement of my organs because Paddy was tapping on the window. I jumped out of my wet skin and then wound down the window.

'Nice car, Miss Evelyn.'

'Thanks, Paddy. It's not mine though,' I explained in case he was about to claim it in lieu of my unpaid bill. I could just see myself trying to explain the incident to Candida.

'No, I didn't think it was,' he replied – a little too swiftly for my liking. 'I just thought I should come round and explain why

I didn't turn up again.' I couldn't help thinking how noble he looked standing there in the rain as a drip ran down his nose to his chin.

'It's OK, Paddy, I understand. After all it's not as if I've ever paid you. I know I've been a lousy loft owner but I'll get some money . . . I promise. I'll change,' I stuttered as a lump of misery welled in my throat.

The chauffeur got out and ran around to open the door – holding, I noticed, a large black umbrella – and wearing his hat! Paddy climbed in beside me, filling the Roller with the aroma of damp wood and fried egg. 'Now there, Miss Evelyn, don't go getting maudlin on me,' he soothed as the chauffeur slammed the door.

Paddy passed me a mangy-looking hanky with bits of plaster hanging off it. 'I won't have none of that. No, miss, it's got nothing to do with your bill. I can't go charging a nice girl like you money anyway. Not after all you've done for me.'

'Done?' I asked dabbing at my face with the hanky out of courtesy.

'Will you be expecting any more guests today, miss?' my chauffeur interrupted.

'Hey?'

'Guests, only I like to know if you'll be expecting anyone proper like – so I can put me 'at on.'

'I thought you said brollies were extra?' I told him.

My chauffeur turned, leant over the divider and said to Paddy, 'Oh, she's lovely isn't she, mate? Eh?' Then he turned to me and gave me a surly look. 'Just because I know me rights like, doesn't mean I've got no manners. You read?'

'Read, write and slap arseholes in the ear,' I warned him – he was really doing my head in now.

'Yes, ma'am.'

'Who's that?' Paddy asked when the chauffeur from hell slammed the dividing glass shut.

'Oh no one, just the chauffeur.'

'*Just* the chauffeur, that'd be right!' His voice boomed through the intercom.

I made a rude sign with my fingers and gave Paddy back his hanky.

'Now, Miss Evelyn, I can hardly be wanting money from a girl who gave me back the most beautiful woman in the world, can I now?'

'You mean the muu-muu woman? I mean your wife?'

'Oh, Miss Evelyn, a man's no man without a missus! Know what I mean?'

'Oh?'

'But that's not what I came for.'

'No?'

'I've got a message here from Rory.'

My heart soared and I looked at him expectantly, waiting for him to pass it over, but he just sat there grinning, making no move towards his pockets.

'Yes, where is it?' I prompted him.

'What?'

'The message?'

'Well that's it see. I lost it.' He looked down at his wet shoes where an ever-expanding puddle was gathering on the carpeted floor.

'Lost it?'

''Fraid so. I've had a lot on my mind.'

'Oh,' I said meekly. 'I don't suppose you have a bottle of temazepam or a sharp object you could lend me, Paddy?'

'You're a funny girl, miss,' he laughed.

'That's what I said,' the chauffeur agreed over the intercom.

'Did you now?' Paddy asked.

'Exact same words. You're a funny bird, I says.' He opened the divider and leaned over to join our conversation. He still had his hat on, I noticed, which made me feel a tad put out.

'That she is,' Paddy agreed, nodding thoughtfully.

I thought about slipping out the door and leaving these blokes to theorise on the virtues of my human comedy but my need for information of Rory held me back.

'How is Rory, Paddy?'

'Who's Rory?' the chauffeur asked.

'Do you mind, this is a private conversation,' I told him curtly.

'Just asking,' he muttered. 'Gees, talk about Miss High and Mighty. Give a woman a Rolls-Royce for a day and she thinks she's Princess bloody Margaret.'

I ignored him. 'So, Paddy, do you think there's much chance he'll come back to London some time?'

'Well, I couldn't say, miss, He's very secretive is Rory.'

'It's just that I spoke to him on the phone earlier,' I explained. 'Well, what I mean is I spoke to him but I didn't really *speak* to him if you know what I mean.'

The chauffeur made a sort of chuckling noise and rolled his eyes at Paddy. 'That'd be right.'

'Do you mind?' I said.

'Didn't say a word.' Then he said la-de-da under his breath and chuckled some more.

'What I mean is, I wish he'd told me everything that was going on about your wife and all the other stuff.'

'Well, whatever he did, miss, I'm sure he did it for your own good.'

Now my blood pressure began to rise – you see, the 'for your own good' argument is one of the seminal points in the feminist fight. It sort of riles us women to learn that all the subjugation and oppression visited on our gender down the ages was done by men who were merely denying us our human rights for our own good. Basically we were meant to buy the argument that chastity and domestic drudgery were good for us.

These days a lot of us girls think that deciding what's best for our own good is all part of adulthood. Call me a rad-fem-bitch, but I kind of like deciding on what's good for me and what isn't. I mean can you imagine the reaction if we girls started laying down the law for blokes like that. As in, 'Sorry, boys, but masturbation isn't good for you so we are going to tie your hands up in little cotton strait-mitts behind your back – trust us it's for your own good!' Yeah sure.

I put this argument to Paddy – and by proxy the chauffeur who echoed my worst fears. 'Think we got ourselves one of them feminists here, Paddy!' He laughed – making the ape face at me but Paddy, bless his soul, didn't engage with our learned friend on this one.

'Well that's true, miss, only I think Rory was trying to take extra care of you because he liked you. Too much he told Rosy. And truth is, Miss Evelyn, he got the impression from you that you didn't think an artist was—'

I cut in. 'An artist?'

'That's right, an artist, miss. Making quite a name for himself in New York now too. The private-eye business was just something he fell into by chance, see. Oh sure he did a bit to make some money but sculpture's his true love. It all looks like a pile o' junk to me but he's been bought by some of the world's best museums, not that he ever boasts. He was only doing me a favour when I asked him to look out for you. He thought you looked down on him, that he wasn't good enough for the likes of you – a professional barrister and all.'

My chauffeur let out a whistle and turned round to us.

'Don't start,' I warned him but my words went unheeded. 'Hey, Paddy, it's like that great Irishman, that Oscar geezer said: "We're all in the gutter but some of us are looking at the stars."'

CHAPTER FIFTY

coming soon: the future – playing at a venue near you.

The next few months dragged by without me. Some mornings I couldn't even get out of bed. Despite my foul moods everyone was very supportive. Sam bailed me out financially while I waited for money from Warren. Charles dropped in regularly to try and cheer me up and they even sent Bruce over to clean the place. Surprisingly, Candida also went easy on me, even to the point of keeping quiet when I missed a conference. Basically I was in a peanut-butter-induced stupor and, on this particular evening, Charles was in an unsympathetic mood.

'But, Evvy, you've got to go out some time,' she entreated.

'Out? Where's out?' It had been such a long time since I'd been out, I'd forgotten the directions.

'OK look, he was cute but there are plenty more Iro/American private eyes in the sea. Get over it, girl. You're a professional woman. It took a lot of Prozac to get you where you are today – are you honestly going to throw all that away on a man who called you doll?' She looked at me and saw that I was.

'He's gone, Evv, you've got to face it. G-O-N-E.'

'But I'm in love.'

'Same number of letters pronounced l-u-s-t, Evelyn. What about this one?' she asked holding up a juicy little Gucci number I thought I'd die without a few months ago – as it was I'd never worn it again – too short for work, too long for clubbing.

'And besides, he wasn't a private eye, he was an artist,' I wailed, putting a sort of spiritual emphasis on the word artist.

'So what, you don't have the mildest interest in art.'

'I went to the Mitchie Wanhato show!'

'You only went there to try and seduce Matt. Afterwards you said, and I quote, "Art is even more boring than law!"'

'I was just hot and bothered. I loved the show, loved it like mad. It, it, sort of had a quality.'

'Hello? Is this the same woman here? Evelyn, you're the original philistine. You thought art was a Garfunekl before I gave you a *Time Out*, remember. Face it, your only interest in art was to get the trousers off Matt.'

'Was not!'

'Was too.'

'Well it might have started that way,' I conceded. 'But once I got involved my views changed. Besides, Matt was just a pretentious crook. Rory's the real thing.'

'No, that's Coke!'

'Look, don't hassle me. Can't you see, I've never felt this way before,' I sulked, waving the said dress away.

'Crap, you only ever have two states of being – wanting to fuck some bloke's brains out, or blow some guy's brains out. Now pull yourself together. You look a mess. If your life was an installation it would be titled "Self-Pity".'

I gave her one of my sarcastic laughs.

'This is *the* dress,' she declared, throwing a white Prada front-zip number on top of my bed which had become the set I'd created for my tragic demise. My duvet looked like something out of Generation X goes shopping at Sainsburys – strewn with saucers, sweet wrappers, an empty jar of peanut butter with a spoon sticking out, the Chanel compact I'd been using to survey my blackhead situation, and empty coffee Häagen-Daz containers. Basically I was eating my way *into* misery, not out of it.

It was grim stuff for a woman not even closing in on thirty.

'God, he's just a man. Think of all the other marvellous things you've got to live for,' Charles insisted.

But my mind went blank. 'Look Charles, let it drop. I'm just not in the mood for this party,' I told her.

'Crap. You were engaged to the bloke yourself last month – the least you can do is to go to his latest engagement party.'

I thought about this for a minute. Even with my brain fogged up with peanut butter I was sure there was a screw loose in this logic. 'Charles – he cheated on me, remember?'

But Charles wasn't having any of it. Somehow she had managed to lure me into the Prada and zip me up. I suppose if I was going to get up for anything it might as well be for a Prada.

'Show him there's no hard feelings,' she urged.

That was one way of looking at it.

Candida and the Duke picked us up at seven. Their own engagement party was to be held in Monaco, although they were having a few close London friends to dinner at the Lanesborough. And let's get this much clear – I wasn't one of them. I might have got the Duke to get down on one knee, but I wasn't to be included on the invitation list for 'the event of the year' as the *Hampstead Gazette* was proclaiming it. Our relationship had improved – but not that much!

Tonight was Orlando's night – a small party courtesy of 17 Pump Court. As I climbed in the Rolls, Candida put her hand out for me to ogle the biggest square-cut diamond this side of a South African Kimberlite pipe.

'Wow, Duke, you really excelled yourself with this little outcrop of faceted splendour,' I cooed appreciatively. The Duke, whose mouth had seized up one more since our breakfast at Claridges, mumbled something about how good it was to see me again.

I climbed in beside Candida and let Charles sit beside the Duke – out of harm's way.

'So good to see you again, Charles,' Candida meowed,

smarming into her Lacroix like only a true duchess-to-be can.

'Likewise my dear, likewise,' Charles meowed – they were trying to out-facetious one another.

'I think it's sooooo wonderful that Orlando is finally getting married,' Candida announced.

'Not soooooo finally,' Charles insisted. 'He is only twenty-four.'

'Well perhaps it will sober him up,' she purred as we drove off.

'I wouldn't bank on it,' Charles muttered to herself. She squawked as I kicked her in the shins.

We arrived fashionably late, which in London during a tube strike was anything from an hour to two hours. Vinny, as you would expect, was waiting at the door to bore people as they arrived. Poor Judge Hawkesbury was there with his wheezing Staffordshire terrier, Margo (named after Margaret Thatcher).

'Meet Margo,' he said, shoving the grizzly dark thing towards me. I am not a dog person or even a sentient-being person. I'm more your inanimate-object person basically but Candida took the creature into her arms and held it aloft like the fatted calf.

'What a delightful little girl she is, Judge – have you had her *done*?' she enquired as the little bitch paddled her legs and squirmed. Candida was always making sure things were *done*. Anything from hair, to seasons, to marriages. I wondered idly if she'd had the Duke done.

'Oh yes. My word yes – I don't want her spawning anything in chambers, absolutely. Good heavens no.'

The Duke smiled in detached appreciation. He had enjoyed the privilege of a lunch in the judge's rooms above the day before and looked as though the sherry was still working.

I wandered over to join all the usual suspects gathered by the canapé tray. A few people from other chambers were there doing a bit of networking. We had a few places going at the moment so we were throwing our doors wide to attract applicants. Vinny had insisted that as part of his new economy drive, there was no reason why Orlando's engagement couldn't provide an excellent social screening opportunity. Just the same I was struck dumb when my eyes alighted on Giles.

That was all I needed, a man in insteps trying to muscle his way into my chambers. That was going to be my new rule – never under any circumstances date barristers, they will always return to haunt you. He was stuffing his face with crustaceans. I hid behind the hellish string quartet who were torturing a medley of Cole Porter numbers. Usually by the end of the night, they could be relied on to enliven things with a few Chuck Berry hits which Vinny and the European Law experts would attempt to dance to.

Bruce and Orlando were already lost to the music, swaying in one another's arms like a couple of geriatrics at a Waldorf tea dance. Orlando was in his bondage trousers and slippers again with a fishnet top and nipple clips, so it was difficult for him to do anything more than sway. Just the same they looked so beautiful together. So romantic. 'No doubt E-ed up to the eyeballs,' Charles whispered as she came over to join me.

Surrounding the makeshift dance floor were a dozen or so men I took to be from Mossad because they were all wearing skullcaps and looking pretty damn furtive with it. Interspersed throughout the gathering were a few Hasidic Jews wandering around like last season's John Paul Gaultier catwalk models off their diets.

There was a bit of a disturbance over by the door I noticed as I grabbed a bottle of Moet from a passing waiter and warned Charles that she would probably be carrying me out of this party. I had no sooner got the mouth of the bottle to my lips when I heard Margo barking. At first I thought the champagne had gone straight to my head but it was just raw elation at the sight of Rory striding towards me without so much as a centimetre of stomach skin in sight.

'Doll, there you are!' he cried. He was wearing black tie and his hair was as sleek and as smooth as if he'd come straight from Trumpers. He was holding Margo, which was probably why Judge Hawkesbury was scuttling along behind him like a manservant.

Before I had a chance to run through my lines, he had me in his arms – Margo and all. 'Gee it's good to see you, doll,' he cried as he spun me round. Margo made a little deflating sound as she was squeezed in our embrace.

'What are you doing here?'

'Shhh, I'm on an assignment,' he whispered in my ear. I felt my clitoris lose consciousness as the aroma of his pheromones paralysed all my senses – bar one. 'Top-secret stuff, doll. This woman barrister's hired me to see if I can cheer up her girlfriend. Apparently she's hung up on some absolute loser of an artist that pissed off to the States.'

'Oh? And what's this girl like?'

'Like? She's just fine. A bit kooky if you know what I mean, but one hell of a kisser.'

I had already parted my lips in order to receive the bounty of his lips as Judge Hawkesbury came panting up alongside us to reclaim his dog.

'There you go, Judge,' Rory smiled as he passed the flattened Margo over. 'Tell you what – you're right to get the dog out before this doll here starts throwing her right hooks about.'

'That's just what I always say,' agreed Giles who must have snuck up on us in his insteps. 'Everything always ends in ABH when Evelyn Hornton's around.' He turned to the crowd and gave one of those sarcastic little laughs I had taught him.

I wanted to show Giles Billington-Frith just how right he was, but I was already being wrapped up in those great big chesterfield arms and I could see Charles winking at me from the corner of the room. The bastard would keep.